PLEASE DO NOT ASK FOR MERCY AS A REFUSAL OFTEN OFFENDS

Paul Bassett Davies

Lightning
Books

Published in 2020
by Lightning Books Ltd
Imprint of EyeStorm Media
312 Uxbridge Road
Rickmansworth
Hertfordshire
WD3 8YL

www.lightning-books.com

British Library Cataloguing in Publication Data
A catalogue record for this book is available from the British Library.

Printed by CPI Group (UK) Ltd, Croydon CR0 4YY

ISBN: 9781785631856

For my son, Theo, and his comrades,
whose passionate commitment to a better future
for our world and its inhabitants is a mighty
beacon of hope

No man is an island, entire of itself;
every man is a piece of the continent, a part of the main.
– **John Donne**

Know all things to be like this:
A mirage, a cloud castle,
A dream, an apparition,
Without essence, but with qualities that can be seen.
– **Buddha**

'Is it about a bicycle?'
– **Flann O'Brien,** *The Third Policeman*

KILROY

Manfred faced his execution in high spirits. He sang snatches of unrecognisable songs with great gusto, and recited peculiar stories that he seemed to be inventing on the spot. It was all nonsense and gibberish, of course. His mind was deranged, and everything was scrambled up. The crowd couldn't have asked for a better show.

But then there was some unpleasantness. Manfred began to blaspheme in the most appalling way, even repeating the odious words and phrases that had brought him to this regrettable termination. Parents covered their children's ears, and Manfred was silenced swiftly. The remainder of the ceremony was conducted in a more restrained atmosphere, and after it was over there were the usual grumbles from some among the dispersing crowd, deploring the outdated custom that allowed the condemned man to say a few words. They asked each other why the courtesy of a final speech should be extended to scoundrels who exploited it as an opportunity to scandalise decent families. There was no excuse for that kind of exhibition, they said, even if the man was bonkers.

People also complained, as they always did, about how long it took to get out of Shadbold Square, owing to the narrowness of the surrounding streets, and the failure of the authorities to lay on extra trams for these occasions, which were always well-attended despite everyone assuring each other, after every execution, that they certainly wouldn't be coming again and things were very much better in the old days.

Manfred's shoes were presented to his family the next day. His son, Roland, was proud of the memento, but Sheba, his older sister, made a mime of vomiting every time she passed the mantelpiece on which the stained footwear was displayed. The children's mother, Wanda, was a practical woman, and a few days later, when the kids were at school, she put her late husband's shoes in the garbage grinder. When the children came home Roland kicked up a fuss, but his mother mollified him with the promise of a visit to the fish museum. As for Sheba, she seemed indifferent to the loss. However, the very next morning young Roland was confronted by a dreadful scene in the kitchen when he came down for breakfast. Blood was spattered on the walls, and was congealing into a sticky pool beneath the body of his mother, which lay on the floor. Her throat had been cut, and a large kitchen knife was sticking out of her eye socket. There was no sign of Sheba, some of whose clothes and belongings were discovered to be missing, along with a backpack.

It seemed like an open-and-shut case of Abrupt Matricide

Syndrome with an absconding culprit, but the authorities naturally asked the police to investigate.

Detective Kilroy was given the job. He was a handsome fellow, and a professional from the brim of his hat to the soles of his shoes. He lived for his police work, and for Creek, the parrot who shared his austere bachelor quarters. It was a gorgeous specimen of the Freakin Grey species, and Kilroy was very fond of it.

Occasionally he wondered if perhaps he should have risen higher in the force by the age of thirty-nine, but he never let the thought linger in his mind for too long. Regret was a useless indulgence, and he wished he'd known that when he was younger.

Kilroy's first task was to talk to the son. Roland was eleven years old, and Kilroy expected him to be flustered. He'd recently lost his father in unfortunate circumstances, and then, before he could catch his breath, came the additional surprise of his mother's death. No boy could be unaffected by seeing his dad executed, then stumbling across the bloody corpse of his mother in the family kitchen on his way to school.

Beneath his gruff exterior Kilroy was a decent man, and he was surprised to learn that Roland had been taken into custody. When he tried to find out who had given the order to arrest the boy, nobody seemed to know. Kilroy didn't claim to be an expert in child psychology, but he figured that being locked up would do nothing to improve the youngster's frame of mind.

His own plan had been to adopt a friendly approach, and perhaps take the boy out to tea, which he imagined a person of his age might appreciate. But now, the best he could do was to bring a glass of spood juice into Roland's cell, and ask the custodian to remove the shackles. He was determined to treat the boy like his own son, if he'd had a son, and assuming he had a good relationship with the hypothetical child.

Kilroy sat down opposite Roland, handed him the juice, and smiled at him. He wanted to show he wasn't a beast, and he began the interrogation by asking the boy how he was feeling. That was a mistake.

To Kilroy's surprise and embarrassment, the youth began to speak, not just of his feelings at the present moment, as Kilroy had intended, but of his emotions in general. It seemed that Roland's tender young heart was a cornucopia of conflicted passions, which he promptly disgorged.

Sometimes, he said, I feel that life's plentiful syrup is erupting through my pipes, and I am almost overwhelmed by a sense of pure, unbounded joy; I fear that I must swoon at the sheer beauty of the world, in every particular, both great and small, and oh, I am undone.

I see, Kilroy said, playing for time, and at others?

At other times, Roland said in his clear, high-pitched voice, I feel the aching sadness of life pervading my weary existence like an eldritch fog, engulfing me in a haunting melancholy that is nigh on unbearable.

Kilroy checked the notes in his file. Was the kid really only eleven? Yes, according to the notes. Kilroy wondered what the hell they taught them in school these days. As it happened, the file contained copies of Roland's school reports. Kilroy glanced at the most recent one and noticed that the boy had expressed an interest in training to enter the priesthood.

Eventually he managed to get the interview back on track, and questioned Roland about the events leading up to his mother's presumed murder, and the disappearance of his sister, Sheba. That was when the mystery deepened.

The forensic specialists had established the time of Wanda's death as between five and eight-thirty in the morning. That fitted with Roland's account, of coming down to breakfast at nine to find his mother's corpse still warm, her blood in the process of congealing, and the onset of rigor mortis only just beginning. It appeared that Roland was gifted, in addition to his eloquence, with an advanced understanding of human biology. But he was adamant that he'd heard his sister packing her things and leaving the house just after midnight. He was absolutely certain of that.

And later, Kilroy asked, did you hear her come back in?

No, replied Roland, but I sleep very heavily between the hours of one and seven. My nocturnal rhythms are rigid to the point of despotism. If Sheba had returned to the house later, I would have heard nothing.

Kilroy asked if Sheba's behaviour had seemed unusual in the days between her father's execution and her mother's death.

The lad furrowed his brow. Hmmm, he ventured, I didn't see much of her, to tell you the truth. I remember she said she'd been reading a lot.

And that was unusual?

What?

Her reading a lot.

Not really. She was always a keen reader.

Kilroy tried to keep the irritation out of his voice. You just implied, he said slowly, that it was unusual for her to be reading a lot.

No, Roland said with a shake of his head, I didn't. That may be what you inferred, but you asked me if her behaviour had been unusual, and I mentioned that I hadn't seen much of her. That was the unusual part. Normally, I'd see her reading. She would sprawl about the place, engrossed in the trashy girls' stuff she liked. But during the period about which you enquired she spent most of her time in her room, and when I asked her what she'd been doing in there she told me she'd been reading. And before you ask, she didn't tell me what. I suspect she didn't want me to know.

I see, Kilroy said once again. But he saw nothing. He was stumped.

Kilroy excused himself and went outside the cell to collect his thoughts. It didn't make sense. Why would the girl leave the house in the early hours of the morning, taking her backpack with her, and then return a few hours later in order to murder her mother? Unless...unless...what?

Kilroy was aware that an alternative hypothesis was lurking just beyond his mental field of vision, like a distant road sign that was unreadable to a man who'd left his glasses at home. Only by approaching closer could Kilroy decipher the message, but for every step he took in its direction, it receded by an equal distance, remaining tantalisingly fuzzy. Experience had taught him that he needed to relax, unclench the mental fist that constrained him, and allow the message to present itself to him in its own good time, perhaps when he was asleep, which sometimes happened.

But sleep would have to wait. Right now he had a precocious eleven-year-old boy locked up in a cell, and limited time in which to question him. At any moment a social advocate could arrive and pester him to either release the boy, or charge him, or put him to the itching test and have done with it. Even if Kilroy let him go, Roland would have to be rehoused with foster parents, and Kilroy needed to put himself out of the picture before he got entangled in the process, thank you very much. The red tape was a nightmare, and Kilroy didn't need that shit in his life.

But something told Kilroy the boy had useful information, if only he could get it out of him. He refused to consider the itching test. He had never knowingly hurt a child, and despised anyone who would do so. Anyhow, Kilroy didn't generally go in for that type of thing. No rough stuff, unless it was strictly unavoidable.

Back in the cell he was about to resume his questioning when Roland forestalled him by bursting into tears. Kilroy wondered if it was just another tactic, like the eloquence and the emotional disclosure, but nonetheless he handed the snivelling boy a handkerchief that he kept in his breast pocket for occasions like this. The storm of tears began to abate, and Kilroy was thinking that perhaps he might try a new approach, based on jovial, man-to-man camaraderie, when the custodian entered the cell, and told Kilroy he was wanted on the telephone.

Kilroy took the call in the custodian's office. It was the Chief's secretary, telling Kilroy to release the boy and come to see the Chief immediately.

He handed the receiver back to the custodian with a sigh.

The man raised his eyebrows. Trouble?

My middle name, Kilroy said.

The Chief was a big woman, as large as a house. Not literally, but whenever Kilroy thought about her he pictured her as an imposing municipal building, inside which he was not welcome. He found it impossible to imagine any type of intimacy with her.

In reality she was a medium-sized woman with an air of competence and efficiency that often made Kilroy feel like he needed a shower. She had a habit of communicating in a series of questions, some of them rhetorical. In this instance, the questions were as follows:

Why had Kilroy taken a juvenile witness into custody?

Was he aware that this could look bad for the department?

As a matter of interest, was Kilroy a fucking idiot?

When was Kilroy going to focus the investigation on finding the girl?

How far away did he think she could have got by now?

Why wasn't he out there right now, tracking her down?

What was he waiting for?

Kilroy decided not to point out that the order to arrest Roland hadn't come from him. He didn't want to appear defensive or whiny. Besides, if the Chief herself had given the order, Kilroy judged it unwise to confront her about it. And if she hadn't, that meant it must have come from further up the chain, or from a special services unit, operating under separate authority, and Kilroy had no desire to open that particular can of worms. It was a sizeable can, into which it was surprisingly easy to fall.

He simply nodded, stood up, and walked to the door. As he opened it, the Chief spoke again. Kilroy, she said, wait.

He waited.

You're a good cop, she said. One of our best. I'm under pressure to find this girl and get the case wrapped up. Certain people are nervous about it, and these are turbulent times, what with social unrest, people going wrong, people dropping dead for no reason, and so on. So, please proceed swiftly, but with caution. I don't want to lose you, and this girl could be extremely dangerous. Look what she did to her own mother.

If you find your safety threatened in any way, slay her without hesitation. Shoot first. I know you can be sensitive – no, don't try to deny it – and you're not as jaded as you like to think. Keep your pistol handy. I know you'll do your best. Thank you, Kilroy.

Kilroy closed the door gently behind him.

CURTIS

Kilroy told me about the case over a drink the following evening.

I was his only close woman friend, probably because we'd never been lovers. I'll admit that when we'd first met there was a strong erotic charge between us, and we seemed to be headed for bed, but for some reason we never got there. Eventually we reached the stage where we knew each other too well for it to happen. Perhaps it was still conceivable that if we'd drunk too much one evening, and one or both of us had been overwhelmingly hungry for that intimacy, we might have made it. But we would have felt bad in the morning, and nothing would have been the same again. You know how it is.

We were accustomed to meet every week or so, but all that was about to end, for reasons that will become clear. Our paths diverged, and it was a long time before I discovered what Kilroy did after he disappeared. By the time I got the full story, the world had changed irrevocably for all of us.

We met at our usual haunt, a bar called The Cobbler. Nobody knew where the name came from. If there had ever been a connection with shoemaking, or shoes, it had long since vanished. The nearest shoe store was half a kilometre away. Someone in the bar once suggested that cobbler was a type of drink, but that seemed unlikely.

The bar was in the basement of an old building on a busy street, and the noise of traffic and trams was a constant background. It was a dive. George, the owner, cultivated the bar's air of squalor, and understood that any attempt to improve it would turn it from a dive – which has a certain allure – into a dump, which is just a dump.

For one night a week I treated the sticky tables and the disgusting bathrooms as the price of the kick I got from drinking in a place like that with a man like Kilroy. I suspect that he, for his part, found me refreshingly unglamorous. In his eyes, my work at an insurance company made me an ordinary civilian, whose thoughts and feelings represented those of the general populace, from which Kilroy felt himself exiled by his police work. I served as a kind of litmus test for him. However, the process worked both ways, and in order to find out what I was thinking it was necessary for Kilroy to reveal what was on his own mind, which I found useful.

On this particular evening Kilroy looked tired. He'd obeyed his Chief's orders, and focused his efforts on finding Sheba, the fugitive daughter and presumed murderer. He suspected Roland of possessing more information about his sister than he'd divulged, but he'd been warned to lay off the boy.

Damn kids, Kilroy said to me, I've had about enough of them. Especially teenagers.

Hold on, I said, you told me the boy's only eleven. That hardly makes him a teenager.

Kilroy took a slug of his drink and regarded me balefully. I'm not talking about him, he said, I'm talking about the girl's friends. I went to her school. But I couldn't get anywhere, and I don't mind admitting it's bugging the hell out of me. I mean, correct me if I'm wrong, but don't kids of Sheba's age like to talk, especially the girls? Once you get them started, the problem is usually getting them to shut up, right? They gossip and chatter about each other, and they tell you who's got a crush on who, and who's their best friend, and who's not – until it all changes the next week, of course – but something screwy is going on at that school, believe me. OK, I know my personal experience of kids is limited, and so is yours, because…you know…

He trailed off and looked down at his drink. The fact that we were both childless was a topic we rarely mentioned, not because we avoided it with any particular sensitivity, but because there was nothing much to say. But now Kilroy seemed to have made himself uncomfortable, and I tried to lighten the mood.

Well, I said, I can understand how hurt you must have been when the young ladies didn't swoon and fall at your feet. Perhaps you should have shown them your gun. Or perhaps they were scared enough already, on account of a big, tough, handsome cop wanting to ask them a bunch of personal questions.

Kilroy threw me a sardonic look. I don't think they were scared, he said. Not of me, anyhow.

Of her?

Maybe. But not in the way you'd expect. It was more like

they were excited.

I thought about that for a moment. OK, I said, I guess it could be pretty exciting if your classmate is wanted for murder, and on the run.

Then why didn't they talk about it the way people usually do? You know how it is: they either say they never imagined the suspect to be capable of doing such a thing, because she always seemed like such a nice, quiet type, or they say they always thought there was something sinister about her and they're not at all surprised to discover she's a depraved, stone-cold killer. But not these kids. They didn't want to talk about the murder, or about Sheba. They were hiding something.

Maybe they didn't want to risk being implicated.

Kilroy drummed his fingers on the table. No, it wasn't that. I can tell when people are trying to cover their tracks and sell me a packet of crap, and these kids were playing a whole different game. That's what's eating me. I couldn't get a handle on what they were actually feeling. It's almost like they were...I don't know...in awe of her. And not just the kids. When I sat down with the woman who runs the place – the head teacher – I could hardly get a word out of her. It was like a bad first date. Eventually she grudgingly divulged that she'd had concerns about Sheba for some time, and when I asked her what she meant, exactly, she huffed something about her being a bad influence on the other students. OK, I said, like what? Naturally, I expected to hear the usual stuff about fooling around in class, neglecting her studies, forgetting homework, answering back, being disruptive, fighting in the playground— excuse me, what's so funny?

Nothing, I said. It's just that you seem very familiar with that kind of scholastic assessment. Are you by any chance quoting one of your own school reports?

Kilroy rubbed his chin. Well, it's true I wasn't exactly a model student, I guess. But anyhow, those weren't the type of problems the head teacher was getting from Sheba. Not at all. She said the girl was almost too quiet – in class, at any rate. But at other times she was always at the centre of a little huddle: everyone whispering, like they were cooking something up, but damned if she could find out what it was.

And how long had this been going on?

That's just it. She'd been this way for weeks, apparently. Maybe months. And check this: when I tried to find Sheba's designated class teacher – the one who had most contact with her – I discover the guy is on sick leave. So, I contact his home, and the wife tells me he's taken off. Gone fishing. Where? She has no idea. But definitely can't be reached. And not only that, but her poor, suffering husband is such a constant martyr to his nerves that he headed for the hills two weeks *before* the murder. Then I hear that a girl who's supposed to be Sheba's best friend is also absent from school, taken somewhere out east by her parents to visit a great-aunt at the end of her span. I did some checking, and it appears the old lady in question is taking her own sweet time about dying, and the family can't say when they'll be back. Now, all this may not add up to anything, and the fact that two people who were exceptionally close to the girl made themselves scarce a few days before she allegedly committed a murder – all that may be a coincidence, although it's the type that keeps me awake at night. But something's not right, I can feel it. I don't know what it is yet, but I'm sure as hell going to find out.

Good for you, I said. Trust your instincts, they're usually reliable.

Kilroy gave me a mock salute. Thank you, ma'am.

You're welcome, I said. But it sounds to me as though Sheba

was up to something, and whatever it was, it started well before the murder, and possibly before her father's execution. Perhaps even before his arrest. Which raises an interesting question, doesn't it?

Correct. Was it premeditated? Kilroy jabbed at the table. Did this girl plan to kill her mother?

I waited, not knowing if he expected an answer. He cocked his eyebrow at me. Well, I said, she packed her bags. That suggests she planned to leave.

She planned to leave, yes. But did she plan the killing?

Search me.

We both took a sip of our whisky. I looked around. It was quiet for a Saturday night, even though the streets outside were still crowded. I could see the ghostly shapes of feet and ankles passing the grime-caked windows that were little more than a series of horizontal slits just below the ceiling along one wall of the joint.

I leaned towards Kilroy. The girl, I said. Is she definitely the killer?

Kilroy gazed at me impassively. After a moment he picked up his glass and drained it. I should be out there, he said. Out there tracking her down, shouldn't I?

I shrugged, and drained my drink too.

When I returned from the bar Kilroy's hat was on the table in front of him. He was turning it around slowly and scowling at it, as if considering the best angle from which to assault it. He looked up as I placed his drink on the table, and moved the hat back onto the bench beside him.

He took a slug of whisky and shook his head. I don't know, he said.

I smiled at him. What don't you know, Kilroy?

Why I'm here.

In the existential sense?

That too, Kilroy said. But I was referring to the investigation. Why aren't I out there, beyond the city limits, trekking through the meadows, scouring the hillsides, scanning the far horizon in search of my quarry?

Because, I said, you're a city cop.

Exactly. I'm a city cop. But I've got my orders, so off I go.

When was the last time you were out there?

Kilroy picked up his glass and raised it to the light, squinting through it as if he were trying to see distant fields and forests beyond it. I'm not scared, he said. I was born out there, you know. I can find my way around.

I'd forgotten Kilroy was a country boy, but it made sense. Nobody loves the city like a hick who was born and bred outside it. That was probably why Kilroy's style was so old-school, with the hat, and the tie pin, and the polished wing-tip shoes.

Cheer up, I said, perhaps you'll come across a recently-widowed young farmer's wife, struggling to make ends meet. You'll help her fight off her predatory creditors, and in return she will teach you the ways of the wilderness, and eventually, after much devout soul-searching, take you shyly into her bed.

Kilroy gave me a deadpan stare. Fuck you, he said.

I stared back at him. He cracked first, and smiled despite himself. These were the moments I cherished with Kilroy.

He took a drink and wiped his mouth. I don't need any help, he said, with the ways of the wilderness. I can easily make it to the coast if I want to.

Which one?

Any of them, but I'm talking about the only one that matters, right? I mean, she's not heading west, is she, unless she's gone crazy, like her father. Even more crazy, she'd have to be, when you think about it.

South? I suggested.

Why? You get through the forest, you reach the sea, you turn around and come home. You're not going anywhere in a damn boat from there, are you? And if she goes north, she runs out of cover pretty soon, and from then on it's just a dull way to freeze to death, unless she packed a lot more than her pyjamas in that backpack. No, there's only one way she's heading.

He was right. She would take the usual escape route. There were forests and fields and settlements and farms to the east, all the way to the long sands before the coast. And then? Well, that was the interesting question.

OK, I said, when are you leaving?

There was a trace of bitterness in Kilroy's smile. Monday, he said.

He drank the rest of his whisky and stood up.

I stood up too and shrugged myself into my coat. I imagine, I said, I'll see you in church tomorrow?

You know you will, Ms Curtis, and I want to see you praying hard.

I always do.

Yeah, so pray for me, and for my skinny backside out there in the wild.

We exchanged a kiss on the cheek and went our separate ways.

KILROY

Kilroy sat at the back of the church, thinking bad thoughts.

Doubt was not a sin in itself, he knew, but it could lead to sin.

The priest himself had just said exactly that. He was only a few minutes into his sermon, but he was in good form. He'd begun with a strong denunciation of sin in general, and you can't go wrong with a reliable crowd-pleaser like that, Kilroy thought, even if it is a little predictable. But as the priest hit his stride it became clear he was going to come down with particular severity on the subject of heresy – and blasphemy, its inevitable consequence. For, he declaimed, is not heresy the wicked usurper of virtue, and blasphemy its handmaiden, capering lewdly at the foot of its foul throne?

This is what everyone had come to hear, and the congregation was attentive.

The priest declared he would be frank with them. There was no point pretending, he said, that blasphemy wasn't on the rise. They were all adults. He corrected himself, acknowledging there were children present. But what he meant, he said, his eyes searching out some of the youngsters in the church, and giving them a special smile, was that he trusted everyone, even the younger members of the congregation – especially them – to be mature about this problem.

It was impossible, he continued, to tackle the issue of blasphemy without putting it into a broader context. And nobody would deny – he looked around the huge church again, as if searching for anyone who cared to try it, and finding no candidates – no, nobody would deny that people were frightened. I myself, he said, am not ashamed to admit I'm frightened. But my faith sustains me! My faith is my sword, my shield, my pistol! And you too, my friends, you may take the same infallible refuge! For do we not have unshakable faith in the boundless compassion of Upstairs Mum and Dad?

He paused, allowing the worshippers to murmur their agreement. When he continued his voice was quieter and deeper. Some people had to lean forward to hear him, despite the loudspeakers placed throughout the church.

And why are we frightened, my friends? We all know the reasons. Even if you haven't seen it for yourself, you've heard that the sea appears to be retreating from our coasts. Naturally, that's worrying. It's happening slowly, but it is surely happening. In addition to this, it appears that skyflies are on the increase. I will take this opportunity, if I may, to confirm this as an official fact. The authorities would prefer you to know the truth. Rumour and fake news are harmful, and must be confronted with fact. Verified fact. Sightings of skyflies are up.

A ripple of unease spread through the pews. Verified: the top level of fact.

The priest held up his hand, and shook his head slowly with a smile. Brothers and sisters and others, he said, let us be of good cheer! Don't lose heart. You know the old saying, "Better the Devil you know than an unfamiliar proctologist with a hangover!" That got a laugh, as always. The priest waited until the congregation had settled itself, and when he spoke again his tone was soothing.

The important thing, he said, is to remain steadfast and calm. There's nothing wrong with asking questions, provided we trust the answers given by Upstairs Mum and Dad through the scriptures, by the grace of the blessed Shadbold. But once you open the door to doubt, my friends, you're on a slippery slope. The seed of doubt sprouts into the parasitic weed of heresy, which grows until it chokes the light and the life out of you.

Have we not seen, very recently, yet another of our dear brothers, who was led astray by doubt, betrayed into uttering the most dreadful blasphemy, and have we not seen the terrible consequence? He was sentenced to death! And was that decision right?

There were noises of assent from parts of the church, but not as many, or as loud, as Kilroy would have expected to hear.

The priest held up his hands and nodded. Yes. Of course it was. And do we regret it bitterly? Again, yes. It is a tragedy when a life does not complete its span. And now, to add to our concerns, foolish voices are raised, claiming that people are going wrong, and dying for no reason, before their time. Pay no heed, my friends. This is falsehood, pure and simple. Disdain it, as all sensible people do. But blasphemy is another matter. Blasphemy must be rooted out. We cannot allow our sacred faith to be violated!

The priest paused, dropped his gaze, and lowered his head. Kilroy couldn't tell whether he was doing it for dramatic effect, or consulting his notes.

When he looked up there was a smile on his lips. Perhaps, he said, it's time for some good news? I have another Verified Fact for you, friends.

The congregation perked up.

Three weeks ago, the priest said, the authorities shot down a skyfly.

He leaned back in the pulpit to enjoy the effect of his announcement. There were murmurs of satisfaction, and the more zealous members of the congregation looked as if they were having a hard time restraining the urge to applaud. Of course, applause was not permitted in the Landmass Church, although people claimed that the Reformers, in their temple on the other side of town, regularly indulged in applause, and even cheering, when they were particularly moved by the eloquence of their lecturers. It was ironic, people said, that while the Reformers were ostentatious in their disdain for the trappings of priesthood, and in their pose of humility, their lecturers were invariably vain men and women who basked in the recognition they so clearly craved. What hypocrites.

Kilroy knew this wasn't true. He'd attended Reform services a few times, when he was trying to ingratiate himself with a woman of that persuasion, and it was just as boring as sitting in the Landmass church. The lecturers were pretty similar to priests, except they wore ordinary clothes, and strode around among the congregation instead of ascending a pulpit to deliver their sermons. Otherwise it was same, and the humility of the lecturers, assumed or otherwise, didn't prevent them from being as well-paid as regular priests. Kilroy had no problem with that. Educators of any type, whether in schools or churches, were important members of society, and deserved to be rewarded. Only a fool would deny that. And while Kilroy may have had a restless spirit and a medium-sized helping of attitude around authority, he wasn't a fool.

When he finally got the Reform woman into bed, he discovered she would have been perfectly happy to fuck him the first time they met, but she thought he must have been a pious type, because he kept showing up at church, and she didn't want to shock him.

Kilroy snapped back into the present moment and tried to pay attention. He already knew about the skyfly, which was old news in the Interior Department. He also knew the authorities had learned nothing from it. They were no nearer to figuring out what the damned things were, and where they came from, than they were two years ago when they managed to shoot down the first one. This was the third, and the technology inside it looked exactly the same as the unfathomable shit inside the first two, according to the gossip around the office, although the insides of the first one had been badly damaged when they were trying to get it open. They'd been more careful since then, but it made no difference: they couldn't even determine whether a particular component was a power source, or a weapon, or a goddam kitchen appliance – or even a component at all. Some of what was in there appeared to be a kind of goop, that flowed around the whole system.

Kilroy became aware that people around him were nodding and smiling to each other with grim satisfaction. The priest was saying something about what the shooting down of the skyfly proved, and how everyone should give thanks.

This victory, he said, is not only a testament to the skill and courage of our brave defenders in the military, but also a sign of divine approval. Think of it! Only two short years ago it would have been unimaginable that we should be able to bring down one of those mysterious objects that streaked through the sky so many thousands of metres above us, beyond the farthest reach of our plucky gunners, and yet now we have succeeded. We have humbled the dark angels, and our doctors are on the verge of unlocking their secrets. This, my brothers, sisters and others, this is the power of faith!

Bullshit, thought Kilroy, but he stood up along with everyone else as the priest raised his arms, and intoned the blessing:

In the Name of our Upstairs Mum and Dad, through the Grace of the Blessed Shadbold, who is with us, and among us, and within us, we give thanks.

CURTIS

I didn't usually seek out Kilroy's company after church, especially if we'd met for a drink the previous evening, but I wanted to see him again before he hit the road.

I followed him out of a side exit, and when I emerged from the church I was accosted by a young man who handed me a leaflet. Everyone was being given one. Some people were standing by themselves, frowning as they absorbed its contents, and others were talking quietly in small groups. Families passed it around, and adults squatted down beside their younger offspring, explaining it to them with bright, nervous smiles. It was a short message on a single sheet of official paper. A decree:

VERIFIED STORY

*Our Upstairs Parents, in their wisdom and compassion,
gave Landmass to their children to shelter and provide for
us. Thanks be to them, and to the blessed Shadbold. But
certain ungrateful wretches have spread wicked falsehoods
concerning the supposed existence of another landmass,
beyond the vastness of the ocean. No such place exists. Those
who are foolish enough to set off in search of it invariably
perish in the limitless sea. Belief in this imaginary place,
commonly referred to as Landmass Two, has grown in recent
times into a dangerous mania, inflaming the passions of
the impressionable, and luring them from the path of Truth.
Therefore let it be known that from this day onwards ANY
expression, public or private, of credence in this contemptible
delusion will be treated as BLASPHEMY, and will meet with
the severest penalties that such a crime deserves.
In the name of our Upstairs Mum and Dad, through the
Grace of Shadbold.*

I looked around for Kilroy and discovered he was standing beside me.

Don't sneak up on me like that, I said.

Force of habit. Sorry.

It's OK, I said. Do you feel like talking?

Kilroy nodded curtly and jerked his thumb over his shoulder, and I followed him away from the church without saying anything. When we got to the bottom of the steps that led down to the riverside we strolled along the path beside the water until we reached a picnic area set back from the pathway. There was nobody around. We sat on a bench beneath a willow

31

tree and stretched our legs out. Just a middle-aged couple relaxing on a Sunday afternoon.

I held up the decree. What do you make of this?

Kilroy gazed at the river. Eventually he said, Why now?

Yes, I said, it's a strange time to be burning bridges. Or is that the right metaphor for what they're doing?

Kilroy made a wavering gesture with his hand. Maybe, he said, but I'd call it more like doubling down. Landmass Two? No way, folks. No way, no how.

You'd think, I said, they wouldn't want to shut that story down quite so firmly right now. I mean, it's just going to make people ask more questions about the skyflies, isn't it? They're going to say, OK, if not from Landmass Two, then where? If they're being sent by the badders, where the hell are they hiding?

That, Kilroy said, is exactly what they'll say. They're already saying it. Have been for some time, and it just doesn't make sense to stir things up like this. The last thing we need is another wave of hysteria about the badders.

The pink peril.

Kilroy frowned. The what?

Pink peril. That's what people are calling them. The latest catchphrase, or meme, or whatever. Because of the old stories about the badders being pink.

Kilroy shook his head in amused disbelief.

And it's not a good time for hysteria, I said, what with so many other things to worry about. Especially these awful rumours of people going wrong, and dropping dead before their span. Have you actually seen that? I mean, in person?

Kilroy pulled a mock-horrified face. You heard what the priest said, didn't you? Disdain such contemptible gossip!

I laughed. He wasn't going to be drawn on that subject, so

I tried another one. What about your fugitive, I said, do you think she'll try to get to the coast?

And do what? said Kilroy. Steal a boat and sail away to fairyland? Fuck knows. I hope not, for her sake.

Poor girl. She may not even know she'd be committing blasphemy now, just by thinking of such a thing.

Kilroy snorted, then we sat in silence.

I cleared my throat. I'm assuming, I said, that you already knew about this latest skyfly they brought down?

Kilroy threw me a what-do-you-think look, and turned back to the river.

Oh well, I said, it's good to know our tech has advanced so miraculously that we can now shoot them down from way up in the blue yonder with such skill. It gives your confidence a real boost, doesn't it?

Kilroy turned to me and dropped his voice: Yeah, we all know that's bullshit, but so what? Those three flies we got were low and slow, and personally I don't believe it was because they were faulty, either. I think something else is going on. But until we find out what they're really for, it's all guesswork. You can't tell much from the innards, that's what I hear.

Perhaps, I said, they're toying with us for their own amusement.

Kilroy turned back to gaze at the water, and began pulling at his earlobe. Maybe it's… he began, but then he stopped, and gave his ear some more punishment. Finally he muttered, It's almost as if…

As if what? I prompted.

He turned to me abruptly. Nothing, he said. Forget it. Look, I've got things to do before I leave.

He stood up.

I got to my feet and faced him. I knew what was coming

next, but I wanted to hear him say it.

Kilroy gave me a sheepish glance then looked down. It would be great, he murmured, if you could find the time to go and feed the bird.

I let him stew for a moment. I wanted him to consider the fact that I was probably the only person he could ask. He had colleagues on the force he was friendly with, but they weren't the kind of people who would respond well to a request to feed his parrot. And there was probably a woman somewhere, as there usually was at any given time. Or a man, or an other. Or all of the above. Kilroy was an all-of-the-above type.

He must have known I still found him attractive. I didn't mind. There were a couple of people I could see if I felt lonely. One of them was a woman I played squash with, after which we took a shower together and gave each other some attention. I also met her for a coffee sometimes, as she was a very sweet, innocent person. The other was a man who happened to be my supervisor, which was awkward, and pretty corny, but he knew how to turn me on, so I made my choices when I needed to.

And I had no real objection to going into Kilroy's apartment when he was away for any length of time, and feeding Creek, his parrot. I didn't particularly like the creature, but it was well-behaved. Whenever Kilroy knew he was likely to be away for more than a couple of days he let the bird out of its cage, and when I made my visits it just perched on the edge of the table, next to its food bowl, and looked at me beadily. If I forgot to replenish its water it would tap on the edge of the cup, and shove it slowly across the table towards me, holding my gaze impassively. Sometimes it would speak. A few times, just before I left, it would cock its head and say, Thank you, and wink, which I found a bit unnerving. But it was no trouble to me really.

No problem, I said to Kilroy, I've got my keys.

Thanks, he said, and moved in for a hug.

I sat back down after he left, and thought over our conversation about the flies, and how he'd almost puzzled it out, and very nearly told me. Kilroy may not have been the brightest candle in the gas leak, but he usually got there in the end.

KILROY

Kilroy took a tram to the city limits and hired a car. The streets at the edge of town offered plenty of options, and he got a competitive price on a reasonably new model that would only need to be recharged every couple of hundred kilometres. He wasn't spending his own money, but he took pride in holding out for a good deal and staying within his departmental budget. As he drove away he noted with satisfaction that the car handled as nicely as he'd expected it to.

Kilroy felt good. He knew he shouldn't really be in a holiday mood, but travelling out of the city and seeing the sky open up in front of him softened the edges of his habitual alertness. Tracking down a murderer was a serious business, no doubt about it, and Kilroy wasn't planning to get so relaxed that he made any foolish mistakes, but the countryside looked good.

The weather was mild, the clouds were chasing each other, and the air was fresh. There was a lot to like about being alive.

Every five kilometres Kilroy passed a public screen that was showing a storyline on a loop. Each time the car came within range, a light on the dashboard flashed, advising him to stop. He pulled in at the next screen and parked in the viewing area. In theory he would have been forced to stop anyway if he'd driven past two more screens, and the car would be disabled until the loop had run three full cycles, just to make sure he paid attention. Kilroy knew how to override the disable signal, but he wanted to watch, and see how they were handling things.

The storyline was about the blasphemy decree. A woman in her thirties and an older male priest were hosting the story. The woman was attractive in a wholesome way, and the priest had a chubby face and a set of whiskers which gave him a comically benevolent appearance. He reminded Kilroy of someone, and after a moment it slid into his memory: the priest resembled Mister Pilliwink from the much-loved series of children's books.

The two hosts were surrounded by a dozen people, selected carefully to represent a full spectrum of the populace. Pigmentation ranged from the typical milky-coffee skin of northerners to the darker shades of the south. Five of the group were a family: mother, father, three kids. The whole thing was staged in a homely domestic setting, with the implication that everyone had dropped by to visit the family.

The priest beamed, and the two parents nodded encouragingly at the children, while the young woman did most of the talking. Her tone was earnest but reassuring. She spoke for a couple of minutes about the need to cherish and protect every member of society, even people you didn't like. She mentioned tolerance, compassion, spiritual hygiene; the danger of doubt and sin, and the threat of heresy expressed through blasphemy.

Then the text of the decree filled the screen, and she read it out, then the domestic scene reappeared.

The priest said a few words about faith, and a few more about how the best way to conquer blasphemy was to deny it a voice. On this cue, everyone made the lip-zipping sign, then the woman smiled and told everyone that everything would be all right. They all recited the manifest, pointing a finger skywards as they said, In the Sacred Name of our Upstairs Parents, Blessed Mum and Dad; then they placed a hand over their heart as they intoned, By the Grace of Shadbold, who is with us, and among us, and within us.

Kilroy was impressed by how they all chanted and made the signs in unison, but not with absolute precision, so it didn't look over-rehearsed.

The loop began to repeat, and he got back into the car.

He drove another forty kilometres and turned off the main road. He was following the most likely route Sheba would have taken, and heading for a small town with a population of around eight thousand. It was the first useful turn-off a fugitive would take, and for that reason unlikely to be fruitful. Too obvious, especially for someone like Sheba. However, he had to check it out.

Before he'd left the city he reviewed the available information on the case. Nearly all of it was inconclusive; much of it was speculative, and some of it was infuriating garbage. There was very little hard data. No record of Sheba hiring a vehicle, and no reports of her ID or likeness from any buses or long-haul trams. No reports of anyone resembling her seen begging a ride at the side of the road. But so what? People could alter their ID, and disguise their image, and find ways to silence those who gave them rides. However, the very lack of a data-trail told Kilroy that Sheba was smart enough, and determined enough, to take effective evasive action. He wasn't likely to find her at the side of the road, defeated and forlorn, with her appearance unaltered, ready to turn herself in. He was hunting a quarry who was resourceful enough to make the job tough for him.

The game was afoot. Whatever that meant. One of his teachers used to employ the phrase, and had once explained its origin, but Kilroy had forgotten it, along with pretty much everything else he was taught at school. The only things he remembered well were from kindergarten. The image of Mister Pilliwink, for example, and the other characters in the series: Slippery Sam, The Dozzlers, and Elmer the Catcher. Damned if he could remember the titles of the books, though. So much useless crap ended up swilling around your mind, while the education that was actually useful, about how to think straight, had to be acquired once you were out in the world.

For half an hour he drove through a monotonous landscape of white sunfields on his left, and food farms to the right, their flat, uniform acres stretching to the horizon. Kilroy remembered this region from his childhood, when it was on the route his family took for their occasional visits to the city. In those days there had still been patches of woodland and meadow between the food farms, and some of the land where the sunfields now stood had not yet been levelled. But the city had grown, along with the population – until recently, if you believed the rumours – and the food and power required by all those people had to come from somewhere.

Kilroy didn't feel nostalgic about the changes. He'd always experienced mixed emotions on those boyhood trips, knowing the excitement he felt on approaching the city would end up being stifled by the frustration of being with his mother, who never wanted to do anything that interested him, while his dad remained taciturn and non-committal, going along with his wife's preferences. Then, on the return journey, his disappointment curdled into a sense of resentment, until Kilroy became sulky and listless, and his parents abandoned their half-hearted attempts to cheer him up, and probably thought he was an ungrateful little nuisance.

It was while Kilroy was in the process of disengaging himself from these memories, having decided he'd spent enough time with them, that he got the distinct feeling he was being followed.

He checked his rear-view mirror. The long, straight road behind him was empty. There had been very little traffic and Kilroy was surprised by how few vehicles he'd seen. He slowed down. A distant speck appeared in the mirror. Kilroy reduced his speed a little more and watched as the vehicle gradually crept closer. It appeared to be a van or small truck. Kilroy kept his speed steady. When the vehicle was only a few metres away it pulled out and overtook him smoothly. The driver made no noticeable effort to accelerate, and as he drew level with Kilroy he glanced towards him and gave him a polite nod, smiling pleasantly. Kilroy inclined his head briefly in response, and smiled back.

Two travelling men, exchanging the courtesies of the road.

As the vehicle pulled away from him Kilroy saw it was a delivery van for a food company, with a sign on the back advertising top-quality mizzet.

And still he had a strong sense of being followed. He slowed down and pulled off the road at the side of a field. When he stepped out of the car he found himself enclosed in a stillness that extended to the horizon in every direction. The only sound was a faint metallic ticking as the car settled down. Kilroy's senses prickled. He trusted his intuitions, and they'd kept him out of danger in the past, and helped him prepare for it when it was unavoidable. He couldn't shake his feeling of unease. Even if he wasn't being followed, he was being watched. He was sure of it. But by whom, and from where? There was nowhere to hide for as far as the eye could see. Not even a distant watchtower.

He got back into the car.

Kilroy arrived in the small town of S— just after midday. It was a strange name for a town, to be sure, but there it was, on the map. Its inhabitants referred to it simply by making a short hissing sound.

There were three hotels in the town. The one Kilroy had booked into wasn't the most expensive, but it wasn't the cheapest either, and he was irritated when nobody emerged to take his case as he carried it up the steps. The case wasn't particularly heavy, and Kilroy preferred to carry it himself anyway, but it was the principle of the thing.

The scene that greeted him in the lobby explained the lack of assistance. It was deserted except for a bellboy who was sprawled in an armchair, fast asleep. As soon as Kilroy's eye fell upon him he woke up, as if alerted by telepathy, and scrambled to his feet. He had the appearance of an elderly child, with the wizened features, diminutive stature, and bow-legged gait common to all bellboys.

Without a word he scampered to the reception desk and

disappeared into a room behind it. Kilroy heard a muffled thud. The bellboy reappeared, closely followed by a prim little man in a tailcoat, stifling a yawn and pushing his spectacles up his nose.

The little fellow took care of the registration process swiftly, and in a matter of minutes Kilroy was handing a tip to the bellboy in a perfectly acceptable room on the third floor. The bellboy gave no outward sign that he was dissatisfied with the tip, and yet somehow he contrived to express his contempt for it.

Kilroy decided to take a short nap before visiting the town's chief of police, and the door to his room was scarcely closed before he was snoring on the bed.

He woke up twenty-five minutes later feeling seedy and disoriented, and set out immediately, on foot, to the police chief's office, hoping to shake off his lethargy by the time he got there.

His destination turned out to be a large municipal building at the far end of the town square. In a final attempt to dispel the languor that still oppressed him he ran up the steps to the seventh floor, where he was escorted into the chief's office, breathing heavily, by a secretary.

The chief gave the impression he'd been waiting for him. He smiled blandly, pushed himself up out of large, well-upholstered chair, and waddled around his desk with a hand outstretched. Kilroy shook it, noting the chief had a surprisingly firm grip for such a corpulent person. Something about his bearing and manner suggested a military background, despite his elaborately coiffed hair and the string of lustrous pearls that complemented his taupe ball gown. He introduced himself as Brogan Livermore – clearly an assumed name, which made

Kilroy suspect the man had spent his military career in the intelligence service.

The chief returned to his seat and despatched the secretary to fetch them some coffee. Kilroy sat down on the other side of the desk, took several folders from his briefcase, and placed them in front of him. The chief matched his bid by removing an equally large number of folders from a drawer in the desk and slapping them down with grim satisfaction. Kilroy gazed at him expressionlessly.

Hell of a mess, the chief said, looking pleased.

Kilroy asked if he was referring to the murder.

Oh, unpleasant, of course, the chief replied with a wave of his hand, but I'm talking about the whole investigation.

Kilroy stiffened in his chair.

I don't mean you, the chief said, giving Kilroy a shrewd glance, I'm talking about all the sightings. I don't know what gets into people.

Kilroy relaxed his guard. He had to agree. Before he'd left the city the reports had already become so numerous that he'd directed a junior officer to sift through them and filter out the more obviously deranged ones, which turned out to be a lot of them. People claimed to have spotted Sheba everywhere, and identified her in a number of highly improbable guises. Some of the informants were clearly trying to settle old scores by casting suspicion on various neighbours or shopkeepers against whom they held a grievance, and a few seemed intent on denouncing members of their own families.

If you want my opinion, Livermore said, the big mistake was to put out information that the girl may have changed her appearance.

Tell me about it, Kilroy said. It wasn't my choice, believe me. But what can you do when people who live behind a desk make important operational decisions that compromise our work in the field?

Livermore sighed and leaned back, shaking his head.

The two men had taken the measure of each other, and now they slipped into their familiar roles. They were cops: tough but reasonable professionals who chafed at the bureaucratic restrictions which hindered them in the exercise of their duty, but loyal to their job and their colleagues, no matter what. They knew how things were. One of them was wearing a dress, and Kilroy had no problem with that. Hell, he himself was partial, on occasion, to slipping into nicely-made, loose-fitting clothes when he got home after a hard day.

Livermore slid a picture across the desk. It was a copy of the photo of Sheba that had been sent down the wires to regional police departments, post offices, churches and schools. Livermore tapped it with a pudgy finger.

It's bad enough, he said, when it's just a regular picture. But some joker in the city department has been sending mock-ups of how she might look now, and they're an open invitation for every crank and headcase in my area to report they've seen her disguised as everything from a postman to a fence post.

I know, Kilroy said, and a ton of that crap has been flooding into head office. And while I'm not surprised by sightings that suggest she's changed her skin pigment, or lost a leg, or grown a beard, the ones that give me a throbbing headache are from people who seem to believe a thirteen-year-old girl, specifically described as being one-point-five metres in height, can somehow grow by fifty centimetres, or shrink by an equal amount. But what can you do?

Livermore chuckled sympathetically. Then they got down to business.

An hour later Kilroy walked out with five folders, each containing a lead to be followed up, representing what remained after he and Livermore had whittled down twenty times that many possibilities. Of the five leads, Kilroy thought two were just about plausible, two might prove worthwhile, and one was a wild card.

The town's municipal jurisdiction extended over a wide area. Kilroy marked the location of each lead on a map, and set off in the car to visit the most distant one first, intending to work his way back by a route that formed a spiral on the map, at the centre of which was his hotel. That shape pleased him.

After driving for more than an hour he reached the homestead where someone had reported the recent arrival of a female farmhand, who, they claimed, was 'acting furtive'. Kilroy had no difficulty locating the girl in question, working in a field adjacent to a ramshackle farmhouse. She was at least twice the age of the person he was seeking, and scarcely possessed the intelligence to answer the simple general-knowledge questions Kilroy habitually employed to break the ice and evaluate a suspect, let alone to try and throw him off the scent. His instinct told him she was being exploited by the farm's owner, and he made a mental note to send a social inspector out there. He would need to put the order through Livermore's office, but he hoped the rapport he'd built up with the chief would stand him in good stead for the request.

His next lead concerned a girl who'd been seen apparently living rough, just outside a small settlement. When Kilroy questioned the locals their descriptions of the girl were wildly contradictory. Eventually the owner of the house nearest the girl's alleged campsite, who had spotted her first, conceded that what he'd seen might not have been a girl at all, but a tree or a bush, moving in the wind. At this, the other witnesses, who had gathered around Kilroy, changed their stories and began suggesting Kilroy should arrest the householder for being a habitual liar and a damned nuisance.

The third folder led Kilroy to a toll-keeper and her husband, to investigate a report that a girl had been seen coming and going from their tiny cottage in the night. It soon became apparent that this girl was the couple's daughter, who'd left the area several weeks previously, and moved to the city. She returned a few days later, having changed her mind, then changed it again and departed once more. The parents showed Kilroy a cramped bedroom, preserved just as their daughter had left it. They were convinced she would soon come home again for good, suitably chastened and disillusioned by city life.

Kilroy's next lead was a dead end, literally. The road became a dirt track, which stopped at the edge of an area of scrubland. The address he'd been given was a derelict building that was little more than a pile of rubble. It was one of a handful of similar ruins, which might once have formed a small hamlet.

This report had been the most detailed and plausible of the five. Amid the desolation Kilroy discerned the phantoms of buildings which the informant had depicted in lively detail, conjuring up a small, thriving community of artisans and traders, among whom the missing girl was hiding. The anonymous informant described meeting a girl whose appearance matched Sheba's with close but casual accuracy, and being worried about the lonely youngster. The account was qualified with disclaimers, saying its author was probably mistaken, and the girl seemed friendly and bright, and perhaps she was guilty of nothing worse than homelessness, or just restlessness, you know how young folks are. The report was a fabrication of a kind calculated to excite a detective's interest, and Kilroy wondered if the informant was an ex-cop. He had long since ceased to be surprised by the elaborate lengths to which people would go in order to perpetrate hoaxes, but their motives for doing so, in cases where no money, attention, infamy or glory would accrue to them, remained as opaque to him as they had always been.

Perhaps, Kilroy thought as he drove away from the ruins, the informant truly believed in the narrative they'd located in an imaginatively repopulated abandoned settlement, and the account was a kind of ghost story.

The final call on Kilroy's schedule was the wild card. The informant had identified himself as someone called Mercury, and provided an address on the outskirts of S—, only a mile from Kilroy's hotel in the centre of town.

He pulled up outside a house in a comfortable suburb, and reviewed the contents of the folder. It contained a two-page letter, carefully handwritten in language that was oddly formal. However, it contradicted itself in several places. The author began by asserting that a girl had been stealing food from his kitchen during the night, but he didn't explain how he knew the culprit was a girl, as he hadn't actually seen the intruder. Then he claimed he'd caught a glimpse of her the following night, from the top of the staircase. The description he provided matched, almost word for word, the details circulated by the police. Then, at the end of the paragraph, he mentioned it was very dark and he hadn't been able to see her properly.

And yet something about the letter had snagged Kilroy's attention. Perhaps it was a single, striking detail: the informant claimed to have heard the girl weeping quietly.

Kilroy got out of the car and stood under a tree that was still in blossom, filling his lungs. It was early evening.

The door was answered by a man of around forty. He had the look of someone just home from work, who was hoping to get a little peace and quiet before dinner.

Kilroy introduced himself and showed his ID.

The man frowned. He gave his name as Frobisher.

Kilroy asked if someone called Mercury lived in the house.

The man shook his head, puzzled. Then his expression cleared, but not in a good way. He turned and called over his shoulder, Honey!

A woman of about his age emerged from a room behind him. When she saw Kilroy she slowed down and approached warily, remaining just behind the man who, Kilroy felt it safe to assume, was her husband. As they both gazed silently at him, Kilroy heard the sound of feet running up a staircase and a door slamming.

The woman sighed. You'd better come in, she said.

The couple told Kilroy that Mercury was the name of their son's imaginary friend, or one of them. It was the son, Julian, who had run upstairs, and was currently hiding under the bedclothes in his room. He had a habit, they said, of writing letters to the authorities, in the guise of his non-existent chums.

Julian's parents seemed more exasperated than angry, and when Frobisher assured Kilroy he would punish his son, Kilroy suspected the punishment would not be severe. As Frobisher's wife, Gloriana, spoke of their son's lively imagination, and the careful research he put into his letters, Kilroy heard more pride in her voice than censure. When the couple went on to speak of their son's sadness that he didn't have a brother or sister, despite their best efforts to provide him with one, it was their own yearning that inflected their voices. Kilroy sensed a wistfulness that seemed to fill the room like mist, as Gloriana turned away to gaze out of the window at the soft evening light.

Tell me, she said quietly, do you have children, detective Kilroy?

No, ma'am.

Gloriana nodded slowly, still gazing out at the fading light.

Her husband cleared his throat. Have you never considered it, sir?

Kilroy hesitated. As it happens, he said, it seems I'm unable to have children.

Oh, I'm so sorry, Gloriana said.

She exchanged a pained glance with her husband. Frobisher turned to Kilroy with an awkward smile, and produced a series of muted humming noises that were undoubtedly intended to convey sympathy.

Kilroy had surprised himself. Something about this nice couple had encouraged him to disclose a very personal matter of which he rarely spoke. Now he regretted it, not because he felt exposed by the admission, but because the delicacy of the topic had left them all feeling embarrassed.

At that moment the street lamps came on, changing the atmosphere in the room.

Frobisher stood up to close the curtains. When he sat down again a small boy was standing in the doorway, staring at his feet. He shuffled forward until he was directly in front of Kilroy. He didn't raise his eyes. I'm sorry, he muttered.

Speak up, Julian, his father said.

Kilroy quickly raised a warning hand to silence Frobisher. He leaned towards the boy and tried to make his voice suitably stern: Don't do it again, son. Will you promise me?

Julian nodded but said nothing. He was about to turn away when Kilroy found himself reaching for the boy's hand, and grasping it gently. It's all right, he said.

The boy shot him a glance from beneath his lowered brows, and Kilroy saw the trace of a smile. He gave the boy's hand a squeeze – which Julian returned with almost imperceptible pressure – before he released it, and the child trotted out of the room.

I'd better be on my way, Kilroy said.

As he walked into the hallway the doorbell rang.

Frobisher edged past Kilroy and opened the front door. An elderly woman with white hair and a plump, pleasant face was on the doorstep. It's time, she said.

Gloriana emerged from the front room. Good grief, she exclaimed, is that you already, Nina? Is it happening?

Yes, the old lady said, he's just getting ready. Are you coming?

Frobisher stepped back from the door and introduced Kilroy to Nina, and told him she lived in the house next door. When Nina heard Kilroy was a police detective her face lit up. Oh, she cried, do come! Please do! My Roger always had great respect for police officers, and he wanted to join the force himself, you know, but… She trailed off, and gave Kilroy a regretful smile.

Frobisher took Kilroy by the elbow and steered him away from the woman in the doorway. Look, he said in a low voice, I don't want to put you in an awkward position. If you'd prefer not to, I'm sure they'll understand.

No, Kilroy said, I'll be happy to drop by.

That's very kind of you, Frobisher said, and you don't have to stay until the end. But it would mean a lot to both of them.

You know how it is with some folks: they like to have a whole bunch of people in for a dying, and old Roger was always a gregarious type. A terrific host. And a very decent man, as it happens, and a good neighbour. He'll really appreciate you being there, even for a little while.

Kilroy nodded. He didn't particularly want to attend a dying, but at this moment he didn't feel he had much choice about it.

It was lucky that Nina and Roger had a large front room. The dying was well underway, and Kilroy estimated there were around forty people present. Roger, the departing man, was propped up in a bed at the far end of the room. He looked radiant, partly because of the natural sheen the skin acquired as the end approached, but partly because he seemed so happy. His dark eyes sparkled, and his smile was full of good cheer.

It appeared that the old man had made it to the very end of his window: the full eighty-three years. His coppery skin was deeply creased and wrinkled but it looked soft, giving his face the appearance of a walnut made of velvet.

Nina made her way to the bedside and whispered in Roger's ear. He peered in Kilroy's direction, and beamed. He raised a trembling hand. What an honour, he said in a quavering voice, to have you in my home, detective. Thank you so much for joining us!

Kilroy smiled at him. My privilege, sir, he said, and tipped his hat, which seemed to tickle the old boy no end. He whispered something to his wife, who glanced at Kilroy, then nodded to Roger.

Roger pushed himself up a little, helped by his wife. On a case, detective?

Yes sir, Kilroy said, I'm on the trail of a fugitive.

A fugitive! The old man was delighted. Imagine that, he chortled, Detective Kilroy is on the trail, and he's right here!

He sank back in the bed and closed his eyes. The effort of speaking to Kilroy seemed to have taken a toll on him. Nina looked around the room, and everyone moved a little closer, murmuring quietly.

That was when Kilroy saw the woman.

She was on the other side of Roger's bed, at the edge of the crowd. She looked about Kilroy's age or a little younger. She was tall, with short hair and light skin. She was looking directly at Kilroy, and he felt penetrated by her clear, steady gaze. Her eyes were extraordinary. They were blue, which was unusual, but there was something about their shape, too, which made them look especially wide, and rounder than most. Kilroy felt a thrill of attraction. She held his gaze for a long time before looking away, turning her attention to the old man in the bed.

Roger's breathing had changed, and his eyes were closed. Nina put her lips close to his ear, but in the stillness that had settled on the room Kilroy could hear her whispered question, asking Roger if he wanted everyone to stay, or just close friends and family.

Old friends, he muttered, and family.

Nina looked up with a smile. Several people began to move away from the bed, some of them calling out to Roger affectionately as they shuffled towards the door:

Sleep well!

See you next time around, you old rogue!

Take it easy upstairs, someone said, then got a laugh by putting on a shrill voice and saying, Don't break anything up there!

Roger chuckled quietly.

The end was near. Kilroy raised his hat to Nina, and she

whispered to Roger, whose lips twitched with the trace of a smile. Kilroy turned away. Frobisher caught his glance, and nodded in the direction of his house, raising his eyebrows. Kilroy shook his head and lifted a hand in farewell, then joined the throng making its way out of the door. He glanced back at the people who remained in the room, and couldn't see the woman among them, and thought maybe he'd find her outside. But when he stepped through the door and looked around he couldn't see her. People were drifting away, to their homes or cars, and there was no sign of her. Somehow he'd missed her.

Kilroy stood there until he began to feel foolish, then made for his car.

It was late when Kilroy got back to the hotel, and the restaurant had just closed. However, the maître d' saw him peering through the glass doors, and arranged for him to be given a plate of cold farge. Kilroy took it to his room, and when he'd finished eating he spent half an hour writing up his notes, then went to bed.

He fell asleep thinking about the woman he'd seen.

He woke up early, and as the inky sleep drained from his mind her image was still there, emerging like a statue exposed by a dark, receding tide.

After a hurried breakfast Kilroy used the phone beside his bed to call to Brogan Livermore, intending to give him a brief account of the leads he'd followed up, and their failure to yield anything useful.

Chief Livermore answered the phone sounding breathless, and explained he'd been doing his morning exercises. He added that he was, at that moment, wearing a tailored silk pyjama-suit in what he described as shimmering dusky orange.

That sounds nice, Kilroy said.

Thank you. I'll be in something more formal by the time you arrive, of course.

Arrive where?

Here, Livermore said with a trace of irritability. I'm expecting you at nine. That's what we arranged when you phoned me last night. Don't you remember?

Kilroy was puzzled. He knew he hadn't phoned Livermore the previous night. He'd been very tired. Just remind me, he said, what we spoke about, will you?

Livermore sighed. You said you'd had no luck with the leads, and I commiserated with you, and said that I, on the contrary, had discovered something utterly extraordinary.

And what was it?

I'm not going to tell you over the phone! As I intimated last night, Detective Kilroy, it concerns your own safety, among other matters. That's why we arranged to meet this morning and speak in person. Are you sure you're all right?

I'm fine, Kilroy said, just a little…hungover. Sorry.

Ah, you investigators, Livermore chuckled. You lead quite the wild life, don't you?

Before Kilroy could reply he heard a commotion on the other end of the line.

Excuse me, Livermore said to him abruptly, something has just come up. It won't take long. I'll see you at nine, as arranged.

The line went dead.

As Kilroy turned the corner into the town square he saw that some kind of incident had taken place. Without breaking stride he veered to his left and entered the colonnaded walkway that surrounded the square. He slowed his pace, and stopped about halfway along, peering around a pillar to watch the scene.

Four uniformed cops were erecting barriers to keep a small crowd of bystanders away from an area in front of the municipal building at the far end of the square. More people were arriving all the time, craning forward and asking those in front of them what had happened. As they received information, they peered up at the seventh-floor balcony, then down at the cobbled courtyard beneath it, where two plain-clothes officers were huddled around something that was being examined by a woman in a white coat. As the woman stood up and the plain-clothes cops took a step back Kilroy saw what it was.

Brogan Livermore had landed at the foot of the steps in front of the building, and what Kilroy glimpsed was not so much a corpse as a mound of flesh with a head near the top. Livermore's ample body, no longer supported by a rigid structure of bones, or constrained by the fragile seams of his orange silk pyjamas, had…spread. It was as if a huge, gorgeous cake had been flung from the top of the building by a pastry-chef in a fit of petulance.

Kilroy saw a man and woman emerge from the building and walk down the steps. They looked completely unremarkable, which was why Kilroy observed them closely. Their ordinariness was contrived to deflect attention, but Kilroy recognised something in their bearing, and the economy of their movements, and the way their eyes swept the area unhurriedly, scanning, absorbing, assessing. He didn't doubt they belonged to a special services unit.

The couple approached one of the newly-erected barriers and a police officer held it aside. They slipped unobtrusively into the crowd, moving through the press of bodies with scarcely a ripple of disturbance.

Kilroy turned away and began to retrace his steps swiftly.

A movement caught his eye on the other side of the square. A figure was keeping pace with him in the colonnaded walkway parallel to his own, matching his stride. It was a woman. As Kilroy watched her, appearing and disappearing between the pillars, she turned her head to look at him. It was the woman he'd seen the previous evening, and whose image had haunted him since then.

Kilroy experienced a sharp blow to his groin as he collided with a shopping cart being pushed by an elderly man, who cursed him genially and walked on. When Kilroy turned his watering eyes once again to the colonnades on the other side of the square there was no sign of the woman.

He returned by an indirect route to his car. He'd taken the habitual precaution of parking a couple of streets away from the hotel, and he didn't go back there to collect his suitcase. Five minutes after reaching the car he was beyond the town boundaries, keeping a close eye on the rear-view mirror.

Kilroy drove east, through a landscape that was still flat and featureless. To his left the outline of distant foothills was visible: the beginning of a curving range whose tail he would cross if he continued all the way to the coast, two hundred kilometres away.

But his next stop was closer. He was heading for a place called Town, whose name originated in the days when there were only two major conurbations on Landmass: a city and a town. Both had increased in size, but Town, with a current population of around three hundred thousand, was still the smaller of the two.

It was bisected by a river that had its source in the hills, and was one of the features that made Town attractive. It was less busy and stressful than the city, but the river was wide enough to support some commercial trade, while being sufficiently placid to offer many leisure opportunities. Among those who found it congenial were both retirees and younger people involved in artistic and cultural pursuits, and this combination also contributed to the town's agreeable atmosphere. It was altogether a very pleasant spot, if you liked that kind of thing.

It also happened to be where Kilroy's father lived.

Strictly speaking his old man lived outside Town, just beyond the suburbs, where the roads narrowed and you began to notice the telephone poles.

The house had a large garden which Kilroy's dad, Sylvester, liked to call a parcel of land, where he grew crops. This caused tension between him and Kilroy, who tried to turn a blind eye to the fact that Sylvester was committing a crime.

It hadn't always been a crime. When Kilroy was at school he'd learned that the ancestors had grown food for themselves, as a matter of necessity, and their resourcefulness was to be admired. But as his education progressed, every mention of this enterprising agricultural spirit gradually disappeared from the curriculum, and from each new edition of Kilroy's textbooks, as they were updated. By the time he left school he was being taught that crop cultivation by individual citizens undermined the integrity of the market. Not long afterwards, such activity was classed as a misdemeanour.

Kilroy's father was contemptuous of these developments. Sylvester was damned if he was going to stop cultivating his little plot, where he grew farge, mizzet and spood.

In his heart Kilroy felt his old man was right. What harm could it do? But Kilroy was a cop – a career he'd pursued in the face of strong discouragement from his father, as he used to remind Sylvester in the days when they still argued about these things. It was easier to ignore the issue now. Kilroy didn't visit very often, and if it meant subduing his conscience as he sat at the dinner table and ate the food that Sylvester sourced from his crops, he could live with it, especially as the meals were generally delicious. That was one thing, at least, which had improved now that Sylvester lived alone.

Kilroy's mother had been killed twelve years ago in a croquet accident, but his father, at seventy-eight, was very much alive. However, there was no getting around the fact that he was three years from the beginning of his window, and during the last couple of years Kilroy had noticed that while his dad was as vigorous as ever when it came to digging the soil, he was less bothered about actually planting any crops. In fact, the act of digging seemed to have become an end in itself. The holes were getting deeper, and some were more like wells, interconnected by a system of trenches. It struck Kilroy that perhaps it was the digging his father had enjoyed all along, and now his hobby had become a mania.

Kilroy came to a decision. He'd been planning to visit the old place after conducting his investigations in the region. But now he realised the prospect would prey on his mind, and distract him. Best to do it first. He took the next turning off the main road, and drove towards the house where he'd been born.

KILROY

It was early afternoon when Kilroy pulled up outside the old house. He killed the engine, opened the windows, and enjoyed the silence.

He tried to identify any changes that had taken place since his last visit, almost two years ago. The borders of the long gravel driveway that extended down to the road were as neatly trimmed as ever. His father devoted a lot of care to the front garden, and Kilroy half expected to find Sylvester working out there, stripped to the waist. It was a sight that had often greeted him upon his arrival in the past. He suspected that, in recent years, whenever his old man heard a car approaching up the driveway he removed his shirt, grabbed a spade, and rushed into the garden, just in time to present a picture of youthful virility to anyone who was arriving.

Kilroy got out of the car and leaned against it. He noticed there were two large holes in the front garden. That was something new. His father had always confined his digging to the land behind the house, but now, it seemed, a line had been crossed. He straightened up and put his jacket on.

As he approached the veranda, the house door opened and his dad emerged. Kilroy trotted up the steps, and they shook hands. Sylvester's grip was powerful, and Kilroy wondered if he was feeling a need to prove something. But the old man seemed as hale and healthful as ever, and only the deepening grooves on his weather-beaten face suggested he was approaching the window at the end of his span.

Kilroy was glad to note that his father wasn't bare-chested, although his shirt was so ragged that its purpose could only be decorative, and his skinny legs, roped with sinew, were exposed by a pair of equally tattered shorts. Sylvester took great pride in his appearance, in the sense that he was proud of not giving a damn about it, as he always told everyone. It was a point of honour with him to resist replacing any garment until it literally fell to pieces, and he was derisive of anyone who spent more than the smallest possible sum of money on such things. Kilroy had long since given up trying to persuade him to wear decent clothes. For his part, Sylvester refrained from passing comment on Kilroy's approach to matters of dress, although he still couldn't restrain himself from looking Kilroy up and down slowly, ending in a deadpan stare from which he broke off after a long moment with an almost imperceptible shake of his head.

Hey Dad, Kilroy said, how's it going?

Sylvester nodded at the car. Drive it around the back, will you?

Why?

I'll tell you inside. Stay on the gravel. Try not to leave any tracks.

Kilroy went back to the car. He drove it slowly around the house and parked close to the back wall. His father appeared in the kitchen doorway and watched him as he got out of the car. With much deliberation Kilroy checked the gravel and the grass verge for any tracks he might have left. Nothing was visible. He raised his eyebrows at his old man.

Sylvester nodded, then turned and went into the house. Kilroy followed him into the kitchen. He closed the door behind him, and his father gestured for him to sit down at the battered old wooden table.

Let's have tea, he said, putting a pan of water on to boil.

OK, Kilroy said. Meanwhile, what's new? Why the dramatics?

I'll tell you in a minute, Sylvester said, and busied himself with the tea.

Kilroy waited until his father was sitting across from him, and they both had a mug of tea in front of them.

So, Kilroy said, tell me about it.

About what?

About what's going on. Why the precautions with the car?

I'll tell you. But first let me ask you something.

What?

How's the bird?

Creek? He's fine, thanks.

Sylvester sucked his teeth. It doesn't make sense to take a bird like that into the city, where he can't fly around. I don't know why I ever let you take him away with you. More fool me.

Kilroy made an effort not to rise to the bait. Creek had

belonged to his mother, and it was she who had given him the parrot when he left home. She sensed a loneliness in him, she said, and wanted him to have some company in the life she imagined he would be leading in the city. The gift had nothing to do with his father, and the old man knew it. Kilroy resisted saying any of this. He'd said it all before, and it had never made the slightest difference.

You're probably right, Dad.

Thank you.

And now please tell me what's going on.

I've got your girl, Sylvester said.

What?

Your missing girl. I've got her.

What the hell do you mean?

Sylvester leaned forward and tapped a horny fingernail on the table. The girl you're looking for, he said slowly, the fugitive you seek, is right here.

Kilroy looked around. Where? Where is she?

Calm down. She's safe. I got her in a hole.

A what?

Out back. In one of my holes.

Kilroy sprang up. What the fuck!

Careful, Sylvester said, you'll knock your tea over.

Dad, tell me what you're talking about. Right now!

Whoa, son! Sylvester leaned back, squinting up at Kilroy judiciously. You see, this has always been your problem. That temper of yours. That's why I wanted you to join the police. I thought the discipline might help you.

Kilroy hardly trusted himself to speak. He swallowed hard. It wasn't you! It was mother! You were always against it!

No, no, son, Sylvester said patiently, you've got it all wrong, as usual. I had to work damn hard to persuade your mother to let you do it. She was dead set against it. She was worried you were too sensitive, bless her.

Kilroy tried to control his breathing. His father had always been like this. For a long time he'd wondered if the old man did it deliberately, to mess with his head, or to test him, or to prove some kind of psychological theory about the subjective nature of reality. Why else would he persistently deny things that Kilroy knew to be true? Why did he consistently assert such outrageously false versions of events? Recently, however, Kilroy had come to the realisation that it wasn't about what was true or false. It was about Sylvester's right to tell the story he wanted. It was purely reflexive: a habit of stubborn contradiction that Kilroy knew he would never be able to challenge successfully. Any attempt to argue the point with his father simply played into his hands.

He knew all this, but it didn't help. A tide of bitterness and frustration swelled within him. He struggled to subdue it.

Sylvester had assumed an expression of grave paternal concern. Kilroy sat down. He'd almost forgotten about the girl. He expelled a long, slow breath.

Dad, he said, tell me exactly where she is. Is she all right?

Oh yes, she's in fine shape.

In fine shape? In a hole?

Sure, Sylvester said, there's a big old mattress down there, and some blankets. And a lightweight tarp over the top, in case of rain. And a lamp she can use in the dark. And a bucket for her bodily needs, which I've already hauled up once, on a rope, and emptied for her.

Holy shit, how long has she been down there?

Since yesterday. In case you're wondering, the mattress was already down in that hole. The only hole with a bed in it, as it happens.

Wait, Kilroy said, I'm confused. Why was there a mattress in the hole?

I sometimes spend time down there. Looking up at the sky.

And she just happened to fall into that one? Or did you push her in?

Nope, Sylvester said, she jumped in.

Kilroy was silent as he absorbed this information.

I knew you were coming, his father said.

How the hell did you know I was coming?

Sylvester stood up and walked around the table. He placed a hand on Kilroy's shoulder. Son, I'm your dad.

Bullshit.

Bullshit I'm your dad?

No, bullshit you knew I was coming. Don't give me that crap about intuition.

You got me, Sylvester chuckled. But it's still true I knew you were coming.

How?

She told me. She said you'd be showing up soon.

Kilroy gazed up at his father's face. He wasn't smiling any more. His hand tightened on his son's shoulder and he dropped his voice. You're not the only one looking for her, and that's why she's in the damned hole, if you really want to know. It's a precaution, in case anyone busts in here.

All right, Kilroy said, let's go and see her.

The plot of land at the back of the house had plenty of holes in it, Kilroy noticed, and some of them were pretty damn big.

His old man led him to the far end of the plot and picked up a ladder that was lying next a canvas tarpaulin spread out on the ground.

Hey there, he called out, we got a visitor! OK to expose you?

No problem, said a muffled voice from below the tarp.

Sylvester unhooked the canvas from some pegs and flipped it back.

Kilroy stepped forward and looked down into the hole. It was about four metres deep and at the bottom was the girl, sitting cross-legged on a mattress. There was a lot of other stuff down there, and she seemed to have made herself at home.

Kilroy didn't know what to say. His dad squatted down beside him and spoke to the girl: Want to come out?

Sheba stood up and gazed at Kilroy. After a long moment she said, Do you think you were followed?

No, I don't think so. Pretty sure.

Sheba nodded.

Sylvester slid the ladder down in one swift movement and its feet hit the soil beside the mattress with a thud.

Coming through, the girl said, stepping onto the ladder.

They sat around the table in the kitchen. Sheba was tall for thirteen, and she seemed remarkably poised to Kilroy.

As he watched her sipping the broth Sylvester had given her, he caught her eye a couple of times, appraising him over the top of the steaming mug. There was a strong intelligence there, but it wasn't like her brother's precocity. She wasn't a show-off. Even before she began to speak, Kilroy could see she didn't need his approval, or anyone else's. It was more like the other way around: something about her made you hope she'd be friends with you.

Sylvester had insisted on feeding her before he allowed her to tell her story, which confirmed to Kilroy that the old man already knew at least some of it, and was enjoying making him wait to hear it. But what the hell, let the old bastard have his fun.

Sheba placed the mug carefully on the table in front of her. She had a vivacious, open face. She glanced at Sylvester, who was beside her. He paused, then nodded curtly. He looked across the table at Kilroy with a satisfied grimace.

Hell of a story she's got to tell you, boy. Hell of a story.

OK, Kilroy said, let's hear it.

A hell of a story was an understatement. The short version was that pretty much everything Kilroy thought he knew, about anything at all, was wrong.

He stopped her after a couple of minutes. Wait, he said, can we just take this one step at a time? Firstly, I have to ask you this: did you kill your mother?

Are you serious? Sheba said. Why are you even asking me that?

Out of the corner of his eye Kilroy caught his father shaking his head disdainfully and it was suddenly too much. He banged his fist on the table, hard.

Because it's my fucking job!

The other two were suddenly very still. Kilroy had surprised himself by the intensity of his outburst. He took a deep breath. Just tell me, he said, so I can have a formal denial from you. Before we get onto this other…story.

Sheba nodded slowly. Very well. No, I did not kill my mother.

Any idea who did?

She shook her head, but something hesitant in the gesture made Kilroy lean forward suddenly and point his finger at her:

Tell me, quickly. Was it your brother? Did Roland do it?

No, Sheba said. But he may have…

May have what?

May have…had something to do with it.

Helped in some way?

Sheba shrugged. She was on the verge of tears.

Kilroy leaned back. Well, he said, that's a terrible possibility to have to deal with, and I'm sorry. But I need to try to solve this case. And you'll admit, helping someone to kill his mother is a pretty unusual thing for a boy to do.

Roland is kind of weird, Sheba murmured.

Even so, Kilroy said, that's a little extreme, although it's not uncommon for people in families to take against each other, and plenty of families have problems, for sure.

Kilroy had made an effort not to glance at his father while he said this, but now he heard the old man snort:

No shit, Sherlock!

Something tugged at Kilroy's memory. Wait, he said, turning to Sylvester, what was that? About Sherlock?

It's just an expression.

I know, but where does it come from?

Sylvester frowned. I don't know. From a story?

Kilroy drummed his fingers on the table. It's funny, he said, I was just thinking about that yesterday. My old teacher used to refer to Sherlock, and I vaguely remember some stories, or proverbs, or something. But I wonder where it was from?

Sylvester spread his hands. Search me, son. Even back when I was at school, that stuff was all ancient history. It's probably from one of the old books they took away, when they cleared out all the rubbish.

It's not rubbish! Sheba said loudly, making Kilroy jump.

Sylvester raised a finger to his lips and glanced around.

Sorry, Sheba said. She leaned forward and continued in a lower voice:

But why did they really take the books away? It's what I've just been trying to tell you. Think about all the questions everyone wants to ask, if only we weren't too scared. And my father found out! That's why they killed him!

What did he find out? Kilroy said.

Sheba looked at him impassively and folded her arms.

All right, Kilroy said, tell the story your own way. But what makes you think your father had some kind of inside information about something important? And how did he find out about it, whatever it is?

Sheba asked if Kilroy had been at her father's execution.

No, he said, but I listened to a recording. Some of it.

Only some of it?

Yes, I stopped listening before…the end.

Sheba gave him a bitter little smile. Surely, detective, you're not scared of a bit of blasphemy, are you?

Kilroy shifted in his seat and cleared his throat. Sorry, Sheba, but your father began to say some very strange things. Not just the blasphemy. I mean, it was nonsense, really, wasn't it? I think he was probably deranged, unfortunately.

Perhaps you should actually listen to what he said.

Well, perhaps I will, in due course.

No time like the present, Sheba said, and reached under her thick jacket. She unclipped something from some kind of belt she was wearing and placed it on the table carefully. It was a small black box.

Kilroy stared at it. He looked up at her. Is that a recording device, Sheba?

Uh-huh.

Where did you get it?

My dad made it.

May I see it?

Sheba hesitated. You can look at it, but please don't touch it.

She pushed the device towards Kilroy. He kept his hands below the table and studied it. It wasn't dissimilar to the government-issue recorders that he and his colleagues used, but this one was smaller and sleeker. It looked more sophisticated. Kilroy exchanged a glance with his father.

Sheba reclaimed the device. If you're ready, she said, I'll play what's on it. Yes?

Kilroy nodded.

OK, this is what my dad wanted people to hear. The thing is, he had to find a way to get the message across before the authorities realised what he was saying. That's why he pretended to be crazy. If he'd just come straight out with it, they would have shut him down right away. They shut him down anyway, when they figured out what he was doing, and they made it seem like it was because he was blaspheming and being a heretic, and all that shit. But it wasn't. It was because he was trying to tell people what he'd found out. Listen.

Sheba pressed a recessed button on the side of the machine.

Suddenly the room was filled with sound. Kilroy was amazed by the quality. You could hear everything – the crowd, the officials on the platform, even the birds singing. And, above them all, Manfred's voice, as audible as if he were standing only a few metres away:

... is most manifest, because upstairs mum and dad are real, as the teachings tell us, lovely bubbly jubilation, have they touched you? They've touched us each and every one, cold hands, warm heart, they care for us, they care so much, they made us in their image, and we are their children, but they didn't have us the ordinary way, that would be too much like hard work, can you imagine?

So, once upon a time, upstairs mum and dad had to go

away on a long journey, and they were sad about leaving the children behind, because they remembered they didn't have any children! Quick, they said, we must make some, otherwise nobody will be here to look after things while we're away, hurry, hurry, hurry, so they made some children and tried to teach them to be good while they were away, but they were in such a hurry it was very hard work. Luckily there was Shadbold, to lend a hand, and they made the children, hundreds and hundreds and hundreds of them and then they said, wait, what about the animals, what if the animals eat them, or what if they eat the animals, oh dear, what a calamity, what shall we do, so they killed all the animals just to be on the safe side, because you can't be too careful. And sometimes you can't be careful at all, it turns out, but what do you expect, they're only human like the rest of us! Yes, upstairs mum and dad are just as bad and just as good as us, and they'll be home soon, and what will they find? Ignorance is bliss, they say, but what the hell is bliss? Search me! So now we must let the secret out and—

Manfred's voice suddenly became muffled, and then it was cut off. Kilroy heard shouts and jeers from some in the crowd, and others shouting them down, then the sound of blows and cries as the police used batons, restoring order swiftly.

The unrest was over almost before it had begun, and Kilroy reflected that the majority in the crowd probably didn't even know it had happened.

The recording ended abruptly.

Sheba looked at Kilroy expectantly.

Remarkably good recording, Kilroy said, but I'm sure you're

aware it's illegal for an ordinary citizen to own a device like that.

Sheba made a sour face. You're playing for time, she said.

Kilroy nodded. True, I'm trying to take it in.

Sylvester leaned forward. I'm convinced, he said.

Convinced of what? Kilroy said.

What he's saying. About the church, and so on.

Kilroy sighed. But what is he saying, exactly? That our religious beliefs are false, or foolish in some way? That Upstairs Mum and Dad are just as human as we are? OK, that's some pretty brutal heresy, if I'm catching his meaning correctly. But where's the evidence? Most people just assumed he was crazy, to be honest.

Kilroy caught his father and Sheba exchanging a swift glance. Sylvester was clearly very taken with her. Kilroy wondered how much time she'd spent in the hole, and how much time she'd spent in the house, with his dad. His imagination began to construct an ugly possibility, and he stifled it immediately. Get a grip, he told himself, you may have differences with the old man, but he's not like that.

Kilroy realised they were both looking at him.

The reason, Sheba said, why they put him on a blasphemy charge, and went big with the craziness angle, was because they don't want people to think too hard about what he actually said. I'll admit I wasn't too sure myself, until I read the notebooks.

OK, Kilroy said, now this is new. What notebooks?

Sheba turned to Sylvester. Can you get the satchel, please?

Sylvester stood up and walked to the old stove in the corner. He smiled at Kilroy and waggled his eyebrows. Kilroy knew what was coming, but he wasn't going to spoil Sylvester's enjoyment. He was seventy-eight, for pity's sake.

Sylvester reached out with a flourish, like a magician preparing for a trick. He grasped the stove's chimney and pivoted on his heel, pulling the chimney around with him. There was a grinding noise and the base of the stove revolved, revealing a recess underneath it. The recess was surprisingly large, about the size of a coffin.

Sylvester grinned. You know, he said, even in the days when we used this thing for heat, I could do that. It's a false chimney, see, and the real one goes up through the wall. Remember I was always telling you to never, ever touch that chimney? You thought it was because it was hot, but actually it was because it was cold, and you might have realised it was a fake.

Kilroy tried to look impressed.

Sylvester reached down into the hole and retrieved a large satchel. He spun the stove's base on its axis again, and covered the hole. He stepped to the table, but paused in the act of laying down the satchel in front of Sheba. He gazed intently at Kilroy.

Wait, he said, did you know about that? That hidey-hole?

No, Dad.

Sylvester narrowed his eyes. Holy shit, you knew!

Kilroy smiled sheepishly.

How long? Sylvester said. How long have you known?

Kilroy shrugged. Quite a while.

Damn! So, all those years ago, when we used to hide your presents in there, for your birthday, and Shadbold Day, you knew about them?

I knew they were in there, and I knew about the hole, but I didn't look.

You didn't? Why not?

I thought it wasn't right.

Sylvester frowned. He looked away, and gazed out of the window. When he turned back his eyes were glittering. You're a good kid, he said quietly.

I'm thirty-nine.

I know, I know.

Sylvester laid the satchel gently in front of Sheba. She'd been looking down, her hands folded in her lap. Now she picked up the satchel, undid the catches, and passed a small blue notebook over the table to Kilroy.

Start with that one, she said.

Kilroy had been reading for only a few minutes when they heard a car approaching along the driveway.

He sprang up, and nearly collided with Sylvester, who was striding across the kitchen, heading towards the front of the house.

I'll deal with it, Sylvester barked as he left the room, and I'll yell if it's trouble.

Sheba stood up. She looked pale. Kilroy took her arm and guided her to the back door. Stay here, he said, and be ready to run if we need to.

He followed his father, and as he reached the hallway he saw him open the front door. Late afternoon light flooded into the hallway, silhouetting Sylvester, and casting deep shadows. Kilroy tucked himself into the darkness beside the staircase and peered through the bannisters.

Oh dear, said a thin, quavering voice, is this the right place?

Sylvester moved to one side and Kilroy saw an elderly woman standing on the doorstep. She was very small, and seemed confused.

Sylvester leaned down to address her. Which place are you looking for?

Is this the place that's for sale?

No, said Sylvester, not that I know of.

Oh dear, the woman said again, I'm awfully sorry, I may have taken a wrong turning. The agency in town gave me directions but I think I got lost.

She unfolded a map, which appeared to be bigger than she was. As she struggled with it Sylvester took it from her gently and folded it to a more manageable size.

OK, he said, indicating a section of the map, this is where the town is, right here, so which road did they tell you to take?

The old woman peered at the map, making uncertain noises.

Kilroy felt someone at his shoulder and turned to see Sheba right behind him. He frowned at her, and she edged back.

Wait, the woman on the doorstep said, which way is north?

Sylvester raised his arm and pointed back along the drive. That way, he said.

The woman looked over her shoulder, then peered at the map again. Oh my goodness, I've come in exactly the opposite direction to where I'm supposed to go! Oh dear, I'm so sorry. I feel such a fool.

Sylvester inclined his head. No problem, ma'am. Here, take your map. You need to turn left at the end of the driveway, then take your second right at the intersection. That'll take you around town on a bypass, and eventually you'll come to a junction where you should take another right. That's the road you want.

The woman began backing away. Thank you, you're very kind.

Mind the step behind you, ma'am. And you can turn your car around where it is, no need to reverse all the way back.

Thank you again. And I'm so sorry I disturbed you and your family.

Sylvester paused for half a second. I don't have any family here, he said.

Oh, I see. No, of course… I'm sorry. Goodbye.

You have a safe journey.

Kilroy heard a car engine start, then the grinding of gears. Sylvester stood in the doorway, watching the woman drive away. He closed the front door softly.

Fuck, Kilroy said, emerging from the shadows.

Fuck is right, son.

Sheba stepped forward. What's the matter, she said, looking from one to the other, are you saying it's not a coincidence? I mean, she's just an old lady.

Old ladies, Kilroy said, can be deadly. Have you ever seen them in action when there's a sale at a hat shop?

Sylvester laughed and clapped his son on the shoulder.

Really, Sheba said, do you think it means something?

Kilroy nodded. I'm afraid so.

But who is she? Is she with the police?

Not the police. But she could be from a special services unit. Or some other outfit. There are units I don't even know about.

It's a bad business, Sylvester said, when the cops don't even know what the hell is going on with other cops.

We live in strange times, Dad. And we need to go.

You're right about that. Which way?

Kilroy turned to Sheba. You were heading for the coast, right?

Sheba nodded.

That's no good. The further east you go, the more exposed you become. The towns get smaller, and then it's just pissy little villages scattered around, and the land is totally flat. There's nowhere to hide.

So, where can we go? Assuming you're not arresting me.

I'm not arresting you. And we're going back to the city.

What!? Sheba backed away. If you're not arresting me, why

75

are you taking me back there?

Whoa, Sylvester said, calm down, girl. He's right. He can hide you much more easily in the city.

Sheba's shoulders slumped. Kilroy figured she'd been living on her nerves ever since she fled. Now she was ready to give up.

He turned to his father. We'd better get going, Dad.

Right. If anyone comes calling, I'll tell them you went east.

Don't get yourself into trouble.

No, I'll make it seem like they tricked the information out of me. I know how to deal with these jerks.

Kilroy glanced at Sheba. Got everything?

She patted the satchel, which was now slung over her shoulder.

Kilroy nodded. Let's go back to the kitchen. Then out of the back door and straight into the car.

They trooped back to the kitchen in silence.

Kilroy opened the back door and stood aside. The car's open, he said.

Sheba turned to Sylvester. Thank you, she said. She lurched towards him, kissed him on the cheek, then darted out of the door.

Kilroy faced his father. They took a step towards each other, reaching for a handshake, but both seemed to come to the same decision simultaneously, and opened their arms. They embraced, and held each other tightly.

Eventually Sylvester patted his son's shoulder, like a wrestler asking for a break, and they released each other.

Kilroy hadn't hugged his dad since he was a kid.

Be safe, he said.

You too, son. I hope I see you again.

I hope so too.

KILROY

Kilroy stayed on the back roads, and a couple of times he took farm tracks to cut between the roads in an effort to avoid the main routes.

Sheba, in the front beside him, said nothing. After driving for half an hour, Kilroy decided it was time to ask her a few questions.

Tell me, he said, how did you get to my dad's place? How have you been travelling all this time?

Bicycle, Sheba said.

Kilroy was speechless for a moment. It simply hadn't crossed his mind. But what could be less suspicious than a teenage girl cycling along country roads? People would assume she was some local youngster, on an errand, or just enjoying a bike ride. He shook his head admiringly.

That was smart.

I don't know about that, Sheba said. It was necessary, that's what it was. I couldn't very well hire a car, could I?

No, I guess not. Hey, where's the bike now?

In one of your dad's holes.

Kilroy took a deep breath. Look, about my father. I know he seems a little eccentric, but he means well. You see–

Yeah, I know. He was kind to me. Congratulations on your nice dad.

Thanks.

You're a lot like him.

Yes, people used to say I looked like him.

And in other ways.

What other ways?

Never mind. We don't have to talk about it if you don't want to.

I didn't say I didn't want to.

Yeah, right.

Kilroy decided to change the subject. OK, he said, but how did you know where he lived? And how the hell did you know I would come there? I didn't even know myself. Well, I guess that's not exactly true. I suppose once I knew I was heading in that general direction it was inevitable I'd call in at some point. But what made you go there?

Because I wanted to contact you, and it was the safest way of doing it.

Me? Why did you want to contact me? I was meant to be tracking you down and arresting you. I still am, as it happens.

Sheba didn't reply. Kilroy glanced over at her. She was chewing her bottom lip. After a while she shifted in her seat and turned to him.

I knew you were OK, she said.

How did you know that?

Roland told me.

What do you mean, Roland told you? Kilroy gripped the wheel and frowned hard at the road ahead. How did you talk to your brother about me? I mean, when was that?

After he was released. He said you were OK, and you weren't mean to him or anything. He said you brought him juice.

Kilroy tried to make sense of what he was hearing. Hold on, he said, I thought you were on the run by then. Are you saying you were still in the city?

Yes. I waited. I didn't want to leave without seeing Roland.

I thought you said Roland helped to kill your mother.

I didn't say that! I said he may have had something to do with it. He does strange things. He's kind of unusual.

Kilroy snorted. Tell me about it!

Fuck off. He's my brother.

Sorry. But you said yourself he's…odd. So, why is he like that?

I guess, Sheba said, it's probably because of all the times he didn't chew his food properly, and my dad hung him up by the ankles and hit him with a stick with nails in it, to teach him a damn good lesson. That may have traumatised him.

You're kidding.

Of course I'm fucking kidding! Look, he's just weird. He was born that way. If you really want to know, personally I think he has a problem with his feelings, like he almost has too many of them, and he can't control them, and the way he talks, all that goofy formal language, I think that's a front, or a way to deal with it, or whatever. Something like that, anyway.

Kilroy nodded slowly. What she said made a lot of sense.

OK, he said, let's get back to the story. Where were you when Roland was in custody? And wait, did he tell me the truth, about you leaving the house and then coming back, and then leaving again on the night your…the night it happened?

Yes. But I can't get into that now. It's too complicated. I had an argument with my mother. About my dad and…other stuff. But when Roland was taken away by the cops, I just waited around. Different places. I slept in the adventure playground behind the school. There's a kind of hut there. But I kept an eye on the house, and when Roland was brought back to pick up some things, and they were waiting in a car outside, I went in through a back window that we used to sneak in and out of, and talked to him. And that's when he told me about you.

You said 'they' were waiting in the car. Who was waiting?

My mother's cousin and his wife. They've fostered Roland. They're OK. Quite nice, actually. Not jerks, anyway.

Kilroy experienced a sense of relief from a pressure he hadn't known was bothering him. He was glad to hear Roland was in a good home. But he still needed more answers from the girl beside him.

So, he said, that still leaves the question of how you figured out that you should go to my dad's place. And how did you know where it was?

Sheba bowed her head. Finally she sighed and said, A friend helped me.

Who? What friend?

I can't tell you.

But what kind of friend are you talking about?

Enough! I don't want to tell you, and that's it.

From the corner of his eye Kilroy saw her making the lip-zipping sign.

They sat in silence for a minute. Then Sheba said, Well?

Well what?

Can we cut to the chase, now?

Kilroy shot her a puzzled glance.

She rolled her eyes. Duh! The notebook I gave you! How much of it did you get to read before the creepy old lady arrived?

Not much, Kilroy said, just the first few pages.

But enough to understand what he was really saying?

I understood what he was suggesting, yes. But to be honest, what I saw wasn't evidence. It was just an idea.

OK, but what did you think about the idea?

Kilroy shrugged. Is it any more plausible than any other ideas? Your father says there was a flood, hundreds of years ago, and now the waters are receding. But we already know about the flood, from the gospel, and now the authorities have confirmed what's happening at the coasts. As for the stuff about Upstairs Mum and Dad being just the same as us, and leaving us behind when they mysteriously went somewhere else, that's not only heretical, it's downright seditious. Why should anyone believe that type of thing?

You have to read the rest of it.

OK, I will.

Sheba turned and gazed out of her window. There were fields on both sides of the road for as far as the eye could see, and they were all exactly the same.

Sorry, Kilroy said, it's not much of a view.

I don't care.

Look, I'm not trying to say your father wasn't onto something.

Sheba ignored him.

Kilroy tried again. So, what about the other notebooks? What's in them?

You really want to know?

Yes. Tell me, please.

It's the whole story. The real one, not the crap they want us to believe. For example, we aren't the first people to exist. There were people here before us, and not only that, there was more than just Landmass.

What people? People like us?

Kind of. Not exactly. Dad figured out they must have been more advanced than us, because they set everything up. Everything. Our whole world.

Kilroy frowned. This was getting pretty wild. What if Sheba was as crazy as her father, and Kilroy was sharing a car, in the most remote and unpopulated landscape he'd been able to find, with a homicidal maniac who had slaughtered her own mother and was about to do the same to him, possibly with an implement concealed in the satchel she was now reaching into?

Kilroy casually took one hand off the steering wheel.

Sheba was looking at him. She was still reaching into the satchel.

What's the matter, she said, do you think I'm crazy, or something?

Kilroy laughed. Of course not, he said, slowly moving his free hand towards the pistol under his jacket.

He flinched as Sheba removed her hand from the satchel. It was holding a bundle of notebooks similar to the one he'd begun to read back at his dad's place.

It's all in these, Sheba said. Perhaps I should have given you one of the others to start you on, but I knew you'd be able to relate to the material about the flood, and the waters receding, and I thought that might make it easier for you to get your head around the more unfamiliar concepts that follow on from that stuff.

Thanks. Very kind of you.

Sorry, I didn't mean—oh, never mind. You obviously don't believe me anyway.

Whoa, Kilroy said, what gave you that idea? I want to believe you, as it happens. But you have to understand, I'm a cop. I start from a position of scepticism. I look for evidence. I don't take anything at face value. I dig for the facts. And I always, always assume the worst – about everything and everyone.

Nice work if you can get it.

Kilroy smiled. Look on the positive side, though. If you can convince a suspicious, mean-spirited old bastard like me, you can convince anyone.

All right, but you've got to give me a chance! I need you to read this shit, and talk about it with me. I spent days and days reading, and thinking, and struggling. It twisted my head, I can tell you. But finally I got it. The whole thing. But you? You expect to make a judgement call after five minutes reading one of the notebooks, and then you spend half an hour in a car with me, wondering if I'm about to stab you up with a knife, or something!

No, I wasn't!

Oh, give me a break. That bulge under your jacket isn't exactly subtle. I saw you reaching for the gun.

All right. Let's agree to trust each other, OK? But we need to make a plan. First we have to put you somewhere safe. Then I'll read the notebooks, as soon as I get a chance, I promise. Hey, talking of which, are those the only copies?

No.

Really?

Sheba hesitated. I…copied them. Most of them.

Bullshit.

It's not!

Sheba, if you want me to trust you, you have to tell the truth.

All right. I started copying them. But I didn't get very far.

OK. So, as soon as we can, we need to get proper copies made. I know where we can do that. Unregistered, off the radar, no paper trail. Thinking about it, maybe we should go there first and—

Kilroy broke off and squinted into the rear-view mirror.

Sheba craned around in her seat. What is it?

Someone behind us. Holy hell, he's coming up fast!

Kilroy considered trying to outdistance the car behind them but the speed at which it was approaching convinced him it would be futile. Instead he undid the clasp holding his pistol in place.

Within seconds the car was right behind them. Kilroy gripped the wheel, steadying himself to prepare for whatever evasive tactics he could come up with. The other vehicle swung out and sped past with a roar. It was a black sedan of a regular make, but the engine must have been tuned up. As the car flashed past him Kilroy caught a glimpse of a male driver who appeared to have no passengers.

The car pulled away from them as quickly as it had approached.

Who was that? Sheba asked. Do you know?

No, but he's in pretty damn big hurry, whoever it is. Uh-oh, wait.

Up ahead in the distance the car began to swerve wildly.

Shit, said Kilroy, what's he doing?

Is he slowing down?

The black car had stopped swerving. Its speed dropped to a crawl.

Kilroy began to apply the brakes as smoothly as he could.

Sheba gripped the dashboard in front of her. Why are we stopping?

Don't get out unless I tell you. Understand?

Sheba swallowed hard. She nodded.

Kilroy pulled up fifteen metres behind the stationary black sedan.

He walked towards the car, his left hand loosely holding the side of his jacket, ready to flip it away from his body if he needed to draw his pistol.

Just before he reached the vehicle the driver's door swung open.

Kilroy stopped. He waited.

Nothing happened.

Kilroy gripped the butt of his pistol with his right hand and walked on. When he reached the back of the car he saw that the driver appeared to be slumped over the wheel. He edged forward until he drew level with the driver, and peered inside. The man raised his head slowly and looked at him. The man's face was eerily familiar. Kilroy took a step back, unable to understand what he saw.

He was looking at himself.

But it wasn't himself, exactly. It was a strange likeness, as if Kilroy was looking at a distorting mirror. But what he saw wasn't a distortion, it was more as if his own features had been fractionally rearranged in some way.

The man was breathing heavily. His eyes were bloodshot, and they skittered around, as if he had difficulty focusing. Very slowly he raised his arm. Kilroy realised the man was pointing a gun at him.

Kilroy willed himself to move. The man in the car seemed to find his target. Kilroy saw the colour change in the skin of his knuckle as his finger tightened on the trigger.

Kilroy drew his pistol and fired.

The man's head snapped back and a section of his skull smashed into the passenger-side window and bounced off, leaving a clump of brain smeared on the glass.

Kilroy felt himself toppling backwards. He staggered, then steadied himself. Slowly he lowered himself to the ground and sat down in the road.

He was aware of a muffled high-pitched noise. He glanced back at his own car and saw that Sheba's mouth was open in a scream.

Then he heard another noise.

A car. In the far distance, a long way behind his car but approaching fast.

Kilroy couldn't move. Was he injured? Had the man shot him? He looked down at his body but could see no blood, no wound.

The approaching car didn't slow down. It sped past his own vehicle, and Kilroy saw Sheba's head turning to follow it. At least she'd stopped screaming.

That car, Kilroy thought, is going to hit me. Someone tried to shoot me, and now I'll be killed by a car instead. What will the impact do? I'm sitting down, so it may actually drive over me. Do I have time to stand up and get clear? No, almost certainly not. Can I do something to reduce the impact? No, nothing effective. Here it comes.

The car came to a halt less than a metre from Kilroy. He could smell something scorched very distinctly. Oddly, though, he'd heard no sound of squealing tires or grinding brake pads.

The driver's door opened and a woman got out.

Kilroy was puzzled to see it was the woman he'd encountered before, and had last seen in the town square of S–, as they both walked away from a shattered body. The woman he'd been thinking about almost constantly.

She crouched beside him. Are you all right? she said.

Kilroy felt his mind unfreeze. He got to his feet. The woman straightened up. They looked at each other in silence for a moment before Kilroy spoke:

What are you doing here?

I've been following you.

Why?

It's a long story. Too long to tell you now.

Who are you?

My name is Cynthia.

They shook hands, which struck Kilroy as faintly absurd under the circumstances. He knew he was staring at her. At close range the intense blue of her eyes was more striking than ever.

I'm Kilroy, he said.

She nodded. He realised he was still holding her hand, and let go. You've told me your name, he said, but that still doesn't tell me who you are.

That's part of the long story too. Are you hurt?

No. But I've just killed someone.

Cynthia nodded towards his car. What about her? Is she all right?

She seems to be. What have you got to do with all this?

All I can tell you, Cynthia said, is that I want to help you. And her. For a number of reasons, and I will explain everything to you, I promise. But not now. For now, you'll just have to trust me. Will you?

For now, yes.

All right. We need to do something about that man in the car. The body.

Do you know him?

Not personally, no. But I have an idea of who he is, and why he looked the way he does. Like you, I mean.

He didn't seem to be in very good shape, Kilroy said, even before I shot him.

Yes, Cynthia said, there's a reason for that.

But you're not going to tell me what it is.

There's just not enough time right now. You and the girl need to keep moving, and get to the city.

Kilroy looked at the car with the corpse in it. He squinted against the low evening sun. Maybe, he said, I could push the car off the road. Into the field. That won't hide it completely, but there's a good chance it won't be found until morning.

Cynthia said, Why not switch cars? Then push yours off the road, and hide it in the field. That would buy you even more time.

Kilroy gazed at her for a moment. He hadn't thought of that. Right, he said, so even when they find it, they'll think it's me, and he killed me?

Cynthia nodded. Until they do tests. I mean his face is a mess, right?

What about Sheba? They'll look for her.

They're looking for her anyway. And you. When they don't find her in the car they may think she's set off on foot, through the fields.

Who are we talking about, by the way?

Cynthia hesitated. Who do you mean?

Exactly. Who do we mean when we say 'they?'

Special services, for one.

And for another?

Cynthia shook her head. It's complicated. There really isn't time to go into it. We need to get this done.

Kilroy slipped off his jacket. I'll get him out of there. Hold this, will you?

Cynthia took his jacket and laid it on the hood of her car. I'll help you, she said, it'll be quicker.

You don't have to.

It's fine. We'll get him onto the side of the road, and then – she glanced back at Sheba – try to clean up in there. Let's go.

Wait a moment, Kilroy said, I just want to tell Sheba it's all right.

Cynthia put a hand on his arm as he was turning away. No time, she said softly. But don't worry, she'll be OK.

Kilroy was glad of Cynthia's help with the corpse. It was damned heavy. Also the back of the head was open, but between them they were able to manoeuvre the body so that not too much fell out. They laid the corpse on the side of the road, face down

I'll move my car, Kilroy said, so it's ready to roll into the field.

He walked back along the road, trying to smile at Sheba, who was gazing at him through the windshield with wide eyes. Poor kid, he thought. He saw Cynthia striding to the back of her own car and popping the trunk. She opened a case and pulled out some items of clothing, one of which she began tearing into strips.

Kilroy got into his car. I'm sorry, Sheba. Are you all right?

No.

Sorry.

Stop saying that.

All right. Look, we're going to switch cars and get out of here. We need to hurry, but you don't have to do anything. Just get in the other car when I tell you.

Why are we switching cars?

I'll explain later.

Kilroy drove the car forward slowly, positioning it so it would roll easily into the bank of tall crops.

OK, just wait in here a moment.

As Kilroy got out he saw Cynthia cleaning the last traces of blood and brains from the inside of the other car's window. She bundled up the rags, then knelt beside the body and wrapped a large piece of material around the head. She looked up and nodded to Kilroy.

He called to Sheba, and kept himself between her and the body on the ground as she got into the other car.

Nearly done, he said to her. Just don't look, OK?

He and Cynthia picked up the corpse and carried it to Kilroy's car. By the time they'd managed to prop it up in the driver's seat Kilroy was gasping. He noticed that Cynthia was breathing hard, but not as hard as him. She unwound the cloth from the corpse's head. It was a bad mess.

That'll help, Cynthia said. His face looks like shit. Ready to push?

Wait, Kilroy said. He exchanged his pistol with the dead man's, then he put his police ID into the corpse's jacket pocket.

Cynthia nodded approvingly, and walked to the back of the vehicle, bracing her hands against the trunk. Kilroy slipped off the handbrake and joined her.

They pushed the car off the road without too much difficulty, and it rolled a few metres into the field under its own momentum. They both stood back. It wasn't twilight yet, but the car couldn't be seen unless you were looking for it.

They turned to each other.

The girl, Cynthia said, have you got somewhere safe to take her?

I hope so. A friend's place.

Someone you can trust?

Again, I hope so.

OK. You need to get going. It'll be dark soon. That's good.

What about you? Where are you going?

Don't worry about me, I'll be all right.

Will I see you again?

You will. I promise. I'll be in touch soon.

How?

I'll contact you. It won't be long.

Kilroy scrutinised her face. She wasn't going to tell him anything else, he could see that. OK, he said, take care.

I will. Be safe.

Kilroy walked to his car and got in. He smiled encouragingly at Sheba. Are you OK?

Not really. But don't worry, I'm not going to freak out.

Good, Kilroy said.

Sheba turned to him. Where is Cynthia going?

Kilroy gazed at her. How do you know her name? Have you seen her before?

Yes. You know that friend I mentioned, who helped me?

That was her?

Yes. She was a friend of my mother's.

Kilroy considered this. On reflection it seemed no more strange or surprising than anything else that had been happening recently. He started the car and smiled brightly at Sheba.

Off on our travels again, he said.

CURTIS

I was almost disappointed when Kilroy and the girl arrived at my apartment not long after I'd woken up. Not because I didn't want them there, but because it felt too easy, like I hadn't earned it. There was another feeling too, but I didn't want to process it immediately.

I held the door open as Kilroy ushered the girl in.

Curtis, he said to me, this is my friend Sheba.

Come in, I said. I shook her hand and smiled at her.

Kilroy moved close to me and dropped his voice:

I need your help, Curtis.

You've got it.

Wait, he said. It might get you into trouble. I need somewhere for us to hide out for a while. People are looking for the girl, and now they're looking for me, too. Various people, maybe the police – my own people – and others. I think I've thrown them off the scent for a while, but I'm still asking you to take a risk for me.

I held up a finger and placed it on his lips. You don't have to tell me the details, I said. Your word is good enough for me, Kilroy, you know that.

He nodded gratefully and gave me a kiss on the cheek. His breath was stale.

They'd been driving all night. Kilroy looked drained and the girl was dead on her feet. Nonetheless, there was something about her – an intensity, I'd have to call it. Not the weird hyper-alertness that often comes with exhaustion; it was more that she was fully focused, on everything and everyone, all the time. She had a compelling kind of presence, and I found her unnerving. When she looked at me I felt she was seeing more of me than I wanted her to. An interesting girl.

I made them some food, and gave Kilroy some bedding for the couch. He'd slept there a few times before. I told Sheba she could use my bed. All day, if she wanted, as I'd be at work.

She asked me what work I did, and I said I worked at an insurance company.

Oh, she said, like my dad. That's what he did.

I noticed a flicker of attention passing across Kilroy's features, then it faded away, like a car engine almost sparking to life on a cold morning just before the battery dies. He was simply too tired to make the connection.

I said goodbye at eight, and on my way out I casually plucked the spare set of keys from the table in the hallway and slipped them in my bag.

I wasn't ready, that was the truth. I was prepared for the practical side of things, but I wasn't ready emotionally. I'd always known what I would do to Kilroy, if the time came, and I believed I'd come to terms with that. But now it was happening I found it confusing. The emotions I'd expected to feel – guilt, regret, heartache – stubbornly refused to report for duty, and instead I found myself feeling angry, mostly.

You may have guessed that I haven't been entirely honest with you.

But it's complicated. Everything I've said about my feelings for Kilroy has been true, likewise the fact that I enjoyed the time we spent together. What I left out was that it was part of my job to spend time with Kilroy.

The practice of embedding the security services inside insurance companies had been going on for many years, partly because the whole industry is, essentially, one big data repository. It was hard to believe Kilroy didn't know about it. On the other hand, over the same period, there was a general policy of keeping regular cops increasingly in the dark about these things. And not only regular cops: I knew perfectly well that my own unit was under surveillance by people higher up the intelligence food-chain, and above them were still more secret, deniable operations, answerable only to the highest echelons of the government and the church authorities. And they, in turn, were watched.

Someone, or something, was watching over all of us, and they were using the skyflies to do it. Everyone in the department, from my level upwards, knew they contained a kind of camera, and communication equipment, even if the doctors hadn't yet been able to understand exactly how they worked, or how the machines remained in flight. I suspected we were being tested, and when we'd finally unlocked the secrets of the machines we'd inevitably try to replicate them, and the game would change.

In my meeting with Kilroy, before he left the city, I'd probed to see how much he knew about all this, or was prepared to reveal. Obviously he didn't know as much as people at my level, but he clearly knew more than the average citizen, or even the average cop, and more than he was revealing to me.

In many ways Kilroy seemed to be an open book, but I had a nagging suspicion the book was in code, and another story was hidden inside it, waiting to be deciphered. There would always be a side to him that was hidden, from me and from everyone. But what I hadn't expected, and was soon to discover, was how much I'd underestimated him. Not his intelligence, exactly. Let's call it resourcefulness.

When I got to my desk, I made the calls I had to make, and began typing up a report. I expected to be interrupted at any moment, and summoned for a debriefing, but it didn't happen. Perhaps, I thought, they already knew everything they needed to.

Finally, at around eleven, my boss stopped by. This was the man I've mentioned, with whom I had a discreet agreement to get together every so often and discreetly fuck each other's brains out. We'd had to cool things down recently, because quite apart from anything else – our professional relationship, his wife, my other arrangements, a general inclination to secrecy for the good of one's health – it happened that Sheba's father Manfred, the man who'd been executed, had been my lover's boss.

That's right: the late heretic and apparent lunatic had been a high-ranking intelligence officer. Which was just one of the reasons the authorities had wanted to get him out of the way as quickly as possible, and, they reasoned, you can't get much further out of the way than being dead. Having reached that conclusion, they used the entire performance of his execution as a timely opportunity to scare the living shit out of the general public, and deliver an unambiguous message about the advisability of watching your step, citizens.

So, there was a certain awkwardness between me and Rudy, my boss. It was nothing that couldn't be dispelled by a few rounds of sweaty sexual gymnastics when we could get around to it, but in the meantime we had to be careful. I knew Rudy had been questioned about Manfred, and about how much he'd known with regard to his boss's surprising decision to go stark, staring mad. Rudy was lucky they'd only questioned him, and stopped short of more extreme measures. They'd probably concluded that Rudy knew enough about those measures, having frequently administered them himself, to need little encouragement to tell them everything he knew. Which wasn't much. Manfred had been remarkably successful in keeping his plans to himself until he was ready.

Rudy now told me he'd stopped by to let me know that our superiors, all the way up the chain to the top, were grateful to me for my dedicated work with Kilroy, which had achieved a good result. The girl was where they wanted her, and would be taken into custody shortly. Meanwhile they were considering what to do about Kilroy. They might arrest him too, or they might wish to speak to me, later in the day, about contriving to keep him in the dark regarding my role, so I could continue the useful relationship I'd established with him. This news threw me into considerable internal turmoil, which I tried not to show. But something else about what Rudy told me was bothering me too.

Wait, I said, did I hear you correctly, and the girl hasn't been taken into custody yet?

That's right.

Why not?

Search me, baby.

I frowned at him and glanced around.

Rudy winked at me. Sorry, slip of the tongue. Which I know you like.

Shut up. Seriously, why haven't they arrested her yet?

I honestly have no idea. But you know what these people are like.

I lowered my voice and said, Which people might that be, exactly?

Rudy shrugged. The usual ones, I guess, although it might be more accurate to call them the unusual ones. They move in mysterious ways, as you know.

And what am I supposed to do?

Wait for instructions. If you don't hear anything, go home as usual. If your guests are still there, just act naturally. They'll come for the girl pretty soon, I'm sure. But don't worry, Curtis. You've done a great job. OK, I have to go.

Rudy gave my shoulder a squeeze that would have looked unremarkable to a casual observer, who wouldn't have seen the way he paddled his fingers, and strode away.

After he left I found it impossible to get my thoughts in order – or I should say my feelings, if I'm honest. I couldn't experience any sense of closure with Kilroy until I knew what was going to happen. Were they planning to arrest him along with the girl, or would I be asked to keep him in play? And even if they did arrest him, what would the story be? Would they reveal I'd betrayed him, or was there some further subterfuge to maintain, so they could keep their options open?

In theory I should have been able to remain objective about all this, but in practice I was having a hard time holding myself together.

As well as feeling uneasy about Kilroy, I was disturbed by the news that both he and the girl were still at my apartment. I'd assumed that Sheba would be taken into custody as soon as I'd made my report – and Kilroy too, if they decided to roll things up with him at this point. But the people Rudy and I had been talking about, who would be the ones to conduct the arrest, did indeed move in mysterious ways. They liked it. They liked going on raids at dawn, or at odd times, and keeping everyone guessing. They were creeps, to be frank. They weren't regular field officers, who tried to behave like normal citizens: people like me, in other words. These types liked to dress in black clothes, and they weren't shy about letting everyone see their weapons. They also liked to manhandle people, and worse. There were times, unavoidably, when we were all were obliged to be harsh with suspects, but these people I'm talking about enjoyed it, the women as much as the men. Creeps, as I say.

Unfortunately, in the last year or so these types had become more active. I couldn't help thinking there should have been other ways to deal with some of the problems they were responding to, although I'm not saying you can allow social disruption to go unchecked, especially if some of the things I'd been hearing were true. Only a week ago I'd seen a report from a small town near the eastern coast where a church had been burned down. Now, I like to think of myself as a tolerant person, but burning a church? That's just straight-up wickedness, no two ways about it.

But to my mind, people shouldn't be treated brutally just for complaining, especially if they had some justification. For example, there was a certain amount of misconduct in the church, and even serious corruption in a few cases. It was inevitable in an organisation of that size. And if your community was plagued by a particularly egregious case, like a priest blatantly on the take, or a local cop abusing people, then I'd understand if you staged a non-violent protest, provided you didn't use it as an excuse to have yourself a riot, or go on a looting spree, or misbehave in other ways that were plainly asking for trouble. But it seemed the authorities had different ideas. They were on edge, and their first response to any disturbance was to crack down. Their attitude was that you had to keep a tight lid on this shit, otherwise it would explode. Of course, you could also take the view, if you were so inclined, that a simmering pot of shit will explode *because* you're keeping a tight lid on it.

But what did I know? Despite my rank I was nowhere near the top of the tree. Certainly not near enough to be involved in these decisions. Not yet.

However, thinking about all this forced me to confront something I'd been trying to push out of my mind, namely that Sheba would very likely face some rough treatment. I didn't know why I cared, in view of the fact she was an unrepentant fugitive who may have killed her own mother – although that was probably misinformation – but I found I did care about her. Just in case my life wasn't complicated enough already.

I consoled myself with the idea that they might go easy on a child, and even if they didn't, it wouldn't last long. As for Kilroy, he would have no illusions about what he faced. Whatever happened, I hoped it would all be over soon.

And maybe it would have been over soon, if it hadn't been for those notebooks. I didn't find out about them until later, of course, but how did we miss them in the first place? Manfred's home had been turned inside-out after his arrest, and nothing was found. There must have been a secret hiding place, and Manfred told his daughter where to find the notebooks, which she read after his arrest.

But there was another factor that prevented the whole affair from reaching a swift conclusion, and it was simply bad timing. Or good timing, depending on your perspective. For me, in the short term, it was a disaster. The nightmare started when I was about to go for lunch.

I felt a hand on my shoulder and looked up to see Rudy again.

Come with me, he said.

Why?

You'd better just come.

He wouldn't look at me directly, which wasn't a good sign.

Actually, I said, I was just on my way to lunch.

Rudy gripped my shoulder, in a way that was very different from the friendly squeeze he'd administered earlier. As I stood up I saw he wasn't alone. An unsmiling man in dark clothes was standing behind him. I glanced over my shoulder to confirm what I already knew – that another goon, equally dark and dismal, was positioned next to the door.

Five minutes later I was sitting at a conference table in an office nine floors above mine, facing a woman wearing a grey suit and a sour expression. She was in her fifties and she looked like a first-class bitch.

Rudy stood against the wall near the door, looking as though he dearly wished he was on the other side of it. The door was glass, and the two goons I'd seen downstairs were now stationed outside.

There was a man of around sixty sitting on the same side of the table as the grey woman, but a little way back, near the corner of the room. His hands were folded over his stomach and he was watching proceedings with a bland smile and an air of polite interest, as though he wasn't really concerned with all this, and was merely paying a courtesy visit. He was clearly very dangerous.

Thank you for coming, the grey woman said, and without waiting for me to make any smart remarks about not having much choice she got to the point, which was to ask me why I'd reported that Kilroy was at my apartment with the girl.

Because, I said, he was there when I left this morning.

She consulted some notes briefly. Then she informed me that Kilroy's corpse had been discovered earlier, over a hundred kilometres from the city, in a car he'd hired.

Whatever I'd expected to hear, it wasn't that. I struggled for a moment, then began to see that it was obviously a mistake. I asked if the identification of Kilroy's body had been confirmed forensically.

Never mind that, she said, I'm more concerned about your story.

It's not a story. If you mean I'm lying.

You're either lying or you made a mistake.

What kind of mistake?

The grey woman hesitated for an instant and cast an almost imperceptible glance at the man in the corner. He appeared to be studying the ceiling light fixtures. The woman leaned forward and addressed me again:

Is it possible the man who came to your apartment – the man you *claim* came to your apartment – wasn't Kilroy, but someone who looked very like him?

Uh-oh, I thought, what kind of flakiness are we getting into now?

Please answer, the woman said.

I recalled Kilroy's slightly stale breath on my cheek as he greeted me. I shook my head. No way, I said.

The woman gazed at me with an expression of sceptical disdain, making me dislike her even more, which I hadn't thought possible.

Look, I said, why don't you just pick him up? Or if you've already got him, bring him up here. Let me talk to him. Have you been to my place yet?

Yes, we've been there, and apprehended the girl. Kilroy wasn't there, and there was no evidence of him having been there. The girl denied that he'd been with her. In due course we shall doubtless discover if she's telling the whole truth, but for now it seems to me that you lied to us, and we shall have to do our best to find out why. Shan't we?

An embryo of panic fluttered to life inside me. What was she suggesting? Why would I tell a lie like that, which could be discovered so easily? And where was Kilroy, if he wasn't at my place?

All right, I said, keeping my voice low and steady, maybe for some reason Kilroy was out when you went to pick up the girl. Maybe he'll be back.

Mrs Greybitch shook her head with a tight little smile. Unlikely, she said. Your apartment was watched for over an hour before the team went in, and for an hour afterwards, and there was no sign of Kilroy. If he was ever there.

He was there, I said. You need to look more closely at that corpse you found.

The woman raised her eyebrows fractionally and said nothing. The man in the corner was looking at me now, and didn't bother to look away when I glanced at him. His expression was as bland as ever. I got a strong impression he was a priest, even though he wasn't wearing vestments, or perhaps a high-ranking church doctor.

As I chewed this over another part of my mind was busy considering how to save my skin. Perhaps it was a mistake to insist so emphatically that Kilroy had been at my place, and it would be better to leave some room for doubt. After all, if you insist you're right, there's only one alternative, which is that you're wrong. Ambiguity can be more useful in certain circumstances.

All right, I said, making a show of looking defeated and puzzled, I guess it's possible I was wrong.

The woman leaned back in her chair. Oh, really, Ms Curtis? You seemed very sure a moment ago.

Yes, but you've got me confused now. I mean…well, you think you know someone, but how well do you really know them?

The woman checked her notes again before she spoke.

Ms Curtis, she said, you've been running Kilroy as an asset for nearly five years now. Is it possible you've developed a romantic attachment to him, and it's compromising your judgement in all this?

Yeah, I thought, good luck with romantic attachments of your own, you frigid old chilblain. What I said was, No, I've been scrupulous. Everything goes into my reports.

The man in the corner uncrossed his legs and tapped his thumbs together, once. That was all, but it was enough. The woman stood up abruptly.

Very well, Ms Curtis, she said, we shall continue this enquiry later.

May I go home?

No, you may not. I'm sorry, but that's not possible.

She walked out of the room without looking at me again. The two goons outside stood aside for her, then they came into the room. Rudy cleared his throat nervously. The man in the corner became fascinated by the light fixtures once more.

I was taken to the elevator by the two goons. Just before the doors closed, a man I'd never seen before stepped inside, and turned around quickly so I barely glimpsed his face. I stared at the back of his neck. He wasn't particularly large, but I found him frightening. I don't know how much you can really tell about a person from the back of their neck, but something about this particular neck made me think of restraints, and gags, and thin instruments, and not in a good way.

The elevator went down past the ground floor and stopped at the basement car park. I assumed they were going to drive me somewhere, but instead I was led to a small door in the far wall, with drab paint flaking off rusted steel. It was the kind of door you never really notice, of the type that generally leads to a utility area, or a boiler room, or somewhere equally boring. But this one, when the man I hadn't seen before opened it with a passkey, led to another elevator. We got in, and it started going down, and I knew I was in trouble.

Kilroy slept for two hours on the couch. When he woke up he could hear Sheba snoring in the bedroom even though the door was closed. He opened it carefully, padded in, and slipped the notebooks from her bag.

On his way out of the apartment he couldn't find the spare keys Curtis usually left in the hallway. He evaluated this information, and decided it wasn't significant enough to make him change his plans. He closed the apartment door softly behind him.

He walked down three flights of stairs and paused in the lobby. He didn't know if the building had a service entrance, but it wouldn't make much difference. Either they were watching the building – in which case they would be covering every exit – or they weren't. He tried to calculate the odds.

Had the car been discovered yet? How long would it take for them to realise the corpse inside it wasn't his? And when they did, how long would it take to find out about his relationship with Curtis, and come sniffing around?

Kilroy knew he was just putting off the moment when he would have to walk out of the building. He had a sudden memory of his childhood, and being a skinny kid shivering in his bathing shorts on a diving board, thinking about how cold the water would be. Delay achieved nothing, except to make your balls shrivel even more. He strode to the door and walked out into the street.

Not too hurried. Brisk, but not jittery. Look around but don't make it obvious. Quick glances. Keep it casual.

OK, he was clear.

He reached the tram stop just as the one he wanted arrived. Nice timing.

Kilroy got off the tram twenty minutes later in an old part of town. He walked two blocks to a quiet, cobbled street, and stopped at a door beside a shuttered storefront covered in faded graffiti. There were six buzzers attached to the door's rotting wooden lintel, screwed down over a mess of exposed wiring. Kilroy unlocked the door, and went inside.

He made his way up a narrow staircase to the fifth floor, each landing more dilapidated than the one below it. At the top of the building, beneath a skylight caked in grime, he unlocked the door to his secret hideout. That, at any rate, was what it amused Kilroy to call it, and as he never spoke of it to anyone else he could call it whatever he damn well pleased.

He'd been renting the apartment for several years. The terms of his lease were highly favourable, and his landlord – a Mr Gladstone – charged a very reasonable rent, mainly because Kilroy was renting the place from himself. He was Mr Gladstone, and had an ID card, bank account, and social security status in the name of Gladstone to prove it. He also had another set of documents in his capacity as a tenant, in the name of Mr Oliver, who paid his rent regularly and never gave any trouble. Originally, Mr Gladstone had taken ownership of only the shuttered store on street level, but soon he discovered that the previous owner held the lease on the entire building. Whenever the apartments on the other floors became vacant, Mr Gladstone installed in them, as a matter of preference, tenants who were elderly (with the exception of that nice Mr Oliver on the top floor, who was rarely seen) and kept their rent very low. In return, his elderly tenants expressed their gratitude by minding their own business, and not asking any questions. True, their landlord was reluctant to make any improvements to the building, and seemed to like keeping it a little down-at-heel, and somewhat nondescript – even unattractive, one might say – but hell, you couldn't have everything, what with the rent being so low.

It was a good set-up, and Kilroy had created the identities of Gladstone and Oliver, and taken ownership of the premises, with the help of skills he'd learned from various forgers, scammers, fraudsters and other criminal types whose acquaintance he'd made in his nineteen years as a cop, and opportunities that had arisen in the execution of his duty.

The apartment he now entered was surprisingly large, and could have been classed as a penthouse if it had possessed a view, and any decent fittings or furniture, and hadn't been such a shithole. Kilroy threw his coat onto the bed and walked through to an area he'd converted into a photographic studio and darkroom, and got to work.

An hour later he'd photographed every page of the notebooks. There were four books, including the one he'd started reading, and each contained thirty pages. Manfred had written on only one side of each page, and Kilroy wondered if the heretic had known that one day someone would need to copy them, and had tried to make it as easy as possible to record everything he'd discovered.

And what he'd discovered, Kilroy was beginning to learn, was astonishing. If only half of it was true, it was profoundly disturbing. Kilroy tried not to read the material as he was photographing the pages, but he couldn't help seeing occasional phrases.

He developed the negatives immediately and created a set of prints. As he worked, he resolutely resisted thinking about the ideas he kept glimpsing. He found it useful to push the words out of his mind by thinking of something different, in an exercise similar to the one he employed to delay his climax during sex. And, just like the technique that worked for him on those occasions, the most effective mental images for the purpose of distraction were grotesque or gruesome. Accordingly, he found himself repeatedly picturing the broken body of Brogan Livermore, smashed onto the cobbles beneath his balcony like a mountainous, misshapen blancmange. It wasn't pleasant, but it did the job.

Finally, in addition to the prints, Kilroy created a microfilm.

When he'd finished he lifted a loose floorboard in the bathroom and hoisted out a sports bag from the exposed cavity. He removed a gun and a box of shells from the bag. He still had the stranger's gun, which he'd swapped with his own police-issue pistol, but Kilroy took the view that when your life is falling apart, and danger presses in on every side, and you don't know what the hell is going on, nothing cheers you up like a bit of extra firepower. He put the gun, the shells and a few other items into a duffel bag, then he replaced the sports bag and repositioned the floorboard.

He closed the apartment and hurried down the stairs. He needed to get back to Curtis's place. He hadn't thought to leave a note for the girl, and he hoped she was still asleep. Time was short, and there was no Plan B.

There was no Plan A, either.

Kilroy acknowledged this to himself as he stood in the swaying tram. Long-term strategy wasn't his strong suit. He was a tactics man. Even the process whereby he'd acquired his hideout, and set up alternative identities to maintain it safely, had been a series of responses to unfolding events, rather than a result of forward planning.

But now he needed to think about the girl, and the material in the notebooks, and what he should do. He found it difficult to think clearly about the future when he was still struggling to understand everything that had happened in the past few days.

As he stepped off the tram, all thoughts of the past and the future vanished from his mind, and he was aware only of the present moment.

A glance at Curtis's apartment building told him something was wrong.

He ducked into the tram stop's pedestrian shelter and positioned himself behind a pillar displaying the timetable. While pretending to study the information he edged his head around the pillar once, twice, three times, and took in the whole street in a series of swift glances:

A big black vehicle parked next to the apartment building. An armed, black-clad guard beside the doorway. Any plain-clothes? Yes, one sitting outside a café twenty metres away on the same side. Any more? Ah yes – there she was: taking an interest in the shops on the other side of the road, moving back and forth between the same three stores, checking the reflection in the windows.

Movement in the building doorway: Sheba, being escorted out by two plain-clothes agents and another armed guard in black.

Kilroy's mind presented him swiftly with a series of options, and their probable outcomes. He saw himself running up to the goons who had Sheba in custody, and using surprise and violence to free her somehow. Then what? He wouldn't be able to help her run, or give her any useful instructions. No good. OK, how about simply marching up to them, identifying himself, and bargaining for Sheba's release? Absurd. Why would they agree? He had no leverage, and he might be detained on the spot. He'd left the photographic prints at his hideout, but he had the negatives and the microfilm in his pocket, and they would be taken from him. He visualised himself in a cell or a basement, being broken, giving up his hideout and his alternative ID, and then they had everything, and he had nothing. No good.

They were crossing the road, leading Sheba towards the vehicle. Was there a last chance to free her? No. Follow the vehicle? He didn't have the means. He saw himself trying to keep pace with it, running through traffic, looking like a lunatic. No way.

He slowed his breathing. The rush of adrenaline subsided, and the images flickered to a halt. He knew there were no sudden moves he could make that would work. It was time to take stock. The first question to consider was Curtis.

Kilroy didn't want to believe Curtis had betrayed him, and he didn't want to believe he was an idiot either, but both conclusions seemed inescapable.

Whenever he was investigating a case, Kilroy would never entirely rule out the possibility of coincidence playing a part. After all, coincidences did happen, surprisingly often. But at the same time, it was foolish to ignore facts that were staring you in the face, and spitting in your eye while they were doing it.

One fact was that Curtis had left for work, and a few hours later the authorities had shown up at her apartment. Another fact was that Kilroy was certain he and the girl hadn't been followed there. OK, that didn't make it a stone-cold fact, but it was close enough. And he'd dumped the stranger's car at a charging station, and keyed in the location so the hire company would know where it was, but he'd chosen a site more than a kilometre away. And if he and the girl had been followed all along, why wait until noon the following day to arrest them, and then come at a time when Kilroy wasn't even there? No, he had to accept that Curtis had turned them in. But she hadn't allowed for the possibility that Kilroy would want to go out, and copy the notebooks, which probably meant she didn't know about them. That was a relief, at least.

But he had to face another unavoidable conclusion. If Curtis had betrayed him now, it was likely she'd been betraying him all along.

He sat down on the bench inside the pedestrian shelter and turned his coat collar up. He kept both plain-clothes agents in view, and he could see they were focused on the doorway to the apartment building. Screw them, anyway. He knew he shouldn't drop his guard, but he needed to think, and to figure out what was bothering him so much.

It didn't take him long. He realised that the reason he'd always trusted Curtis was because they'd never been lovers. How fucked up was that? What did it say about him, that he expected a lover to betray him, but not a friend? That was why the betrayal by Curtis was so hard to take: because he valued friendship so much more than whatever existed between him and the women he slept with. Then it turned out Curtis couldn't be trusted even though he *hadn't* slept with her. She'd been using him, that was the truth. How had he missed the connection with her job at an insurance company? The answer was that he hadn't wanted to see it, because he hadn't wanted to consider the idea that she was working for an intelligence agency, and was cultivating him as an asset.

As he continued to chew things over, Kilroy was interested to find that his feelings towards Curtis were unchanged. He still liked her and cared about her. He just needed to recalibrate their relationship, that was all. He knew she could be in trouble if she'd reported that he and Sheba were both at her apartment, and then he'd slipped the net. He hoped she would be OK, but there was no immediate action he could safely take that would help her. She and the girl were both beyond his reach for now.

Shit, Kilroy said softly, and stood up. He walked away from the bus shelter without looking back at the plain-clothes agents, thinking about what to do next. His mind always worked better when he was on the move.

He'd taken only a dozen paces when his attention was drawn to a young couple standing in a doorway on the other side of the road. They were entwined in a passionate embrace, kissing and cuddling with great enthusiasm. The show they were putting on was transparently bogus. It was clear to Kilroy that they were engaged in surveillance, and their elaborate performance, far from concealing their intentions, only drew attention to what they were up to. Kilroy's first thought was that they were plain-clothes agents, like the pair he'd spotted closer to Curtis's building, but he decided they were too inept to be professionals. And too young. The man was lanky and angular, with a mop of curly hair, and he couldn't have been older than twenty. The girl looked even younger. The way they were clutching each other as they smooched allowed the young guy to look back along the street towards Curtis's building, while the girl could keep an eye on the other side of the road – and Kilroy. When she realised he'd spotted her, Kilroy could have sworn she actually blushed. She looked away and buried her face in the boy's shoulder, and whispered something. He kissed her, and swung her around so that his back was towards Kilroy, protecting the girl from his sight. Unbelievable. It was almost like they were little kids, who thought that as long as they covered their eyes, and couldn't see you, then you couldn't see them either.

In other circumstances, Kilroy might have laughed out loud at such hopeless amateurs, but in his current predicament, anyone keeping watch on him – no matter how inexpertly – posed a potential threat.

But if they weren't agents, who were they? It took a lot of nerve, or a lot of innocence, or both, to run the risks they were taking. It was one thing to keep Kilroy under surveillance, but spying so conspicuously on an operation by the state security apparatus was asking for trouble. When the goons had been escorting Sheba from the building, it was noticeable that everyone in the vicinity had studiously ignored what was happening – but not these two. Kilroy was almost inclined to go and confront them, and ask them what the hell they thought they were doing, but he walked away. He was thinking about some reports he'd been seeing over the last few weeks. The intelligence they contained was fragmentary and uncoordinated, but when you put them together it seemed that a general sense of dissatisfaction among the civilian population was being expressed – in a few isolated cases – as civil unrest, and this was being exploited by a handful of criminal elements, or simply reckless individuals, who were attempting to organise some kind of opposition to the state. Very few people in the Interior Department seemed to be paying much attention to this stuff, but Kilroy had a feeling the intelligence was being taken more seriously at the top of the department than at his level, where his colleagues tended to be contemptuous of the idea that a bunch of civilians would be able to pose any real threat to the equilibrium of the state. But Kilroy wasn't so sure.

He kept walking, and tried to thrust everything out of his mind except the immediate challenges he faced. He refocused on Sheba. There was nothing he could do for her right now, but he would find a way to help her somehow. He knew she would be facing a tough interrogation, at the very least. He'd told her in the car he could get the notebooks copied, but he hadn't provided any details about how or where he'd do it. Under interrogation she would reveal what she knew, but it wouldn't get them anywhere. Wait, he thought, what about my dad? Sheba would almost certainly reveal, under duress, that she'd been at Sylvester's place. Oh shit.

Kilroy walked faster. He needed to contact his father somehow, and warn him to make himself scarce, and arrange to meet up with him somewhere safe. He pictured the sleek, dark cars pulling up outside his old man's house, and the black-clad figures spilling out, eager to do violence, and he heard his own voice running through his head, telling his dad to scram, get going, leave. He needed to get a message to him, and fast. But how? He didn't trust the phone lines, not now.

He felt a plan forming in his mind, then began to see its outlines. It was sketchy and incomplete, and involved a fair amount of risk, but it was the best he could come up with at short notice.

He needed to get home – to his regular apartment, not the hideout – and he didn't know how much time he had. His apartment could already be under surveillance if the authorities were looking for him. It all depended on what Curtis had told them, and whether they still believed the body in the car to be his.

He decided to take a precautionary measure he'd been holding in reserve. He went into the next public toilet on his route, locked himself in a cubicle, and removed his disguise kit from the duffel bag. First, he brushed out a shaggy wig of black, synthetic hair. He wore his own hair short, and when the wig was on his head it created exactly the impression he wanted. He looked like a man wearing a cheap wig.

Which was the point.

Over the years Kilroy had encountered plenty of criminals who'd attempted to disguise themselves, and one of the most important lessons he'd learned was that it rarely worked. If it had worked, he wouldn't have caught so many of those who tried it. Often they went to great lengths to change their appearance, and spent money on surgical implants, pigment dye, prosthesis, and all manner of painful and costly procedures. But more often than not a good cop, looking hard enough, was able to penetrate even the most elaborate efforts. Because that's what good cops did: they looked hard. A clever disguise might thwart a casual glance from a civilian, but cops were scrutinising every face they saw, searching for any sign of the person they were looking for.

But cops are only human, and embarrassment is a powerful inhibition. A cop's reaction to seeing a man wearing a cheap and obvious wig is likely to be the same as anyone's. Holy shit, they think, that poor fool is either bald, or trying to hide a hideous disfigurement, but whatever the problem is, someone could at least have told him he looks like an idiot in that terrible hairpiece.

The cop, like anyone else, takes in the man's appearance at a glance, cringes in shame on his behalf, and *tries not to stare*. Either that, or they stare at the wig. The same insight prompted Kilroy to glue a large carbuncle on the side of his nose. Like the wig, people try not to look, but at the same time they can't tear their eyes away. They get fixated on the detail – the bizarre artificiality of the wig, the hideous gleam of the boil on the nose – and in the struggle to subdue their own compulsive gaze they overlook the big picture, and fail to consider the entire face.

When Kilroy emerged from the public convenience, the nervous glances directed at him by passers-by confirmed to him that the disguise was working perfectly.

He walked several blocks out of his way in order to reconnoitre his apartment building from both ends of the street. He didn't spot anyone keeping watch, but he was experienced enough to know he could be mistaken.

He entered a coffee shop three doors away from his building and made his way past the tables to a passageway at the back that led to the bathrooms. He glanced behind him, opened a door that was marked for the use of staff only, and slipped through into a service area. People were working in the kitchen directly ahead of him, but they didn't notice him as he ducked through an open doorway at the bottom of a stone stairwell.

He took the stairs to the top floor, where he climbed out of an unlocked sash window, and hoisted himself onto the roof. He made his way across the flat rooftops, stepping over the low walls separating them, until he reached the roof of his own building. He headed for the fire escape at the back of it. A quick glance over the edge told him that nobody was lurking in the rubbish-strewn enclosure behind the building, five floors down. Kilroy climbed down the fire escape to reach his own kitchen window, two floors below the roof. He paused and peered in through the dirty glass pane.

He was struck by how drab his kitchen looked. He imagined for a moment that the apartment belonged to a suspect he was investigating. Detective Kilroy would probably conclude, from the evidence he could see through the window, that the occupant was a single man, not well-paid, with few interests or friends, and an aversion to the use of cleaning products. A lonely figure, perhaps even pitiable.

Kilroy allowed himself a brief smile. OK, that's me. What of it?

He used his clasp knife to slip the catch of the window, and pulled it open. Squeezing through the small aperture, he lowered himself awkwardly down to the floor in the narrow space between the sink and the refrigerator.

A sudden eruption of noise and pain engulfed him as he was violently assaulted by his parrot.

Kilroy tried to protect his face from the furious, squawking bird as he sank to the floor under a storm of beating wings and vicious pecking.

Good boy! he shouted, Good boy, Creek!

The parrot recognised Kilroy's voice and executed a wild reverse-flapping manoeuvre to cease hostilities. It circled the kitchen twice at low altitude, then swooped up to perch on top of the refrigerator, from where it regarded Kilroy with what looked, to him, like a mixture of shock and remorse.

Kilroy held out his hand and the parrot fluttered down to settle on his wrist, then moved up his arm in a series of graceful little hops, lifting each delicately scaled leg with scrupulous deliberation, swaying and bobbing in a hypnotic kind of dance, until it was on his shoulder. It craned forward and bowed, gently bringing the top of its head to rub against Kilroy's cheek.

It's all right buddy, Kilroy said, I forgive you. You did good, you idiot.

He walked into the living room with Creek nestled beside his ear. The bird's food bowl was nearly empty. Despite what he'd learned, Kilroy was still confident that if he hadn't returned, Curtis would have come over within the next day or so to feed Creek.

At that moment the parrot squawked in his ear. Sorry! Sorrysorrysorry!

Kilroy recoiled, attempting to stifle a burst of obscenities that rose to his lips. Creek already possessed an extensive vocabulary of unsavoury language, which he happily unleashed at the slightest provocation, and Kilroy was currently trying to encourage the bird to tone it down a bit.

He shifted the parrot down onto the table, next to its open cage, and set about replenishing its food and water. When Creek seemed to have eaten and drunk enough, he hopped into the cage, settled on the perch, and admired himself in a small, round mirror.

Kilroy placed his bag on the table and unzipped it. The parrot caught the movement from the corner of its eye, and swivelled around. It looked at the open bag and froze. Slowly it raised its gaze to meet Kilroy's. It glanced down at the bag again, then looked up and stared fixedly at Kilroy. Attempting nonchalance, it shuffled away along the length of the perch, until it was pressed up against the bars at the back of the cage. It cast another swift glance down at the open bag, and the dark, yawning aperture it presented, then regarded Kilroy with a steady, unblinking gaze.

It's all right buddy, Kilroy said, I'm not going to put you in there.

The parrot didn't seem reassured. Kilroy inferred that it was still stricken with guilt over its assault on him, and was expecting punishment, and assumed it was facing imprisonment in the bag, perhaps followed by execution or exile.

Kilroy took a fermented mizzet stalk from the can of treats that lived on a shelf above the cage, and held it out to Creek. The bird hopped forward and happily took the peace offering in its beak. A mizzet treat had always been the seal upon a solemn bond between them, and the possibility that Kilroy might violate that trust was plainly beyond Creek's imagination.

Kilroy left the bird to enjoy its food.

He took a small notebook from the bag and carefully tore a thin strip of paper from one of its pages. Using a pen with a fine point he wrote a message on the slip of paper, then sealed it on both sides with clear adhesive tape. Next he fished a canister out of his pocket and removed the microfilm from it. Using more adhesive tape he sealed the microfilm on both sides.

Kilroy returned to the birdcage and lifted the parrot out gently. He was able to feel the beating of its heart beneath the soft feathers his hand enclosed. He placed Creek on the table, and drew up a chair. Now for the difficult part.

Kilroy rolled the note into a thin tube around one of Creek's legs, and used a small elastic band to keep it in place, adjusting it to be tight enough to prevent the tube from slipping, but not so tight it would be constrictive. He covered the tube and the elastic band loosely with another layer of tape. Then he repeated the process with the microfilm on Creek's other leg. The bird remained still throughout, and was patient when Kilroy fumbled. Creek seemed to sense the seriousness of what Kilroy was doing, and what would be required of him.

When Kilroy was finished he held the bird in both hands and lifted it up so its head was level with his own. He looked into its eyes and pursed his mouth. Creek hesitated for a moment, then tilted forward and rested the front of its beak against Kilroy's lips. It was a gentler kiss than they customarily exchanged.

Kilroy walked to the open kitchen window and reached through it with Creek in his hands. Go to Dad, he said, and released the bird.

Creek flapped away, then circled back, hovering outside the window.

Dad, Kilroy said, then closed the window and turned away.

When he looked back the bird was gone. He waited a couple of minutes then reopened the window and climbed out onto the fire escape.

KILROY

Kilroy needed to acquire a vehicle in a hurry without leaving a data trail. That ruled out hiring a car. Public transport was out of the question – too slow and too risky.

He recalled the solution Sheba had adopted when she went on the run. Not that he had any intention of riding a bicycle, but a motorbike was another matter: it would allow him to travel fast, and go off-road if necessary. He could also wear a helmet with a visor, and dispense with what remained of his disguise. It had deceived his parrot so successfully that the wig was in tatters, and there was no sign of the carbuncle that had decorated his nose. It was possible that in all the excitement, Creek had eaten it.

Kilroy walked for an hour until he reached a quiet residential area. It was early evening, and he spotted a few motorbikes parked on the streets or in driveways. He chose one that was chained to a garden fence and secured by a padlock. He picked the lock and hot-wired the bike in less than ten seconds.

He rode slowly through the suburbs until he found what he wanted: another motorbike of the same model as the one he'd stolen. He unscrewed the license plates of both bikes and swapped them, then he got back on the machine he'd stolen, revved it up, and took the fastest route out of the city.

He hoped he'd bought himself some time by exchanging the license plates. When the owner of the stolen bike reported its theft, the cops would simply add the registration to a list of missing motorcycles. Meanwhile, there was a good chance the owner of the second bike wouldn't notice immediately that its license plates had been changed. And when the mismatch was finally reported it might take several days for the two incidents to be connected, and a couple more before the trail led back to Kilroy. If he was lucky.

He drove past the entrance to his father's place just before dawn. He continued for two kilometres and took the next turning on the same side of the road. It was little more than an overgrown track, and he drove along it until he reached a broken wooden gate, where he parked the bike and continued on foot.

The field beyond the gate had belonged to his dad. After the laws prohibiting private citizens from growing crops came into force, Kilroy's mother became nervous about Sylvester's horticultural activities on the land around the house. Unable to reassure her, he simply relocated to the field Kilroy was now crossing, which was screened from the road by woodland. His wife knew perfectly well what he'd done, and where he went when he disappeared three mornings a week, but the couple maintained an unspoken agreement to pretend it wasn't happening. After Dora's death Sylvester abandoned the field, and recultivated the land around the house.

Picking his way carefully through tangled scrub in the pale early-morning light, Kilroy made for a rickety shack at the top of the field. He'd spent a lot of time there as a boy, having been brought along by his dad to help him dig, and plant, and tend his crops. But Kilroy found the work boring, and eventually Sylvester gave up trying to interest him in it, making his disappointment obvious by the transparency of his attempts to hide it. Kilroy had been allowed to pass his time in the shack, nailing old pieces of wood together and taking them apart again, never quite satisfied with his constructions.

He skirted the edge of the field and plunged through a hedge at the top so he could approach the shack from the rear. There was no sign the place had been visited recently, and when he peered in through a cracked window he saw it was empty. He walked around to the front and pushed at the door, splintering some of the warped, rotten wood as he forced it open. The shack smelled damp and mouldy, but it contained two old armchairs that were reasonably dry, and a few blankets in a wooden chest. Kilroy settled down to wait.

Sun was shining through the grimy window and into his eyes when he woke up.

It was ten in the morning. He hadn't intended to sleep. The warm sun was unleashing a pungent miasma of decay from the blanket in which he'd wrapped himself. Even after he stuffed it back into the chest his clothes still stank.

He stepped outside and looked around. It was a nice day.

He tried not to be too pessimistic about his father's failure to appear. For one thing, there was no guarantee that Creek had made it back to the house, and even if the bird had arrived, his father may not have noticed the message that was attached to its leg. He was an old man, after all.

But Kilroy had a good nose for bullshit, especially his own, and he couldn't shake the ominous feeling that was weighing him down.

He walked across the field and found the motorbike where he'd left it.

He cut the engine immediately after he turned into the driveway, and wheeled the bike in among the trees where they grew most densely. He parked it out of sight and walked towards the house, keeping to the edge of the treeline. Where the driveway opened out he stopped and crouched down behind some bushes.

Kilroy watched the house and waited. After fifteen minutes he was certain the place was empty. He didn't know how it worked, but somehow he was always able to determine whether a house he was watching was occupied or not. Sometimes he wondered whether the brain had an unconscious ability to detect subtle vibrations, capable of travelling through brickwork and glass, that betrayed the presence of a living person inside a building.

He stood up and walked to the front door. He felt like shit.

The front door was unlocked. Kilroy walked through the house to the kitchen. He didn't even bother to check upstairs.

He opened the back door and saw Creek. The bird was standing at the edge of the large hole where the girl had been hiding, and he was shifting restlessly from one leg to the other, looking tense and unhappy.

Kilroy drew his pistol and stepped through the doorway.

The parrot noticed the movement and backed away, its eyes

darting between Kilroy's face and the gun in his hand. Kilroy slipped his hand back under his jacket, but it was too late, and Creek took off. As the bird flew away Kilroy noticed that its feathers looked tattered, as if it had been mistreated.

He walked slowly towards the hole. His legs began to tremble and his heart felt like a stone that grew heavier with every step.

His father was lying face-upwards on the mattress in the bottom of the pit. His eyes were closed, and his brows were slightly furrowed. You might have thought he'd gone down there to relax and soak up the morning sun as he mulled a few things over, were it not for the small round hole in the middle of his forehead.

Kilroy sat on the ground, his legs dangling over the edge.

At least, he thought, I won't have to dig a hole to bury him in.

He laughed briefly. He had no intention of leaving his old man down there.

The ladder was propped up against the side of the hole. Kilroy climbed down it and lay on the mattress beside his father.

After a while he became irritated by the way the tears tickled his skin as they slid slowly down his cheeks and into his ears. It was difficult to cry when you were lying on your back. He rolled onto one side and put his arm around his father, holding him in a way he'd never done when he was alive. He nuzzled his head into the crook of his dad's neck, feeling the stubble against the top of his head, and closed his eyes.

When he opened them again he thought he might have slept, but he checked the time and saw that only five minutes had passed.

It was hard work getting Sylvester up the ladder, and at one point he considered the possibility of hauling him up with a rope, but he didn't like the idea. He hoisted his father's body onto his back. He used one hand to clamp the old man's arms around his own neck, and held onto the ladder with his other hand as he ascended, rung by rung.

After he got the body out of the hole he sat next to it on the ground, getting his breath. A movement caught his eye and he saw Creek, perched high in a nearby tree, ruffling his feathers. As he watched, the bird flew down and landed a few paces away. It looked ragged and distinctly unwell.

Kilroy felt a hot surge of anger at whoever had mistreated his friend. Then he saw Creek dip his head repeatedly, and he realised the bird was plucking at its own feathers, damaging itself.

He raised his arm slowly and held it out. C'mon buddy, he said quietly.

Creek hesitated. Kilroy waited, unwilling to stand up in case he scared the bird off. Just when he grew too weary to hold his arm out any longer, the parrot flew up and perched on his wrist. Kilroy waited for it to hop up to his shoulder, but it didn't. The message he'd written for his father was still rolled around Creek's left leg, but the microfilm was missing from the other one. It was possible, Kilroy thought, that if the bird had taken to pecking and plucking at itself it might have undone the tape and discarded the film of its own accord. Possible, but unlikely.

Creek clacked his beak, which was his customary prelude to delivering a pronouncement. He opened his mouth wide.

All fucked up, he croaked, and flew away.

Kilroy laid his father's body on the double bed in the main

bedroom. He didn't know if Sylvester had continued to sleep there after Dora died, and wondered if the old man had relocated to the cot in his study, which would have been like him. But a quick inspection of the bedroom revealed enough of his dad's things in there to suggest he hadn't abandoned the marital bed.

Kilroy was exhausted. It had taken him over an hour to get the body out of the hole, into the house, and up the stairs.

In the corner of the room there was a small armchair that his mother had liked. He pulled it into a position at the side of the bed from where he could see both the corpse and the door, and sat down.

Darkness and silence. Three in the morning.

Kilroy knew he hadn't been woken up by any sound or disturbance, and yet he also knew with absolute certainty that someone was in the house.

The blackness became less dense. He saw the shape on the bed and in the same instant he remembered what had happened.

He remained still for five minutes. Ten minutes. Nothing betrayed the presence of the person Kilroy knew was downstairs.

He stood up and walked to the door, and was aware of the floor creaking beneath his feet. But in the absence of a handy system of ropes and grappling hooks that would have enabled him to swing silently across the room, there was nothing much he could do about it. Except take his gun out.

As he stepped onto the landing he saw a faint light coming from somewhere below him. He went down the stairs slowly, gun in one hand, the other against the wall, ready to duck and roll if he needed to.

The light was coming from the kitchen.

A memory stirred in Kilroy's mind.

He stopped in the doorway and saw a woman sitting at the kitchen table with her back to him. The light was emanating from something on the table in front of her, hidden from his view.

It was his mother. The thought lasted only an instant, but it nearly undid him. He steadied himself against the door frame, then switched on the lights. Time seemed to slow down, and as the woman turned her head he recalled his mother sitting at that table, reading late into the night by candlelight, and how sometimes when he couldn't sleep he would come downstairs and find her, and she would turn towards him with her kind, concerned smile.

The woman wasn't his mother, but Kilroy couldn't have been more surprised if she had, in fact, been sitting there.

Hello, said the woman he knew as Cynthia.

Hello, Kilroy replied. Why are you here?

I came to meet you.

Kilroy gestured at the object on the table in front of her. It was the size of a book and had a glowing screen. What's that, he said.

It's a kind of…lightbox. That's how I'm using it right now, anyway.

For what?

Checking some pictures, Cynthia said. She held up the roll of microfilm that Kilroy had last seen when he'd taped it to Creek's leg.

Where did you get that?

I took it from your parrot. I found him wandering around outside. He seemed pretty traumatised, and I tried to soothe him, but he flew away. I'm sorry I didn't arrive in time to do anything about what happened to your father.

Kilroy said nothing. He tried to remain professional.

Look, Cynthia said, why not sit down and put the gun away?

Kilroy sat down opposite her, but he didn't put the gun away.

Cynthia glanced at it. No? she said.

No, Kilroy said.

Why not?

Because, Kilroy said, in the last forty-eight hours I've been in close proximity to two men who died violently. One of them was killed by me, but only because he showed worrying indications of wanting to shoot me. The other was my father. On both occasions you've also been in close proximity to those violent deaths. Now, I'm not one to jump to conclusions, and infer causality from correlation, and all that, but you being around these events seems suspicious to me right now. So, if it's all the same to you, I'll keep you covered, and if you make any sudden moves I'll shoot you in the shoulder. OK?

Cynthia smiled. Suit yourself.

Thank you. Now, I'm going to ask you some questions. I'd like straight answers, and I'd like them promptly. If I don't get them that way, I may just shoot you anyway, even without the sudden moves, because I'm in a strange mood, what with my father's corpse lying on a bed upstairs.

I'll do my best. But there are some things I can't –

No, Kilroy said. Not what I want to hear. Let's get started.

Cynthia nodded.

Kilroy noticed she didn't seem particularly concerned about the gun pointing at her, or his threat to use it. Perhaps it was this lack of concern that unsettled him, or perhaps it was the fact that he found her extremely attractive, or perhaps it was both, but he was shaking. Not on the outside, but something inside him shivered like a leafy sapling in a summer breeze.

He told himself to get a grip, and tried to clear his mind.

First, he said, tell me who you are.

I'm a scientist.

What kind of scientist?

I'm a geneticist. Or I was. My field of study has changed recently.

That's lucky, Kilroy said.

Why?

Because I don't know what the fuck a geneticist is.

Cynthia laughed. It doesn't matter.

Good. So, what's your new field, Cynthia? What are you studying now?

I'm studying you.

Kilroy didn't hear any irony or mockery in her voice, or see it in her eyes, which remained fixed on his own in a frank but unchallenging gaze. He frowned.

Studying me personally, or people in general?

Both.

That doesn't tell me anything.

Look, I'm just trying to be as honest as I can.

Kilroy placed his free hand flat on the table. So, he said, you're studying. And how are you doing that? Are you using the skyflies? I know there's a surveillance thing going on. That's what they are, right? And are you one of the people who's sending them?

The drones? Yes, kind of. I'm kind of involved.

Drones? Why do you call them that? Do they make a noise?

They used to. A long time ago. And I guess the name stuck.

You know we've been shooting them down, don't you? Or maybe that was the whole idea. You're trying to send us some kind of signal. Is that it?

Cynthia cocked her head and looked at him thoughtfully.

It's weird, she said, how you haven't developed real flight technology of your own by now.

What, like those things? Drones, or whatever? We don't have the science.

But you could have.

What do you mean?

You were on track to develop flight, even air travel, at one point.

At one point? What does that mean? At what point?

A few hundred years ago.

How the fuck do you know that?

Cynthia's expression became serious and she dropped her gaze. After a moment she looked up at him again and reached out across the table.

Give me your hand, she said. Not the one with the gun in it, obviously.

Kilroy liked that. Slowly he took her hand, but he kept the gun trained on her. She said nothing. He felt her fingers twitching slightly against his own, almost unconsciously it seemed, and he realised she was nervous.

OK, he said, why are we holding hands?

I don't know. Want to arm wrestle?

Maybe later.

They both smiled. Kilroy placed the gun on the table, but not where she could reach it. She glanced at it.

Even if I did, she said, it wouldn't help.

Even if you did what?

Swipe the gun.

Think you could?

She looked down again. She seemed to be making a calculation. Finally, she sighed, raised her eyes, and looked around the room.

What do I have to do to get a cup of coffee around here?

Don't change the subject. I'll make one in a minute.

OK.

I'm guessing, Kilroy said, you're not from around here, are you?

Ha! You could say that.

Right. So you're…what? A…badder?

Cynthia shook her head in amusement. I love how you all use that word. It's so… I don't know…

Infantile?

She shot him a shrewd glance. Yes. But I didn't want to say that.

It's all right. We're not idiots. Using a word like that helps people to be brave about it. Seriously. Like, it's a way of dealing with all the shit that's been going down, all the things we don't understand. Which I'm hoping you're going to tell me about.

I will. But please can we have a coffee first?

Fifteen minutes later Kilroy still hadn't touched the mug of coffee in front of him. What he was hearing had made him forget about everything else.

She began by talking about history. How much did he know? Not much, he confessed. History wasn't his strong suit. She told him it didn't appear to be anyone's strong suit, and she wondered why that was. Why did nobody know much about what had happened even a couple of hundred years ago, let alone five hundred years, seven hundred? And why didn't they seem interested in finding out about it?

Kilroy told her he hadn't devoted much thought to the topic. But he confirmed that history as a subject had disappeared from the school curriculum, and the few books that were available were bland and boring. The church had all the information you needed about the past. It was enough to know that Upstairs Mum and Dad were watching over us, and to be grateful to the blessed Shadbold, who had interceded for us in the turbulent, sinful times after the Creation, and had thus redeemed all who lived on Landmass. If you wanted history, there it was.

Cynthia said she begged to differ, and told Kilroy that Landmass had been created nine hundred years ago by scientists. Kilroy, and everyone else, was a descendant of people who had been put there by those scientists.

Kilroy didn't say anything for a full minute. Then he said, What do you mean when you say we were put here?

Perhaps it would be more accurate to say you were left here.

Along with Landmass?

Not exactly. This is where the history comes in. Are you ready to hear it?

Sure. Why do you ask?

You look pale. And you keep glancing at that gun.

Kilroy wasn't aware he'd been doing that. He thought perhaps there was a part of him that wanted to kill Cynthia, because of what she was saying, and the threat it posed to his grip on reality. But there was another part of him that wanted to hear more about what she was telling him, and suspected it made more sense than the beliefs he'd grown up accepting. He reflected that these very different impulses – the urge to kill Cynthia, and the need to listen to her – explained the sense of internal conflict he was experiencing.

Cynthia snapped her fingers at him. Hey, where are you Kilroy?

Sorry. Existential shit. Carry on.

All right. But look, I've finished my coffee and you haven't even started on yours yet. Do you want to make some more?

No thanks.

I meant for me, but never mind. We'll take a break after this next part.

Fine. On with the history lesson, Miss Cynthia.

OK, Cynthia said, here's the thing. Roughly a thousand years ago a major catastrophe began to happen around here. The level of the oceans had been rising steadily, and then not so steadily, and everyone knew it was happening, and some people were trying to stop it, but suddenly – boom, the change became exponential. It looked like everyone and everything was going under.

Wait, Kilroy said, that was the Flood. That's in the scriptures.

Well, it wasn't exactly a flood. It was slower than that. But still fast enough to make everyone freak out. Finally.

Finally?

Right, finally. Because even though it had been clear to pretty much everyone for some time that the world was heading for the edge of a cliff, you'd be amazed by the number of people who still didn't want to admit it publicly, and even when they admitted it, they didn't want to do anything about it.

Why? What was wrong with them?

They were worthless pieces of shit, that's what. Some people are just bad, and there's not a lot you can do about it. Or perhaps you have different views on the matter? I imagine you've come across a few bad people in the course of your work, Detective Kilroy. But perhaps you've reached a different conclusion, and you're convinced there's some good in everyone?

Personally, I think there's some of everything in everyone.

Cynthia pushed her hair back from her face. Perhaps you're right, she said. It's just that I can't talk about all this stuff without getting angry. Sorry. I just cannot believe that we – they – that they left it until it was too late.

All right, Kilroy said, so the flood happened, or whatever you want to call it, but clearly it didn't drown everyone. You know what it says in the scriptures, right? It says Shadbold saved us, and sacrificed himself doing it, and that's why Upstairs Mum and Dad changed their minds and didn't destroy us.

Shadbold, Cynthia said. That motherfucker.

Kilroy raised an eyebrow. OK, he said, that's some pretty fierce blasphemy right there, Cynthia. Fierce enough to get you executed.

She gave a short, bitter laugh. Like I care, she said.

Kilroy didn't reply. Cynthia seemed lost in thought.

A soft chiming broke the silence, startling Kilroy. He realised it was coming from the book-sized device Cynthia had been using, which was now emitting a pulsing glow. She snatched it up, angling the screen so Kilroy couldn't see it.

Oh shit, she said, staring at the screen. We need to hide.

She slipped the device into the pocket of her coat and stood up. Where can we go? Is there an attic or something? A basement? Anywhere!

Kilroy strode to the stove and swivelled the base aside to reveal the recess underneath. He stepped back and looked at Cynthia. She seemed afraid, and it was the first time he'd seen her lose her composure.

She peered down into the hole. Dear god, she said, it's small. But it's good, it's better than a basement. I just hope they haven't got thermals with them.

Thermals?

Never mind, get in.

They heard the first footsteps two minutes later. After that Kilroy found it difficult to calculate the passage of time. He and Cynthia were pressed together so tightly they took it in turns to breathe, one in, the other out. They'd nearly suffocated until they came up with that system.

There wasn't room to lie side-by-side. Kilroy was on his back and Cynthia was half on top of him, with her legs scissoring his. Her face was mashed against his neck, with her mouth slightly open, as if she were giving him a long, brutal kiss. One of her arms was pressing against the other side of his face, and a button on her sleeve dug into his flesh. He could even feel the stitching on the sleeve's fabric. With every breath she took he felt her ribs shifting, even through their clothing, and he knew she was equally aware of every movement of his own body.

Kilroy tried to calculate how many people had entered the house. He knew there were probably fewer than it seemed to him down there, where every step was amplified in the hollow spaces beneath the floorboards, but he was sure there were at least four of them.

He became aware that Cynthia's sweat was mingling with his own where their flesh touched. The heat was stifling.

The footsteps came and went. It seemed the intruders were roving all over the house. At a certain point one person, or it could have been two people, came into the kitchen, or back into the kitchen, and then stood perfectly still, almost directly above them. For how long? A minute. Two minutes. Then they went away, and joined the other sets of footsteps, roving, roaming, up and down, in and out.

Twice it seemed they'd gone, only to return after a few moments. Finally, everything was still. A minute passed. Two minutes. Longer.

Kilroy thought they should move, but they didn't move.

He wondered if Cynthia felt the same way he did – that even though the danger had passed, or probably had passed, there was something about the two of them lying there so close together that was comfortable, even in their extreme discomfort.

Cynthia's breathing changed. Let's get out, she whispered.

They stood facing each other. Kilroy had been surprised by the light when they emerged from the hole. He realised it must have been nearly dawn when they hid, and now it was morning. They'd been down there about half an hour.

They were close. It was as if they'd been pressed together so tightly that some kind of alteration had taken place in their bodies, which now needed to touch each other in order to feel whole, and they couldn't break apart.

Kilroy moved towards her and she seemed to flow into his embrace. They clung to each other as they kissed. Cynthia let go and stepped back.

We can't, she said.

Kilroy said nothing. He focused on his breathing.

Something was wrong. The house felt emptier. He sensed an absence, and he knew what it was even before he spoke:

I need to check upstairs.

He took the stairs fast, the blood pounding in his head, and then he was standing in the open doorway of the bedroom, looking at the slight indentation on the covers where his father's body had lain.

No, he said. Why did they take him?

He heard Cynthia's voice behind him. Maybe to make you feel bad, she said.

But where have they taken him?

I have no idea, Cynthia murmured.

Kilroy lay down on the bed and buried his face in the covers, trying to fit himself into the indentation, and to mould himself to the contours of his dad's absent body, and to smell him.

He heard the bedsprings creak as Cynthia lay down beside him.

She began to stroke his hair. He rolled over and she held him.

CURTIS

They left me alone in a cell without telling me why I was there, which came as no surprise to me. Standard procedure. But I suspected I'd have company before too long.

The man who'd got into the elevator at the last moment had walked ahead of me on the way to the cell, continuing to provide me with a good view of the back of his neck. As the cell door was being closed I finally got a look at his face, which was pretty similar to his neck, frankly, in that it was basically a slab of creased flesh, although the face had a small, punchable nose in the middle, and the neck didn't. He made sure I saw him staring at me impassively as the solid metal door swung shut.

Something told me I'd be seeing that face again soon.

He returned after what I estimated was a couple of hours. They'd taken my watch, of course. I didn't have a belt they could take, but they took my shoes, in case I found an ingenious way to do myself in with them, like perhaps swallowing them.

I was lying on the bunk when Slab-face returned. He sat on one of two chairs that were either side of a small metal table. Everything was bolted to the floor. The custodian asked him if he should stay, and my friend dismissed him with a curt gesture, implying it was absurd to suggest he'd have any trouble with me. He placed both hands on the table and looked at me.

I liked the way he moved. His body was heavy but there was a nice precision and economy to his gestures, and even the way he sat. He knew exactly how much energy to expend in order to achieve what he wanted. I enjoyed his solidity.

He didn't tell me to get up off the bunk, but I did, and sat down opposite him, as he must have known I would. There was no advantage to be gained from talking to a man like that while lounging on a bunk.

He told me his name was Pascal and he was the senior information officer on my case. I knew what that meant, and he knew that I knew. To people in our line of work, saying you're a senior information officer is equivalent to putting on a black hood and pulling out your monogrammed thumbscrews.

He began by asking me questions about Kilroy to which he already knew the answers. Then he got interested in whether we'd slept together, but not in a creepy way. That wasn't the point. All in good time. At this stage of my interrogation he was playing the role of a skilled, objective professional. It was all about establishing a baseline: a house style, a rhythm, a sense of familiarity – which he would then, at some point, suddenly disrupt, and break out of, to throw me off-balance. Then the fun would start.

I tried to use my answers to find out as much as I could, but Pascal was too experienced to give me anything. I particularly wanted to know why my superiors seemed to think Kilroy was dead, when I'd seen him alive a few hours ago. And if he wasn't dead, whose corpse had they found in the car? If, on the other hand, he *was* dead, who the hell did I let into my apartment this morning? A vexing question.

And my superiors seemed equally vexed by it, if Pascal's line of questioning was any indication of where they found themselves. He made me go over everything several times, from my first sight of Kilroy and the girl when I opened the door to them, to the moment I left the apartment. He picked up on tiny details in my account, and tried to make me contradict myself when he asked me to repeat them.

No matter what he asked me, behind it all was a single question: how could I be certain the person I'd seen this morning was really Kilroy? He asked me to describe the sequence of events again. I began to get exasperated, as Pascal doubtless intended.

I hadn't mentioned to him that I'd noted Kilroy's slightly stale odour when we'd embraced, but I kept telling him I knew it was Kilroy, and he kept asking me how I could be so sure, until I lost my temper and said, He even smelled the same, dammit!

Pascal leaned back a little. He gazed at me expressionlessly, and I got the impression complicated machinery was at work behind his eyes.

All this time his hands had remained flat on the table, but now he brought them together and intertwined his fingers. He nodded slowly.

That's interesting, he said.

There was a knock at the door of the cell.

Come in, Pascal said.

The door opened and the custodian poked his head inside.

Excuse me sir, he said.

Pascal didn't take his eyes from mine. What is it?

Call from the top floor, sir. They'd like a word.

Pascal stood up and walked out without saying anything. The custodian gave me an odd look as he closed the door.

It was a pretty corny tactic. The interrogator arranges to be called away, either after a certain amount of time, or at an agreed signal. In this case it may have been when Pascal moved his hands. I couldn't see a camera in the cell but that didn't mean there wasn't one. Either way, the suspect is left to stew for a while. After a suitable interval the interrogator returns. Their manner is different. Something has changed. They exude confidence, possibly a hint of triumph. They have news for you, which can be adjusted according to how savvy you are, what you're accused of, and what they want from you:

We've found the evidence we need to put you at the scene of the crime.

Your accomplice has told us everything.

We've just heard your mother has been admitted to hospital after collapsing when she heard of your arrest.

If you confess to the crime, and a few others we'd like to clear up, we'll try to ensure you get a lighter sentence.

Several witnesses have come forward to swear you are a habitual liar, thief, murderer, cannibal, poltroon, bed-wetter, etc.

It's all laughably transparent, even to someone unfamiliar with the tactics of interrogation, and I couldn't believe Pascal was planning to try something like this. As it turned out, I was right. The interruption, for once, didn't seem to have been a contrived move, and when he strode back into my cell about twenty minutes later his manner had indeed changed, but not in the way I'd expected.

As before, he sat down and placed his hands flat on the table, and once again I admired his solidity, his economy of movement. He seemed a little subdued. He didn't say anything for a while, and once – just once – he drummed the fingers of one hand on the table, until he caught himself doing it. He glanced at me with what might have passed for a smile in a more prepossessing face. Then the questions started again.

But now it was all about the girl. He mentioned Kilroy only in the context of his relationship with Sheba: how close they were, what she might have told him, what she might have given him, where they'd been and what they'd done.

Wearily, I began to repeat my account of the morning's events, but he cut me off:

All right, he said, but what about the last time you saw Kilroy? That was on the Sunday, after church. What did you talk about at that meeting?

It was all in my report, I said.

I know. But think back. What did he say about the girl? Did he tell you how he was planning to track her down?

No, I said, he didn't go into details. He told me he'd be heading east, and said he hoped she wasn't planning to steal a boat, but he was kind of joking. As it happens, we'd talked about it the night before, over a drink, but that was more of a personal thing, about Kilroy being a city boy, and how he was feeling about going out to the country.

Pascal narrowed his eyes, which made them almost disappear, given they were about as narrow as a pair of eyes can get in the first place.

So, he said, what *did* you talk about on the Sunday, there on the bench beside the river, if not the girl?

I shrugged. We talked about the decree that had just come out, mainly.

And detective Kilroy expressed no opinions about the girl? Did he say he thought she was guilty, or not?

No, but he didn't say he thought she wasn't.

Did he give you any indications that he might go rogue on this?

No, he didn't.

And how did you think he was planning to proceed?

The usual way. I assumed he'd be methodical, and liaise with the local police chiefs in the areas he visited, that type of thing.

Pascal got thoughtful again. Yes, he said softly, the police chiefs. I don't suppose you know anything about that, do you?

I spread my hands. Sorry, you've lost me.

Never mind. Did Kilroy mention his interrogation of the brother?

The brother?

The boy. Roland. Sheba's younger brother.

Oh, right. No, he just said there was a misunderstanding.

What kind of misunderstanding?

About his chief telling him he shouldn't have taken the boy into custody, and should have been focused on Sheba from the start, but it wasn't Kilroy who'd ordered Roland's arrest. So I guess you'd call that a misunderstanding.

Yes, Pascal said, I guess you would. But did he refer to Roland's testimony about his sister's reading habits? That she had her nose in some kind of book?

No, he didn't mention that.

And do you yourself know anything about a book?

No, I don't.

Pascal stood up abruptly. The door opened behind him immediately, confirming my suspicion that there was a camera watching us.

Once again he left without saying anything.

I thought I'd probably be seeing him again.

Some time later a strange thing happened.

I was woken up by the cell door being opened. A figure was silhouetted in the doorway by a dim light. I realised it was the custodian.

I asked him what time it was.

Late, he replied. About four in the morning.

For a moment my insides tingled and felt liquid. It's the middle of the night, I thought, and I'm about to be taken to my execution. But something about the custodian's manner dispelled that notion, and I could see he was alone.

What do you want? I asked him.

Sorry, he said, I didn't mean to frighten you. Can you come with me?

Why?

It's easier if you just come. It's all right.

What about the cameras?

I've adjusted them. It will be all right, I swear. Just come with me.

I couldn't think of a good enough reason to refuse, so I got up and followed him out into the passageway.

The lights were low. They were recessed into the ceiling, and created a series of illuminated pools on the floor, stretching away into the distance.

I asked him where we were going.

Just along here, he said.

He was a few steps ahead of me and he stopped abruptly next to a cell door. He pushed at it gently and it swung open.

I glanced up at the ceiling.

The custodian caught my look and said, It's all right, I've taken care of the cameras, and nothing will happen. Believe me.

I nodded. He beckoned to me and I walked to the open doorway.

Inside, sitting at a table like the one in my cell, facing the door, was the girl. Sheba.

The custodian ushered me inside and I sat down opposite her.

Sheba looked up at him. How much time?

He glanced back into the passage. I don't know, he said. Half an hour? Just tell her what you told me.

OK, she said. Thanks, Alexander.

Want me to stay?

Whatever you think.

Best if I stay outside, the custodian said, and keep an eye on things.

He closed the door gently, leaving me alone with Sheba.

She looked a little haggard, and I wondered what she'd been through since I'd last seen her, but whatever it was, it didn't seem to have broken her. The sense of extraordinary vitality that had struck me so forcefully when I first met her was undiminished. She looked me steadily in the eye, and she seemed perfectly calm, but her gaze was almost painfully intense. It was uncomfortable to be under her scrutiny, but you couldn't look away.

Have they hurt you? I said.

A little.

My heart went out to her. When it came back it brought

unwelcome news for me. I had to admit to myself that I knew she hadn't killed her mother. I'd been able to ignore the truth – or distract myself from it – by following my professional drill, but it was impossible to maintain that self-deception in her presence. She was like a truth serum.

If it's all right with you, she said, I've got something I need to tell you.

Go ahead.

Thanks. I'll try to keep it short. I just need you to listen, and not ask any questions until I've finished, is that OK?

I nodded. I wouldn't have dreamed of disobeying her.

I didn't say anything for the next half-hour while she was talking.

I didn't say anything after she'd finished either.

What she told me was unbelievable, but I knew it was probably true. If someone else had tried to convince me of the story it might have been different, but by the time she stopped speaking, everything she wanted me to know was inside me and couldn't be removed, like a stain in my bloodstream.

After I'd been silent for more than a minute she asked me what I was thinking. I shook my head. I wasn't sure what I thought. But I knew what I felt, which was afraid.

OK, I said finally, who else have you told, apart from the custodian?

I can't say.

Why not?

It's not safe for them.

And why did you tell me?

Because I trust you.

Wait, I said, you know I betrayed you and Kilroy, right?

She nodded. I don't care.

147

Why not?

Because you believe what I've just told you. I knew you would.

Before I could think of anything to say, the custodian reappeared in the doorway. He said he couldn't risk giving us any more time, and he needed to fix what he'd done to the cameras. He looked at me apologetically.

I'd better get you back to your cell, he said.

As we walked along the passage he whispered, What do you think?

My mind is numb, I said.

That girl is something else.

I know. What did they do to her? Did they put her to the test?

Not the full strength, but it was still hard.

And?

Nothing. She reacted to the pain, but she didn't tell them anything. I've never seen anyone like her before.

We reached my cell and he turned to me. I took you there, he said, because she asked to see you. I did it for her. I have to trust you.

You can trust me, Alexander.

We shook hands, which I found strangely moving. Then he locked me in my cell.

I didn't think I'd sleep any more that night, but I must have dozed off eventually, because when the cell door was opened it took me a moment to remember where I was. As I did, I also recalled my encounter with Sheba, and what she'd told me, and I felt a hollowness in the pit of my stomach.

The custodian jangled his keys. He shot me a glance whose meaning I understood, and I gave him a quick nod to let him know I wasn't about to snitch on him and get him killed. I hoped that would brighten his day.

Pascal appeared behind him, but he didn't come into the cell.

Come with me, he said.

We were back in the top floor office and the old gang was all there. The atmosphere seemed even chillier than on my last visit.

The hatchet-faced woman glowered at me from her seat at the head of the table. Rudy looked as uncomfortable as ever in his post next to the door, and the addition of Pascal to the group failed to introduce any element of levity to the proceedings. Even the older man in the corner looked unhappy, insofar as his expression betrayed any readable emotion.

The woman, whose name I later discovered was Allardyce, got straight down to business. We've established, she said, that the body in the car wasn't Kilroy's.

That's good news, I said.

Why?

Well, because at least you know I was telling the truth. About Kilroy being at my apartment, and it really being him.

That may be the case, Ms Curtis, but it doesn't help us. Or you, for that matter. It just means it's more urgent than ever that we apprehend Kilroy.

I frowned and nodded, like a good girl. I didn't want to push my luck, but I thought I saw an opportunity to find out a few things – especially how much they knew about what Sheba had told me, and what they planned to do with her. I took a breath, and tried to sound reasonable:

But can you tell me, I said, what Kilroy has done, exactly? I mean, he showed up at my place with the girl, when presumably he had orders to capture or kill her, but I didn't ask too many questions. To me he was still an asset, and I didn't want to scare him off.

The man in the corner gave a little cough.

Perhaps, he said in a silky voice, it might be more fruitful to focus on the young woman you've referred to. She is, after all, the main object of our concern. I think we can all agree on that, can we not?

Pascal and Rudy murmured in respectful assent. Allardyce didn't. It's true, she said, that the girl is of concern to us. But she, at least, is in custody, whereas Kilroy is not. Until we find him we won't know what his motives in this whole affair were, and how much of a threat he poses. I believe we can all agree on that as well.

There was silence in the room. Unless I was very much mistaken, Allardyce had just told the older man to keep his nose out of her business and go fuck himself. Perhaps, I thought, I might have to change my opinion of her.

I heard Pascal breathing heavily, and if it were possible to hear a person perspire I was pretty sure I heard Rudy, beside the door, doing just that.

Allardyce had maintained eye contact with me throughout her exchange with the older man, and now she continued:

Ms Curtis, she said, it's imperative for us to know what the girl told Kilroy in the time they were together and whether his decision to disobey his orders was a result of it. Did he mention anything about that?

No, he just told me he wanted my help to protect her, and said he knew that doing so could put me in danger. It's all in my report, and I've been over it several times again down in the cells.

Allardyce pursed her lips. All right, and what about the girl?

Did she say anything to you about Kilroy?

No, nothing.

The older man leaned forward. May I ask, he said to me, what you made of her? I appreciate, of course, that you only met her for a very short time.

Little do you know, I thought to myself, but I frowned, as if I were trying to remember.

Allardyce tapped the table with her fingernail. Come along Ms Curtis, you've simply been asked for your general impression.

I found her quite…striking, I said.

The old man raised an eyebrow. Striking?

A strong personality.

Persuasive, would you say?

I imagine she could be.

Interesting, he murmured to Allardyce, don't you think?

Yes, Allardyce said testily, and she will be dealt with in due course, but for now, we need to keep her…with us. As I've said.

The man inclined his head in a gesture of acquiescence that was clearly ironic, and calibrated to assert his status in whatever game was being played here.

If Allardyce was even aware of the nuance in his attitude she didn't appear to give a shit about it. Instead, she lobbed me a bombshell.

Ms Curtis, she said, we believe Kilroy may try to contact you.

I looked around the room. What, here?

No. You're being released.

I felt suddenly breathless. I tried to show no emotion, but Allardyce knew the impact her announcement was having on me.

The fact is, she said, we're not sure how much Kilroy knows.

Wait, I said, are you telling me you don't know whether Kilroy is aware that I betrayed him?

That's correct.

Let me get this straight, I said. You're asking me to sit tight, and if Kilroy shows up I'll have no way of knowing if he's going to give me a bunch of flowers or shoot me in the legs and laugh while he watches me bleed to death.

I appreciate we're putting you in a difficult position, Ms Curtis.

Thanks.

Look, she said, we wouldn't ask you to do this if we didn't have to. But the girl, Sheba, may have been in possession of extremely subversive material. We must know whether any or all of this material has passed into Kilroy's possession and if so—

She was interrupted by a positive storm of coughing from the man in corner. She turned slowly to look at him.

I beg your pardon, he said, but I feel it's unnecessary for Ms Curtis to know more details than is required at this stage.

I beg to differ, Allardyce said, and if you'll permit me, Doctor Glibbery, I believe I'm in a better position than you to make a decision about what is and isn't appropriate for a diligent operative of my apparatus to know. I'm asking her to risk her life in this instance.

He didn't reply to that, and the party broke up soon afterwards. I left the room with a higher estimation of Allardyce than I'd had before.

Rudy tried to speak to me as I made my way downstairs, but I brushed him off.

I was free, but I felt far from safe.

I had a lot to process. If my impression was correct I'd just witnessed a significant breach in relations between the church and the security services. Allardyce had referred to the man in the corner as Doctor, confirming my suspicion he was a scientist at the highest level of the church. As for her, she was clearly in the top echelons of the security apparatus.

As far as I could make out, Allardyce was doing her best to keep Sheba alive, even if her motives were far from charitable. Glibbery, meanwhile, seemed to have reached the conclusion that the girl should be disposed of, the sooner the better.

I could see his point. What Sheba had told me represented a convincing refutation of everything we'd been taught to believe. Furthermore, the ideas she proposed could, in the wrong hands – or the right ones – effectively overturn the established social order and the system of authority that maintained it. They were revolutionary.

But it wasn't just about ideas, it was about her as a person. I'd never come across anyone quite like her before. It was more than just charisma, or allure, or an exceptionally forceful personality. What she had was power, and it was clear to me she would destroy the state unless the state destroyed her first.

Such were my cheerful conclusions as I rode the elevator down from the top floor. But it wasn't quite that simple, as I was about to discover.

KILROY

Not for the first time, Kilroy awoke with tender feelings for a naked woman beside him in bed, and thought perhaps he was in love. He was determined to behave like a gentleman.

Cynthia's eyes were open and she was looking at him.

Good morning, she said. She sat up in the bed and leaned back against the headboard, making no attempt to cover herself. She looked very good, Kilroy thought.

About last night, he said.

What about it?

I enjoyed it very much.

Cynthia smiled. You did? I'm glad to hear it. I enjoyed it too.

But maybe I should apologise.

For what?

Well, I was pretty shaky last night, before one thing led

to another, and I didn't try to hide it. Maybe you felt sorry for me, and I should have been aware of that. I mean, the vulnerability, you know? I'm not saying it wasn't real, because the truth is I was knocked sideways about my dad, but maybe it made things a little unfair, and me being like that ended up kind of…exploiting your feelings. Not that I meant to, but maybe it did.

Very nice speech, Cynthia said, but has it not occurred to you that perhaps I just felt like a fuck?

Oh. Right.

Cynthia rolled over and kissed him. Kilroy felt himself becoming aroused, but she disengaged and moved back to her previous position.

If you really want to exploit me, she said, you'll make me some breakfast.

Cynthia finished the last of the food on her plate.

It's amazing, she said, what you can do with this stuff.

Kilroy had found some marinated spood in his dad's icebox and fried it with herbs.

I'll take that as a compliment, he said.

Sorry, I didn't mean—

None taken. But not what you're used to, right?

Not really, no.

Because you have a different type of food where you come from.

Right.

Which is where?

Which is a long distance away.

Landmass Two?

OK, Cynthia said, let's call it that. But I haven't been there all the time. And neither has what you call Landmass Two, for that matter. It was submerged until pretty recently.

So where were you before?

Before that I was somewhere else entirely. Not on any landmass.

Are you telling me you were underwater? There are stories about submerged cities, and even whole countries down there. It's mostly a bunch of lies that fishermen tell when they're drunk. Which you'd have to be, because talking about that type of thing is seriously discouraged. There are laws against it.

No, Cynthia said, not underwater. Not down there. Wrong direction.

What, you mean…in the sky?

Keep going.

Like…on another planet?

Not exactly. But something similar.

Holy fuck.

Let's go outside.

Why?

You look like you could use some air.

They sat on the back porch, in a pair of creaky old chairs that had been there for as long as Kilroy could remember.

He gazed at the trees. Occasionally he shot a glance at Cynthia, who smiled at him. He opened his mouth to speak a couple of times, but he couldn't seem to find the right questions to ask.

Cynthia reached over and stroked his hand.

You OK?

I'm sorry, Kilroy said, I'm just trying to…understand. So, from what you're saying, and what I've read in those notebooks, everything hereabouts went to shit around a thousand years ago, but some people got away. They escaped, yes?

Escaped, survived, whatever you want to call it.

How many?

Several thousand to begin with, then another few thousand, then the ones who stayed behind until the last moment. Those were the scientists, mainly.

All the scientists stayed?

God, no. Just a handful. A few hundred. Maybe a thousand or so.

Why did they stay?

Let's just say we wanted to ensure life survived here. They, I mean. The original scientists. Nine hundred years ago.

How did they do it?

Cynthia took a breath. This is going to sound weird to you, and probably a little creepy. But they kind of…took what makes everyone human, the basic material, and adjusted it, so it had a better chance of surviving what was happening here. They changed the design in a couple of small ways. Nothing very dramatic.

Hold on. Are you talking about building new people?

No, not new people. Not at all. I mean, when you look at us, you and me, we're almost identical. In most ways. Like, what happened last night. We couldn't have done that, let alone enjoyed it, if we weren't biologically compatible.

That's true. I personally felt we were very biologically compatible.

Cynthia laughed and patted his hand. Me too, sweetheart.

But you're saying we're different in *some* ways? Our bodies, our minds?

Look, even if they'd wanted to, they couldn't have changed things in a big way.

And did they want to?

Make bigger changes? No. The whole purpose was to ensure

the survival of the species, in this place, with the minimum of genetic deviation.

The minimum of what now?

Genetic deviation. I'll explain another time. But this wasn't some type of ghoulish Frankenstein experiment.

You've lost me again.

Sorry. Specific cultural reference that was omitted from the starter pack.

Starter pack?

Oh hell, this is going to keep happening. Just accept it doesn't matter. Please?

OK. I'll have to take your word for it.

Cynthia didn't reply to that, and Kilroy remained silent. After a couple of minutes, she gave his hand a squeeze. He turned to her.

She raised an eyebrow. What's on your mind, Kilroy?

Just thinking. These scientists, right? The ones who stayed. They were all good people? All dedicated, selfless, committed to doing the right thing?

Why do you ask?

I'm just wondering. A thousand people? With that many, there must have been some conflict. There always is. Everyone has their own agenda, even dedicated scientists. Especially them. Some of the worst mayhem I've investigated has been caused by very bright people working together until they start working against each other. I can't believe that out of a thousand people there's nobody who loses the plot, or goes rogue.

Cynthia let go of his hand. She hugged herself as if she were cold.

Of course, she said, there were different views. There still are. That's one of the reasons I'm here. But whatever happens,

Kilroy, please believe that I'm doing what's best. For you, and for all of us. Please.

OK, I'll give it a shot.

Cynthia smiled, a little sadly it seemed to Kilroy, and was about to speak when her attention was caught by something behind him.

Hey, she said, it's that bird of yours.

Kilroy saw Creek flying towards them. The parrot circled a couple of times, then settled at the edge of the same hole in which Kilroy had discovered his father's corpse.

He still looks unhappy, Cynthia said.

But Kilroy was already on his feet, walking towards the hole, then running. Before he got close to the bird it took off and made for the trees. Kilroy reached the edge of the hole and looked in.

He dropped to his knees.

Cynthia was running towards him.

Fuck! Kilroy yelled. What the fuck is happening?!

Cynthia reached him. She looked down into the hole and saw the corpse.

This is wrong, Kilroy said. Why would they do this? Why put him back down there?

He felt Cynthia's hand on his shoulder. Slowly he got his breathing back under control. He stood up and gazed around. Things seemed unfamiliar to him.

For what it's worth, Cynthia said quietly, it's possible the people who took the body from the house aren't the same people who killed him.

Why? What do you mean?

Somewhere along the line, my people could be involved.

Your people? What people?

People like me, who come from where I'm from.

What are they doing here? I thought you wanted to help.

I do. But some of my people don't want me to be here. They're looking for me.

Kilroy recoiled and took a step back.

Careful!

Kilroy looked over his shoulder. He was right at the edge of the hole. He turned back to Cynthia.

Shit, I nearly fell in.

Cynthia nodded.

Kilroy began to laugh. That would be perfect, he said. Just perfect.

Cynthia held her hands out to him. He took them and allowed her to draw him towards her. I'm sorry, she said.

Me too. I'm sorry, and I'm totally confused. I don't understand any of this. It's all too much. What the fuck is happening?

Cynthia didn't answer him.

He'd enjoy this, Kilroy said, nodding towards the hole.

You think so?

Sure. He loved to keep me guessing. And to have the last word.

What do you want to do? Cynthia said. Want me to help you get him out?

Kilroy thought for a moment. No, he said, I'm not moving him again. Not now, anyhow. Let's just cover the hole with the tarp. Take the other end, will you?

Cynthia walked to the far end of the rolled tarpaulin and picked up the corner.

Kilroy squatted down beside the hole. He leaned over and dug his hands into the side wall and pulled out a clump of earth. He stood up, and after looking down at the corpse for a few more moments he dropped the soil onto his father's body.

See you another time, Dad. Don't go anywhere.

They unrolled the tarpaulin to cover the hole.

A few minutes later Kilroy was back in the chair on the porch, trying to think straight.

Cynthia came out of the kitchen with a glass of water and handed it to him. Kilroy drank all of it without seeming to notice. She took the empty glass gently from his hand and placed it on the ground.

Want something stronger?

No, not right now. Thanks.

She stood beside him, gently stroking the back of his neck.

Hey, she said, want to find your parrot?

Kilroy looked up at her. You're very sweet.

Me? Why?

Thinking of something to distract me. Trying to cheer me up.

I'm serious. We can locate him.

You want to go for a walk in the woods? Climb some trees?

Uh-uh. We can use this.

She reached into her coat and took out the book-sized device she'd been using when Kilroy found her in the kitchen. This, she said, can connect us with an eye in the sky.

What *is* that thing?

It's a number of things, she said, pressing her finger against something under the corner of the object. Its screen sprang to life with a pulsing glow.

Kilroy held out his hand. Can I look at it?

Maybe later. Right now, do you want to see something cool?

How can I say no?

OK, I'm bringing her in. Look up there.

She pointed to an area of the sky high above the treeline

opposite them, then she used both hands to operate the device.

Kilroy kept his eyes on the area she'd indicated. A tiny speck appeared. It grew in size, then began to swoop down.

It was a skyfly. Within seconds it was hovering at the height of Kilroy's head, so close he could have taken a couple of paces and touched it.

He'd never seen one of them at such close range. It was around two metres long and a metre wide, with a depth that was slightly less. Black and sleek but not glossy. At this distance Kilroy could distinctly see what looked like a camera in its nose, and several recesses in its underside that appeared to contain more cameras, or other devices.

It was almost silent, hanging in the air like the solid ghost of itself, emitting a faint humming sound.

He glanced at Cynthia. She seemed to be enjoying herself.

OK, she said, let's send her back up to find your friend.

Cynthia used her device to send the skyfly soaring up again, but after a couple of seconds it appeared to stall, and dropped down to its previous position. It moved slowly towards Kilroy. The camera in its nose swivelled fractionally and Kilroy could see an iris inside it dilating and contracting, finding focus.

Shit, Cynthia said.

He turned to see her frowning at the controls.

What is it?

Oh fuck! Someone's overriding me! Shoot it!

Shoot it?

Yes! Quick! Shoot it, Kilroy!

Kilroy scrabbled for the gun he'd placed on the floor beside his chair, and by the time he raised it the skyfly was swooping up and away, rising rapidly. He shot five times in quick succession, finding his aim as he fired. The third shot struck it, throwing it off-balance, and the fifth shot ripped into its belly.

The object remained motionless for an instant, then it began to disintegrate.

Look out, Cynthia said, grabbing Kilroy's arm and pulling him back so they were both underneath the porch canopy.

Kilroy saw the machine separate itself into a cloud of components, as if he was watching an explosion in slow-motion, or an expanding three-dimensional diagram. The fragments hung in the air for a moment, then all at once they plummeted down, some of them connected by viscous strings of phlegm-like gloop. For several seconds, pieces of debris thudded and pattered onto the porch canopy.

When it was over Kilroy stepped forward to look at some of the pieces strewn on the ground, but Cynthia tightened her grip on his arm.

No, she said, we have to go!

Go where?

Your motorbike – now!

She shoved him forward so hard he nearly lost his balance.

Wait, he said, let me—

He scooped his bag up from the ground and allowed Cynthia to propel him to the steps. She continued to clutch him until they were on the grass, then she let go and ran as fast as she could towards the treeline.

Kilroy kept pace with her and they reached the edge of the grass and plunged into the woods. Kilroy took the lead, weaving between the trees until they reached the motorbike.

Cynthia jumped on the pillion.

Kilroy handed her his bag, straddled the bike, and pressed the starter. The engine came to life instantly.

Put the helmet on, Kilroy shouted, and keep your head down. He swung the bike around in an arc, crashed through the bushes, and accelerated along the driveway towards the road.

A black saloon car rolled to a stop up ahead, blocking the way out. Kilroy calculated he had room to get around it.

Lean with me, he yelled over his shoulder, and watch your legs!

The car doors opened and two people emerged. Kilroy began to lean into a tight turn to get past the front of the car.

As he drew level with the car he saw one of the figures raise an arm. Kilroy felt a light stinging sensation in his shoulder and began to lose his balance. He fell off the bike and hit the ground, and kept falling, into darkness.

The pattern on the carpet seemed familiar.

Kilroy realised he was back in the house, in the good front room. That was what they called it – the good room. It was on the other side of the hallway from the living room, and they used it only for special occasions. There was a dining table with eight chairs. It was like a waiting room, and Kilroy had never wanted to spend any time in it when he was young.

His shoulder still stung a little. He and Cynthia were sitting in armchairs on either side of a large window.

A man and a woman were facing them, seated on a pair of high-backed dining chairs they'd pulled away from the table. Kilroy recognised them as the pair who'd emerged from the car, and he understood the seating arrangement was deliberate. If he or Cynthia made a move the other couple could be on their feet much more quickly than they could.

Not that Kilroy planned on making any sudden moves. Partly because he felt groggy, and partly because both his guns were on the table. The man's hand was resting casually on the polished wooden surface, close enough to the guns to make his point. The man was about thirty, and he was dark, like a Southerner.

The woman's skin was lighter, more like Cynthia's. She too had a weapon within easy reach, although it wasn't one Kilroy recognised. It had the shape of a pistol, and was about the same size, but it was slender and appeared to be transparent. Kilroy could see some type of dart lodged in the barrel, and a row of similar dart-like capsules standing upright on the table, next to the weapon.

The woman was speaking quietly to Cynthia, but now she turned her attention to Kilroy, and the man followed suit. Kilroy waited.

Hi, the woman said, how are you feeling?

I'm OK, Kilroy said. How long was I out?

Just a few minutes.

Who are you?

I'm Gabrielle, she said, and this – indicating the man – is Benedict.

The guy nodded at Kilroy and cleared his throat. We're sorry, he said.

About what?

About sedating you. Technically it's an assault.

I've had worse.

That's not the point. There are implications for us. We don't interfere.

Kilroy heard Cynthia make a snorting noise.

Bullshit, she said. Let's not play these games.

The woman – Gabrielle – turned to Cynthia sharply:

That's rich, coming from you, doctor.

You think I'm playing games here?

Yes, and dangerous ones.

Cynthia stared at her for a moment, glanced at Benedict, and shook her head. You two, she said.

The man leaned forward. You've done untold damage here,

Cynthia.

You know my position.

Oh yes, we know. You and your deluded friends.

If you're referring to the committee for—

Not any more, the man said. Your committee doesn't exist any longer, Cynthia, and you know it. You knew it before you came here. Your arrogance is breath-taking.

No, I'll tell you what's arrogant, Ben. Standing back and doing nothing, and waiting to see what happens while people – actual living people – are going to hell in a handcart, and watching it happen because you find it interesting, like it's some mad, sadistic experiment for you.

Benedict spread his hands. What, he said, gives you the right to do this? Tell me! I really want to know. What gives you the unilateral right to break the one rule that everyone agreed on, the only damn one, and come and do this?

Cynthia spoke as if to an infant, spelling it out: I…changed… my…mind.

Benedict slapped the table. You can't! Don't you understand that? You people are as bad as Shadbold!

How dare you, Cynthia said, struggling from her chair, how dare you compare me to that evil fucking monster, when all we—

Enough! Gabrielle was on her feet and her weapon was pointing at Cynthia.

Sit down, she said. And Ben, let's not go there. Get a grip.

Sorry, Benedict said.

Gabrielle kept her eyes on Cynthia. You know what's in here, she said, indicating the weapon in her hand, and if you want to make an issue of all this I can always replace it with one of those other slugs on the table, and you can have a nice sleep all the way home. Your choice, doctor.

Cynthia sank back in her chair. You think you're taking me back?

You know it, Gabrielle said.

Cynthia nodded towards Kilroy. What about him?

We've agreed all this, Benedict said.

You've agreed it, I didn't.

Benedict pointed at her. Don't start with me, Cynthia.

It's all right Ben, snapped Gabrielle, we have a plan and we'll stick with it.

She sat down and placed the weapon carefully on the table.

Don't mind me, Kilroy said, I'm right here but please go ahead and talk about me like I'm dead. See if I care. Anyone want a coffee? Something stronger? A punch in the throat? Just say the word.

Benedict sighed. We're truly sorry about all this, he said. He placed his hands on his thighs, smoothing the fabric beneath his fingers.

Kilroy noticed that Benedict was well-dressed. The woman, too. It was all very understated, but it looked as if their dark, reserved clothes had been made by an expensive tailor.

So, Gabrielle said, do you have yourself under control, Cynthia?

Don't talk to me like that. You know you have no real authority. We'll win in the end, no matter what you do. You may as well accept it. If you want to be useful, go home and leave me here to do my work.

Gabrielle raised the weapon again. I swear to god, Cynthia, I will put you so far under it'll take you a year to think straight again.

You'd like that, wouldn't you?

You're damn right. It may happen anyway, once the team decides the best course of action. That would be nice, to have you out of our hair for a while. And meanwhile, I think there's something you need to say to your friend Kilroy.

You think so?

I do. And if you don't comply with what we've suggested it could have a very negative impact.

Cynthia pulled a mocking, puzzled face. Wait a minute, she said, that sounds like a threat. Is that right, Gabrielle? You're threatening my people on the committee?

Your people? Sure. And not just them.

Who else?

People here.

Cynthia said nothing. She lowered her head.

Well, Gabrielle said, are you going to tell him?

Cynthia seemed to sag for a moment, then she sat up and looked at Kilroy. Her face was expressionless.

I owe you an apology, she said. I've misled you. I'm not supposed to be here. I've been acting selfishly, and against the best interests of your people.

Kilroy raised his eyebrows. What about my best interests? Or any interests that you and I might share?

Gabrielle made a tutting noise.

Kilroy glanced at her and she gave him a sour look.

Did Cynthia sleep with you? Gabrielle asked.

A gentleman never tells, Kilroy said. But I'll break the habit of a lifetime. The answer is no, she didn't.

Benedict leaned forward. Why should we believe you?

Do me a favour, Kilroy said, and fuck yourself.

Break it up boys, Gabrielle said. And you, Cynthia, keep going.

Cynthia took a breath. I was wrong to involve you in all this, Kilroy.

In all what?

The whole thing. The subversive stuff. The heresy, or whatever you'd call it. With the girl, and what she's trying to do.

I was already involved, Kilroy said. You forget, I'm a cop. I was given a case and I did what I had to. You didn't involve me in anything.

But I was wrong to try and change the course of what you're doing, and to influence the outcome, and to, you know, get involved myself.

Interfere, Benedict said. That's the word you're groping for, Cynthia. The most important word in the charter. We do not interfere.

Cynthia pressed her lips together. She was breathing heavily.

Leave it Ben, Gabrielle said. She's got the message.

Ben nodded towards Kilroy. And him?

What else does he need to know?

Actually, Kilroy said, since you're asking, there is something I need to know.

Go ahead, Gabrielle said.

Did you kill my father?

Your father?

Yes. Did you kill him?

What? No, of course not!

Wait, Benedict said, when did this happen?

Yesterday.

Shit, Gabrielle said.

Kilroy looked from one to the other. They seemed genuinely puzzled. Either that, or they were terrific actors.

So, he said, you didn't kill my father? How about moving his body around? Did you do that?

Sorry, Benedict said, but we don't know what you're talking about.

He's right, Gabrielle said, but if someone killed your father, that's terrible.

Yeah, Kilroy said, that's how I feel about it too.

The dynamic in the room had changed. Not enough for Kilroy to feel good about the odds of grabbing Cynthia's hand and sprinting out of there with her, but enough to open up the possibility of a little leverage with the strangers, whoever they were. Regardless of the answer to that question, Kilroy was convinced they knew nothing about his father's death, or the weird relocations of his corpse.

He considered his options. His priority was no longer the need to tear these people apart with his bare hands, rip their hearts out, and stuff them down their throats. Right now he needed to focus on preventing them from taking Cynthia away.

Gabrielle stood up. We should leave immediately, she said to Benedict.

The man picked up one of the guns on the table and put it in his pocket.

Kilroy noticed that it didn't seem to spoil the cut of his suit.

Benedict glanced at him, then said to Gabrielle, What about him?

You're not suggesting we take him with us?

Of course not. But he'll know about us.

There you go again, Kilroy said. You know I can hear you, right?

Benedict was about to reply to him, but Gabrielle held up her hand. She studied Kilroy for a moment, then addressed him in a voice that reminded him how much he hated schoolteachers:

This is extremely awkward, and we've been put in an impossible position. Ethically, we've crossed a line even by being here. The responsibility for this lies with the person who

left us no choice but to come here once she transgressed a strict moral boundary. She doesn't belong here, and any blame for what happens is entirely hers.

As Gabrielle paused for breath Cynthia broke in:

Jeez Kilroy, I know just how you feel. They're at it again, right? I mean, what am I here, chopped liver? Hey, do you have that expression?

No, but I get the idea. And personally, I don't need this shit.

Same here, sweetie.

For god's sake, Gabrielle said, get a hold of yourself, Cynthia. Do you have any useful suggestions about the best way to deal with this?

There's nothing to deal with, Cynthia said. What has Kilroy found out that he didn't already know, or wouldn't catch up with pretty soon? The truth is out there, as the old saying goes. You can't un-ring that bell. Now it's all about the narrative, and the battle for hearts and minds, and perhaps I should remind you that this whole scenario was modelled and gamed, along with all the others. All I did was shove it along when it was stalling, and try to minimise casualties. The commitment to reduce suffering at all costs, remember that?

Thank you, Saint Cynthia, Benedict said. Thank you for your blessed and compassionate intervention.

At least I tried. More than you've ever done, you pussy.

OK, Gabrielle said, that's it. Time's up. Cynthia, you're coming with us, and your friend can stay here and fend for himself. That's all we can do.

Benedict picked up the remaining gun from the table and got to his feet. He looked down at Kilroy.

Sorry friend, you're on your own.

Wait, Kilroy said. There's just one thing I need an answer to. Can you at least do that, before you leave me in the shit?

Benedict glanced at Gabrielle.

What is it, she said, what do you want to know?

It won't take long. In fact, the quickest way is to show you.

Show us what?

It's easiest to just take you there, really. It's on your way out. Just outside. Is it OK if I get up?

Benedict stepped back and raised the gun. OK, but don't do anything unexpected, you know what I mean? Don't make us do anything that gets us any deeper into this mess. We need to be out of here.

Kilroy got to his feet slowly and raised his hands up high, exaggerating.

Yeah, Benedict said, no need for that, chief. Just remember I'm behind you and be sensible.

No problem, Kilroy said. I'll lead the way, shall I?

Kilroy walked out of the back door and down the steps. He took a few paces, then paused and glanced over his shoulder. Benedict was behind him and to his right. Gabrielle was still on the porch, her weapon pointing at Cynthia, waiting for her to reach the ground before she descended the steps herself. Not taking any chances.

Follow me, Kilroy said.

Where are we going? Benedict asked.

Kilroy pointed to the treeline.

Benedict squinted against the sun. Into the woods? We don't have time.

No, just at the edge there.

Kilroy glanced behind him again and saw that Gabrielle and Cynthia were now both down the steps. He walked on, keeping his gaze level, trying to make it look like he was focused on the trees. He reached the edge of the tarpaulin.

Just there, he said, and raised his arm again to direct their attention away from the tarp, and the hole it concealed. He hoped to hell Cynthia knew what was on his mind.

He veered closer to the edge of the tarp. He was about halfway along it now, and the sun was in their eyes. He slowed his pace slightly, and before Benedict had time to adjust he spun around and charged into him with his shoulder as hard as he could.

Benedict lost his balance as he was raising the gun, which Kilroy grasped by the barrel and yanked away, giving him a shove with his free hand.

Benedict windmilled his arms frantically, trying to keep his balance, teetered for a moment, then he toppled back onto the tarp, which was anchored so lightly to the edges of the hole that it began to sag immediately.

From the corner of his eye Kilroy saw Cynthia drop to the ground, supporting herself on her fingertips as she extended one leg and swept it around in an arc, catching Gabrielle's ankles.

Now Benedict was falling into the hole, the heavy tarp wrapping itself around him like a blanket and swaddling him as he fell, struggling and cursing. He hit the bottom with a thud and Kilroy hoped he hadn't landed on his dad. The rest of the tarp slid down and flopped over him like huge, exhausted wings.

Kilroy ran towards the women. Gabrielle was on one knee, trying to aim the dart-gun up at Cynthia, whose hand was clamped around Gabrielle's wrist, struggling to prise the weapon from her grip.

As she twisted and pulled at Gabrielle's wrist Kilroy stopped in his tracks.

Gabrielle's arm was turning black. As the blackness spread

to her neck Cynthia twisted the gun from her hand. Without pausing she levelled it and fired, hitting Gabrielle in the chest. She toppled over and her eyes were glazed before she hit the ground.

Cynthia stepped away from Gabrielle's body and turned to Kilroy.

He pointed at the gun. Will that thing work again?

Cynthia glanced down at it. Yes, three more slugs in there.

Let's shoot your other friend.

They ran to the edge of the hole. Benedict was struggling to his feet, still hampered by the thick canvas bunched around his ankles. He looked up at them. He seemed to know what was coming.

The dart hit him in the throat. His eyelids came down like shutters. He remained upright for a second then collapsed.

Good shot, Kilroy said. Let's go.

The intruders' car was parked in the driveway outside the house. Kilroy reached it first and opened the front passenger door.

Cynthia hesitated when she saw him.

You drive, he said, and got into the passenger seat.

She ran around the front of the car and got into the driver's seat.

Freeze, Kilroy said.

She saw the gun he was holding, levelled at her. She froze.

Now, he said, put both your hands on the wheel.

She did as she was told.

Very slowly, he said, use your right hand to reach across and take that weapon out of the pocket you put it in, holding the barrel.

Cynthia curled her right arm around her torso and dug

her fingers into her left-hand coat pocket. With difficulty she extracted the dart-gun and held it up.

Slowly move your arm, Kilroy continued, and put that thing on the dashboard in front of me. That's it. Good. Thank you.

Kilroy picked up the weapon with his free hand and put it on the floor between his feet. Now drive, he said.

Cynthia turned to look at him. Where are we going?

Take a right onto the main road.

All right. And after that?

Just drive.

CURTIS

Even before I stepped out of the elevator I began to suspect I would need to reconsider the conclusions I'd reached on my way down.

The doors to the basement parking level slid open to reveal Allardyce standing in front of me. I'd last seen her sitting in her office less than three minutes earlier. Either she'd taken fifteen flights of stairs at superhuman speed, or there was another elevator somewhere for the exclusive use of high-level personnel.

As I stood there gawping at her the doors began to close again and she reached out a hand to stop them.

Come on, she said.

I followed her. For an awful moment I thought we were heading for the door that led down to the cells, but she veered away to a corner near the exit, where a dozen sleek official cars sat in the shadows.

She opened the back door of one of them and gestured for me to get inside. I did so, and she went around the other side and slid in beside me.

We closed our doors, which made the nice muffled thud of solid, well-made components fitting themselves together with satisfying precision.

She half-turned to me and draped an arm over the back of the seat.

I'm sorry I had to give you such a hard time, she said with a rueful little twist of her mouth and a tone of sympathy in her voice. This, apparently, was a very different Allardyce from the harsh bitch I'd met upstairs, although that didn't make her any less dangerous. More so, if anything. I knew where I was with the bitch up in the office, but now we were just two gals in the back of a car, and all bets were off.

I shrugged. Just doing your job, I suppose.

Exactly. And believe me, I would not have sent you down to the cells earlier on if I could have avoided it. But I needed to make a point.

I got the point, thank you.

No, not to you! Hell, no. I'm talking about Glibbery. That man scrutinises my every move. If I hadn't made a point of treating you with the severity he feels you deserve I would have been in trouble myself.

I smiled and made sympathetic noises. She slid a little closer to me and I leaned back casually, wondering if the door beside me was locked centrally.

Look, she said, I'm not asking you to like me, Curtis.

Smart woman, I thought. She knew the odds were against her there.

Liking me, she continued, doesn't matter. What matters is what we can do for each other. I meant what I said upstairs, about you being a diligent agent. You're one of the best. Your private life is a little spicy for my liking, but as long as it doesn't interfere with your work I don't care very much.

I try to be discreet, I said.

She unveiled a smile that I found deeply disturbing.

I know you do, she said, but never mind about that. I need your help, Curtis. And if you can do what I ask, your career will benefit immensely. I'm talking about a fast track to the top. But this particular assignment must be clandestine, and you will report directly to me, bypassing the conventional chain of command. Do you understand what I mean?

I understand, and it seems that you're putting me in a compromising position.

Yes, it does, doesn't it? She leaned back and gave me another smile. This one was less chilling than the last one. Or perhaps I was just getting used to them.

Why the secrecy? I said.

I'm concerned about certain people in positions of authority within the security apparatus who can't be trusted.

You mean traitors?

That's correct, she said.

So, I'm to answer directly to you, in what may prove to be a dangerous mission, or even a rogue operation for all I know, and if it falls apart I'm deniable and disposable. All I have is your word that we're doing the right thing. Is that a fair assessment?

You could put it that way. You'll just have to trust me, Curtis.

And if I don't?

I believe we have a convenient metaphor to hand.

She gestured towards the steel door leading down to the cells.

Think of it this way, she said. You could go all the way down – she tilted her chin at the door – or all the way up. Is that clear enough for you?

OK, I said. You'd better tell me what you want me to do.

The girl, she said. I need her dead.

I tried not to look too shocked. Very well, I said, but can you tell me why?

She's dangerous, and the longer she's alive the more people are going to be exposed to the insurrectionary subversion she's peddling. The network will only grow, and it could get out of hand.

There's a network?

Yes. We fell down on the job when we took care of the parents. We didn't fully contain the situation. As a result, some of these subversive ideas are spreading, and a kind of cult appears to be growing around them, and around the girl. But we may have been too late in any case. There's evidence that she began disseminating her insidious doctrine before her father was executed – possibly even before he was taken into custody. We've had to shut down the school she attended, and arrest several students and teachers, but it's becoming obvious that the damage had been done already, and now the problem is expanding like a poisonous gas we're unable to neutralise. It's unfortunate that Sheba appears to have a strong personality and a gift for narrative, albeit simplistic. The fact is, her stories seem to be striking a chord with a certain type of person in these troubled times, and they risk inflaming an already volatile public temperament. People are eager to believe in something new, no matter how destructive it may be.

Excuse me, I said, can we just rewind a moment here? Are you telling me it was we who killed the mother? Our apparatus?

Allardyce looked uncomfortable for the first time since I'd met her.

It wasn't my idea, she said. Somebody was trying to be clever. Too clever for their own good, it turned out. You see, after Manfred, the father, had been tried and sentenced, we learned that the mother was also involved in some way, although we still don't have all the details. And as if that wasn't bad enough, it emerged that the girl was a threat too. So, it was decided – not by me, as I say – that both problems could be solved by disposing of the mother and blaming the girl. But the entire operation was mishandled from beginning to end. So much so, that I've begun to suspect there was more than mere incompetence behind it. I believe treachery was involved.

That's unfortunate, I said. But what about the plan you outlined to me upstairs? That I'm to function as some kind of bait, and lure Kilroy to me so that he may, or may not, take the opportunity to eliminate me. Is that still operational?

Allardyce waggled her hand in a 'maybe-maybe-not' gesture.

That's still a useful role you can play, she said, although I can assure you we will minimise the possibility of exposing you to any danger.

We? I said. You told me this was off the books.

No, that's the other operation. Remember, I was quite open with everyone upstairs about sending you back into the field to await contact from Kilroy, and the risk it might expose you to. Quite open, and very firm with any opposition.

I studied her face as I recalled the conversation upstairs, and it dawned on me that it had been a piece of theatre. The big display of defiance towards Glibbery over my mission – sending me out as bait for Kilroy – was intended to be dramatic, to deflect attention from what she actually wanted me to do, which was a little freelance assassination.

Allardyce glanced at her watch. I'll continue, if I may.

Yes, of course.

Very well. And I hope I don't have to remind you that everything I tell you is confidential. If I even suspect that you've breathed a word of it to anyone I'll make sure you're put away for the rest of your life, and never see the light of day again. Clear?

Clear.

Good. Now, if I have my way, the girl will be moved soon. This will appear to be a step taken on compassionate grounds. It may involve a visit to her brother, which would be useful for various reasons, not least because I'm by no means satisfied that he hasn't been mixed up in this from the start. In any event, I anticipate that an attempt will be made to rescue the girl while she is being moved.

I raised my eyebrows, and was about to speak but she cut me off:

How can I be sure about the rescue attempt? I can't reveal that at present. But you will be involved in an operation to thwart it. During that operation the girl will be terminated. If we can make it appear that she was killed, perhaps accidentally, by the people attempting to free her, that would be ideal. If such an outcome is not achievable, don't worry. Your role, if discovered, will expose you to no censure. Quite the opposite. It will be the first stage of your accelerated promotion. If the whole operation fails I won't hold it against you – unless, of course, I suspect sabotage on your part. In which case, you know the consequences. Any questions?

I couldn't think of a single thing to ask her.

She nodded, and unleashed another smile. This one froze my blood, especially as she accompanied it with a pat on my knee, which made me very tense.

She put away the smile and gave me an evil look.

It's all right, she said, you're not my type.

That, I reflected, was probably the closest to anything resembling good news that I was going to receive in this encounter.

She opened her door. I suggest, she said, you go home, carry on as normal, and wait for my next instruction.

I got out of the car.

Remember, she said, over the top of the car, I genuinely respect you, Curtis, both as a person and a professional. There aren't many people I'd entrust with a mission like this.

Thank you, I said, I'm grateful for your confidence in me.

*

It was good to be home. I allowed myself to collapse a little. I'd only been away for a couple of days, but it felt like much longer.

Although strictly speaking it was still the afternoon, I felt I deserved a drink. I changed into a pair of silk pyjamas and poured myself a generous shot of whisky, then I sat down to think a few things over.

Among the topics that occupied my thoughts was the possibility that everything Allardyce had told me was a lie. Even if some of what she'd told me was true, or even if all of it was true, I could be certain there was a lot more she wasn't telling me.

Allardyce could, for example, be concealing the fact that

she knew about my supposedly clandestine visit to Sheba's cell. I only had the custodian's word for it that the cameras were switched off. What was his name? Alexander. I needed to consider the possibility that Allardyce was setting me up, and I was the one she wanted dead, perhaps along with the girl, perhaps not. Alternatively, what if this whole thing was some kind of test? Loyalty was a valuable commodity in the current situation.

All of this was familiar enough territory, and my speculations and suspicions roamed around it with sure-footed confidence. But there was a new feature in the landscape, through which I needed to tread with caution, in case it collapsed beneath me and I tumbled down a deep, dark hole.

This potential hazard was the idea that a network of conspirators was forming itself around the girl and her weird, subversive doctrine. Like all sensible people, I'm wary of conspiracies at the best of times, especially when they come wrapped up in heretical ideas, but when a conspiracy becomes a cult you're in uncharted territory. The habits of a lifetime are abandoned, and the rules no longer apply. People cease to be rational actors (to the extent that they were rational in the first place), and normal behaviour is replaced by messianic conviction and fanatical devotion. Self-interest – that reliable human calculus – stops working the way it should. People get unpredictable, and I get unhappy.

There was still whisky in my glass when the doorbell rang. I threw on a dressing gown and put the security chain on the door before I opened it. I like to think it takes a lot to surprise me, but seeing Pascal, my erstwhile interrogator, did the trick. He stood there impassively while I stared at him. After a moment he peered theatrically around the hallway, and exposed the tips of his teeth in what I guessed was a smile.

As you see, he said, I am alone. May I come in?

Give me a moment, please. I'll just get the chain.

I closed the door and leaned my back against it. By professional standards I was underdressed. I fastened the top button of my pyjamas. Then I undid it again. I'd been taken aback to find Pascal at my door, and he was as ugly as ever, but I still found myself stimulated by the erotic undertone I detected in our relationship.

I unclasped the chain and let him in.

He accepted my offer of a drink, and made himself at home on the couch.

After I handed him his whisky I sat down beside him, taking care to keep a meaningful distance between us. Nice place, he said.

Thanks. Why are you here?

Sorry if I surprised you. There's something I wanted to show you.

He extracted a folded piece of paper from his pocket and gave it to me. It was a handwritten note: 'Do you suspect surveillance devices here?'

I shook my head. No, I said, not as far as I know. I check regularly.

Good. Then let's assume we're OK to talk.

Yes, let's. What's on your mind?

I know what the girl told you.

Oh shit, I thought, so much for Alexander, the noble custodian. If I hadn't been so scared and disoriented at the time maybe I wouldn't have fallen for his story about being a spellbound convert to Sheba's message, and fixing the cameras, and so on. It did seem a little far-fetched, on reflection.

It's all right, Pascal said, you weren't betrayed, if that's what you're thinking.

It did cross my mind, I said.

I have other ways of finding these things out.

I bet you do.

He chuckled and shook his head. I'm not a savage, you know. Much of my work is mundane, and it's mostly about analysing data. It just so happens that sometimes it's part of my job to extract important information from people who are reluctant to provide it. If it has to be done, so be it, but it's not a vocation with me, I assure you.

I don't really care, to be honest.

I believe you. And that's certainly not why I'm here. I'm here because of what Allardyce told you in the car park.

This time I couldn't hide my surprise. He regarded me with satisfaction.

Congratulations, I said, I'm impressed. You know everything. You're omniscient.

Sorry, I can see you're irritated. I apologise if I'm coming across as a bit of a prick.

You are, a bit.

All right, I'll stop showing off and get to the point. But first…

He drained his glass and held it out. Any chance of a refill?

Pascal took a sip of his fresh drink and angled himself towards me on the couch.

You, he said, are far from being a fool, and you certainly understand how dangerous that girl is. I expect you can see why Allardyce wants her dead. But she's not really thinking this through. Especially when it comes to the existence of the network she must have told you about. She did tell you about that, didn't she?

Why ask me, I said, when you know everything about it already?

I don't know *everything*, just a summary. But she told you about the network?

Yes, she told me.

Good. So, my concern is that killing Sheba may actually be counterproductive, if we don't deal with the people she's already reached – the true believers – and get rid of them too. If we don't, the danger is still out there, and, what's worse, we may create a martyr, which is not a gift one should hand to a fanatical cult. Don't you agree, Curtis?

I can see your point, but what do you expect me to do about it?

It's tricky, I admit. We need to find a way for you to sabotage your mission without tipping off Allardyce that you did it. The advantage we have is that you've been told to dispose of the girl during the rescue attempt, which will inevitably involve a certain amount of chaos and confusion. Those elements are required, in fact, in order for you to do what Allardyce asks, and make it look as if Sheba was killed by accident, or by her own people – her rescuers.

Hold on, I said, everyone is talking about this rescue attempt as if it's a done deal, but who is actually meant to be pulling it off? How can we be sure Sheba's followers – or her network, or whatever it is – are going to make a rescue attempt at all?

We can't be sure. All we can do is provide the right conditions.

But how will they even know she's being transferred?

Pascal chuckled again and took another sip of whisky. I noticed he'd shifted slightly closer to me on the couch. Look, he said, I'm sure Allardyce told you about traitors in our midst, and all that kind of thing?

Yes, she seemed slightly obsessed by the idea.

On the contrary, she's quite right. In fact, we're relying on it. There are definitely people within our apparatus who are converts to Sheba's cult, and so we just have to make sure it's common knowledge, internally, that we're going to transfer Sheba to another location. Then we simply ensure the security plans are sufficiently flawed to encourage a rescue attempt.

Who are these people, I said, these mysterious traitors in our midst?

If I knew that for sure, we could perhaps go about this in a different way. As it is, one of the reasons I want you to subvert the operation, and to keep Sheba alive, is because I want you to infiltrate the network.

Are you serious?

Very much so.

What the actual fuck?

Pascal regarded me thoughtfully. I would have assumed, he said, you would see the necessity of what I'm proposing. We need to catch everyone in the network, and that includes anybody within our apparatus. I'm surprised Allardyce is so keen to have Sheba killed, given that such a step may leave those people untouched. So surprised in fact...

He trailed off.

Now it was my turn to laugh. Oh my, I said, that's just great. Now you're telling me Allardyce is a traitor, is that it?

Certainly not, Pascal said. I'm simply observing that it would be very foolish to kill the girl without rounding up *all* her associates, whoever they may turn out to be.

So, I said, all I have to do is subvert a badly-planned operation, cover my tracks, infiltrate a group that may or may not attempt to rescue the girl in the intentional chaos, arrest or kill everybody involved, one of whom may be a high-ranking apparatus officer, and somehow walk away from the whole demented farrago in one piece.

That's about it.

And what would you like me to do in the afternoon?

Pascal laughed with what seemed like genuine amusement. He leaned over and patted my knee. I kept my eyes firmly on his. He removed his hand, and took a slug of his drink.

I'm glad you find it funny, I said.

He nodded. Fair enough, I can see why you perhaps don't. But I think you're exaggerating the difficulty of what I want you to do. It's true that any plan to transfer the girl will need to have some *apparent* flaws in it, which will encourage a rescue to be contemplated. But an opportunity for the rescuers is an opportunity for us, too. It's a chance for you to convince them you've gone rogue, disobeyed your orders from Allardyce to kill the girl, and thrown your lot in with them, the renegade network.

My head was beginning to hurt. I lifted my glass and squinted through it. Wait a minute, I muttered, I thought you said Allardyce *is* one of the renegade network.

He shrugged. She may be, or not. It doesn't make any difference, don't you see? If she's a traitor, you'll expose her by infiltrating the network. If she isn't, you'll still be destroying the network, and she can't complain about that, if you succeed.

And you, I said, where do you fit in? Are you senior to Allardyce?

We work in different branches. I hold the same official rank as her, but my branch takes operational precedence in matters that arise from data collection and assessment.

I waved a hand at him. That's meaningless crap, and you know it.

He patted my knee again. Perhaps I do, but it makes no difference to you. As far as you're concerned you answer to me in this.

Before I could reply, he surprised me again, this time by standing up, draining his glass, and making for the door. When he reached it, he turned and waited.

I walked over to him.

Thanks for the drink, he said.

You're welcome. But I still have questions.

I know. But the overall plan – about moving the girl, and the rescue – will be evolving over the next couple of days. Let's wait until we have more details.

All right, how about just one question?

Go ahead.

What if I don't agree to do what you want?

Pascal's expression became grave. Let's not even go there, he said. You wouldn't like it. Believe me.

He opened the door and walked out. As I closed the door he half-turned in the corridor without breaking stride, and smiled at me briefly, then he was gone.

Fifteen minutes later, as I was lying on the couch finishing my third whisky, there was a knock at my door.

I smiled to myself. I'd been wondering whether Pascal would come back.

I slipped out of my dressing gown and strolled to the door. As I opened it, ready to deliver the wisecrack I'd prepared, I froze. It wasn't Pascal.

It was Dr Glibbery, the older man from the meetings with Allardyce.

Sorry to disturb you, he said, but I need to speak to you.

Even though I was standing squarely in the doorway, and I

didn't move, a moment later he was in my living room. It was as if he'd rearranged the laws of nature to suit his convenience, and had somehow *flowed* past me.

He stood in the middle of the room and watched me as I struggled back into my dressing gown. When I'd got it on he gave me a bland smile.

I picked up my glass and finished my whisky. I was damned if I was going to offer him a drink, although I was pretty sure he would have refused. I didn't offer him a seat either. I focused on my breathing. I needed to regain some control of the situation, and myself. I was badly rattled and halfway drunk.

Glibbery cleared his throat. Once again, he said, I must apologise for coming to your home, and at such an unconscionable time of night. However, I feel my rudeness is at least partly mitigated by the fact that your last visitor left you scarcely fifteen minutes ago, and I have the consolation of knowing that that you keep relatively late hours.

How dare you—

Glibbery held up a hand to stop me. No, he said, please spare me any histrionics. I assure you I have no wish to make this interview longer than necessary, for both our sakes. I would not be here if it weren't unavoidable. Why don't you sit down, Ms Curtis?

I made a sour face and sat down on the couch, landing a little harder than I'd intended. Fuck. My judgement was cloudy. I needed to clear my head.

So, Glibbery continued, I'm aware that our friend Pascal was here, and that his mission was to persuade you to undertake a certain course of action.

Persuade me? I didn't notice any persuasion. He gave me an order.

Quite so. An order that, in some respects, countermanded the instructions given to you by Allardyce in her car earlier today.

I leaned back and closed my eyes. I felt like going to sleep. That wasn't an option, so I sat up again and fixed Glibbery with my best deadpan stare, the impact of which was ruined because I'd forgotten about my drink, perched beside me on the couch where I'd placed it during my brief rest, and which now splashed the leg of my pyjamas as it toppled over. I caught it before it fell onto the floor, and wiped at my leg ineffectually.

Glibbery took a step towards me. May I offer you my handkerchief?

No thank you.

I can see you're tired.

I am, I said. I'm exhausted by all the instructions I'm getting. And now I suppose you're going to give me an order that contradicts Pascal's order, which countermanded Allardyce's order, and after you've left someone else will barge in and override your instructions, and so on, until Shadbold himself floats in here on a cloud of ineffable grace and finally reveals my true mission.

No, Glibbery said, I simply wish to elaborate on what Pascal asked you to do. And by the way, I advise you to moderate your speech, even in this informal setting. There's no call for blasphemy, and it could get you into trouble.

Thanks for the tip.

You're welcome. Now, I understand Pascal instructed you to keep the girl alive, and to do so, if practicable, in a way that will ingratiate you with the subversives, and enable you to infiltrate their network. Is that correct?

Yes, correct.

Good. My instructions diverge in only this respect: after

infiltrating the network I wish you to stay in place, and to make no attempt to denounce its members or to have them arrested. Instead, you are to use your position to discredit the movement, and the girl herself. It's not enough to kill Sheba, as Allardyce suggests, or to roll up the network, as Pascal wishes. The danger at the heart of this whole business is a set of ideas, animated by the forceful personality of the girl, and her mystique. That is what must be destroyed.

I gazed at him impassively. He remained inscrutable. I gave up.

OK, I said, whatever you want.

Thank you. Obviously we shall need to talk again soon. The only other point I need to make at this juncture is that you should trust no one except me. There is treachery afoot, believe me, and we must root it out. Accordingly, you will answer to me alone throughout this entire operation, in every respect, and my orders supersede any others that you may have been given.

Really? Funny how everyone keeps telling me that.

Whatever they may tell you, Ms Curtis, I assure you that I outrank them.

What, you run the whole security apparatus?

He gave me a thin smile. No, that's not my role. I am the senior church doctor with responsibility for liaison between all branches, and I hold a permanent seat on the State Management Committee. I also occupy the post of Procurator of the Faithful.

I took a moment to absorb the implications of what he'd said. That put him right at the top of the tree, among only a handful of people. Five, at most.

He raised an eyebrow. Anything else?

I stood up. What do I tell Pascal? Or Allardyce, for that

matter?

I'm sure you'll think of something. After all, you're a clever and resourceful officer, or so we keep hearing.

He turned and walked to the door.

Good night, I said.

And to you, he replied without turning around. He closed the door softly behind him.

I weighed up my situation. Within the space of a few hours three powerful and dangerous people had given me three sets of conflicting instructions. Each suspected at least one of the others of being a traitor. Which one was right? For all I knew, all three of them were traitors.

And where was the evidence of the mysterious network they'd each referred to? What if the only people in the network were actually Allardyce, Pascal and Glibbery? What if they'd seen which way the wind was blowing, and seized upon the girl, and her subversive doctrine, as a way to exploit the social and political upheaval they anticipated? Each of them mistrusted the other two, and perhaps wanted to test their allegiance, or to trick them into betraying themselves, in order to eliminate them from whatever power structure would eventually emerge from the chaos. And they were using me to do it.

I sat down and considered my options. As I saw it, there was only one thing to do, which was to pour myself another drink.

KILROY

Cynthia glanced down at the gun Kilroy was pointing at her.

Is that really necessary?

We're about to find out, Kilroy said. Slow down and take this turning coming up on the left.

Cynthia nodded, but she didn't slow down by much as she swung the big car smoothly onto a narrow country road with fields of mizzet on either side.

Handles nicely, she said.

Yeah, now let's see how the suspension holds up. Take this gap on the left.

Where?

Here. Here!

Cynthia caught the turn at the last moment and the car fishtailed as she threw it into an opening between the rows of crops, raising clouds of dust. They jolted and bounced along a rutted track. The gun in Kilroy's hand didn't waver.

Don't fuck around, he said.

Cynthia grimaced. Yes, boss.

Up ahead. Just drive in. And stop, obviously.

The dirt track led to a structure like an open-fronted barn. Cynthia nosed the car into it. She cut the engine and looked around. The space was empty except for a few dozen bales of mizzet stacked along the back wall.

Out, Kilroy said.

The bales were surprisingly soft, and the way they were stacked provided a good place to sit, like a deep couch that ran all along the wall.

Cynthia made herself comfortable, and Kilroy perched a couple of metres away. He kept the gun on her. She shook her head in exasperation.

Come on Kilroy, she said, I was sitting on your face with your dick in my mouth less than ten hours ago.

And less than two hours ago, Kilroy said, I still thought that meant something.

Cynthia burst out laughing.

Kilroy made a dismissive gesture with his free hand. All right, I don't mean it like that. I meant… I don't know. I don't know what to think. For all I know, everything about you could be fake.

Are we still talking about sex?

I'm talking about everything. The whole story. The spellbinding tale of an intrepid scientist with a mission to save the world, and the bad guys who show up at just the right moment for you to put on a convincing performance for my benefit, and for me to prove what a hell of a hero I am. I think

195

maybe it's all bullshit.

Why would I go to all that trouble to deceive you? Think about it, Kilroy.

I have been. That's why we're here. Me with the pistol, and you with a lot of explaining to do.

Why? Who do you think I am?

Maybe just another agent from the security apparatus. I wouldn't put anything past them. There are people in those departments who devote their lives to constructing elaborate plots and conspiracies to dupe ignorant bastards like me, probably just for the depraved thrill it gives them.

I agree, Cynthia said. Your security apparatus is quite capable of anything. But remember, those people are government employees who need to justify their budgets and their use of resources.

Meaning I'm not worth it?

Probably not.

But I am to you?

Maybe I like you.

Maybe you do. But if I'm not important enough for my own government to take all that trouble over, why are you making such an effort?

Cynthia hesitated.

Go ahead, Kilroy said, tell me.

Look, it's complicated –

Kilroy got to his feet and took the dart gun from his pocket.

Cynthia edged away. What are you doing?

How about a test? How about we find out if this thing works on you, or whether those two friends of yours, after we finished that exciting fight we had, just stood up as soon as we were out of sight and started laughing their heads off. How about that?

Be careful with that thing! Seriously, Kilroy. You're not

thinking straight. It worked on you, remember. It put you out like a light.

Kilroy pointed the weapon at her. Cynthia tried to make herself small and raised her hands, cowering behind them.

Wait! I'll prove it! Just give me a chance.

What will you prove?

That I'm who I say I am. Look, I get it. I get how you could believe the whole scenario has been cooked up by the security apparatus. Maybe you can even believe they're controlling the drones, because yes, they could have developed flight technology in secret, it's within the realms of possibility. But what if I do something nobody here could do? Would that convince you, if I show you something like that?

Kilroy lowered the dart gun. Try me.

I need to get something that's in my top pocket. OK?

Do it slowly.

Cynthia fished out a small tubular object like a lipstick. She raised it to her eyes and examined it, making a small adjustment to it. She seemed satisfied. But instead of applying it to her lips she inserted it slowly into her left ear.

To Kilroy's astonishment Cynthia began to change colour.

The pigment from the flesh around her ear began to leach, and to be replaced by the shade of pallid redness that results from stirring a drop of blood into a cup of water. The effect spread across her face, then down to her neck and shoulders. In a few seconds the transformation was complete.

Holy shit, Kilroy said, you're pink.

White.

What?

We called ourselves white. Those of us who shared my... tone. Caucasian was actually the official term.

Kilroy was aware his mouth was hanging open. He shut it.

Cynthia stood up. Sorry, but I had to do something to convince you.

This is weird, Kilroy said.

I know.

Are you all like that? Pink like you?

No. Remember what happened when I grabbed Gabrielle? Where I squeezed her arm and it began to get darker?

Yeah.

She's black.

Black? What do you mean black?

Her skin is a different colour to mine. Some of us were white, like me, and some were black, and some were other colours and other shades. We had different races. But we wanted to spare you all that. The original scientists, I mean. They didn't want you to have to deal with that.

Why not?

Cynthia smiled. It caused us a lot of problems.

What, like fighting? Like wars?

In the past, yes. There was a lot of baggage. Troublesome legacies. Those weren't the only reasons behind the decision to minimise the differences with you, and to make everyone the same, more or less, with only minor variations of pigment – darker in the south, lighter in the north, and so on – but basically the same. Other factors were involved, but our troubled history played a big part in it.

I can't imagine people being black, Kilroy said. How do you see them at night?

Sorry, Cynthia said, I shouldn't have used the word black. Just imagine your people from the south, and then think of them being several shades darker.

Kilroy put the dart gun back in his pocket carefully. When he looked back at Cynthia he still couldn't quite believe it.

She moved towards him and he flinched. She stopped.

Is it really that bad? Do I look so weird?

I need time to get used to it.

Close your eyes.

Why?

Just do it.

Kilroy closed his eyes. He sensed her moving closer. She put a hand on his upper arm and another behind his neck. He felt the heat of her face, and then her lips on his. She kissed him for a long time. When she gently pulled away he opened his eyes. Her face was still so close that he saw nothing but her eyes.

OK, she said, what kind of kiss was that?

A good one.

But what colour was it? Was it a pink kiss, a brown kiss?

They both cracked up at the same moment.

Maybe, Kilroy said, that's not the best phrase to use.

Cynthia stifled her laughter. Seriously, she said, it's the same as before, right?

Kilroy nodded.

She took his hands gently and placed them on her body, slipping them up under her shirt. Kilroy moved one hand further up and cupped her breast.

And that, Cynthia whispered with a catch in her voice, what colour is it?

Kilroy didn't reply. He moved his other hand around her, pulling her closer, and ran his fingers down her spine to her waistband. She pushed him back so he sat down on the bales, straddled him, and began to undo his belt.

They both knew where this was going, and went there.

After they got there, they lay in each other's arms for a while, then they rearranged some of the bales into a makeshift bed, and went there again.

An hour later they were lying on their backs beside each other.

Kilroy squinted at the roof. Can they see us up there?

What, with the drones?

Right. I mean, can they see through buildings?

Some of them. If they use thermal cameras that detect body heat. Then you can see a kind of fuzzy outline of a person. Like a coloured ghost.

Is someone watching us right now?

I doubt it.

So they didn't see us?

Cynthia laughed. You sound disappointed.

Well, they missed a pretty good show. Am I right?

Cynthia leaned over and kissed him lightly.

Absolutely. World-class performance. You want me to hold up a score card?

Nah. Just make a note. But how can you be sure they're not watching?

Cynthia propped herself up on one elbow. Because, she said, you shot the hell out of the drone that was in this district.

But there are others, right?

Yes. But none around here.

How many of those things are there?

In total, for all of Landmass? A couple of hundred.

Wow. But can't those two, Gabrielle and whatshisname—

Benedict.

Yes, him – can't they, like, call one down or something?

Nope.

Why not?

Because of what's in there.

Cynthia kicked her bare foot against the pocket of her coat, which was among the clothing they'd spread out on their makeshift bed.

Kilroy raised his head and squinted down at the coat pocket.

Is that your control pad?

Not just mine. I took theirs too.

I didn't see you do that.

When I was fighting with Gabrielle I took it from her.

And what will those two do when they wake up? Unless they're already awake. Are they? How long will those dart shots put them out for?

Cynthia thought for a moment, calculating. They're awake, she said.

Will they try to find us?

We've got their car, their weapons, and their pad. I'm guessing no.

Where will they go?

That depends on what happens. How things pan out. They may stick around here for a while, or they may head for the place you call Landmass Two.

And where is that, exactly?

On the other side of the world. Literally.

That figures. But how will they get there?

They'll have some kind of transport available.

What, like a boat?

Like a boat, yes.

And when they get there, what will happen?

Cynthia sat up and clasped her knees.

When they get there, she said, my problems will start again. There are plenty more people like those two, who don't want me here, and are trying to stop me and everyone else who thinks like me.

And how many people are on your side?

A lot, and it's growing. There are more of us than them in

fact, but they've got more power. At the moment. There's a major struggle going on between people like me, who believe we need to intervene in what's happening here, and people like them, who think it's fine to sit back and watch, no matter what happens, or how many people get hurt, or destroyed. Because it's all science to them. Actual living people don't matter.

Gee whizz, they certainly sound like the bad guys.

Cynthia glanced at him sharply then rested her head on her clasped arms. After a few moments she looked up and gave him a wan smile. When she spoke she sounded weary.

You're right, she said, it's not that simple. Of course it's not. Debates about ethics are as old as science itself. But that was the problem, back when the disaster happened: they didn't have a chance to develop a robust ethical framework for what they were doing. It was all new. Some things happened faster than expected, and some things happened slower, or didn't happen at all. And the hardest thing of all to predict was how people would behave. The end of the world was full of surprises.

It sounds like you're speaking from personal experience.

Does it? Sorry, I didn't mean it to sound that way. But it was only a few hundred years ago, and I feel close to those people who worked on the project. You feel connected to your predecessors in a particular field of work. I know it wasn't easy for them.

Kilroy said nothing. He gazed around at their surroundings.

What are you thinking? Cynthia said.

I came out here to save my father. I was too late for that, but I have to get back to the city and try to do what I can for the girl. I can't leave her where she is.

You're not to blame, Kilroy.

Sorry, but I think I am.

Cynthia studied his face. She nodded. OK, let's get moving.

She started to swing herself around, but Kilroy grasped her wrist.

Wait, he said. We'll leave when it's dark. That car can pass for an official vehicle, especially if people don't see it too clearly. Where did they get it, by the way?

They have ways of doing these things.

What a surprise.

Hey. What's bugging you Kilroy?

I need you to tell me about a couple of other things.

Cynthia looked down at her wrist, which Kilroy was still gripping. He released it. She leaned back and gazed at him levelly.

Is it about the guy you shot, and why he looked like you? I was going to explain, but there hasn't been time.

There's time now.

You may not like what you hear, I warn you. But I can see you're not going to trust me until I tell you, and I don't want you pulling a gun on me every ten minutes, so I'll do my best. But I have to ask you one thing.

What?

Can we get dressed first?

They sat with their backs against the bales, facing the setting sun.

It was total chaos, Cynthia said. But it was also weird, because even when it changed from being an emergency to being a disaster, it wasn't as bad as it could have been. A lot of people expected the worst possible scenario. Like, Armageddon. That was a cultural thing, I think, because of all the books and movies. And when it happened, some people did fall to pieces. Not everyone. It wasn't like some kind of zombie cannibal apocalypse. But it was bad. Basically, the weather went crazy, the water started rising, and a lot of people died. Which was just fine with certain other people, who said it made the task of selecting survivors easier. They said it was fortunate so many people died from what they liked to refer to as a natural event. Unbelievable. The world was drowning and burning, and still people were talking about weather cycles, and self-rectifying systems.

Hold on, Kilroy said. Selecting survivors? Selecting them for what?

For the satellites.

We don't have those, whatever they are.

I know. We nearly didn't have them ourselves. But it's amazing how much money people in government can find when it's a matter of life and death for them personally, to say nothing of all the private money that came into it, too. But all the money in the world couldn't make enough satellites for everyone. Not by a long way.

It must have got ugly, Kilroy said.

Cynthia nodded. There was conflict. There was horror. But there was never any serious disagreement about the need to keep human life alive on this planet. It helped that the team who did the work were mostly volunteers. In return, they were all promised a place on the last ship out, after some tough negotiating. And through it all, as time was getting shorter, they worked harder and harder, trying to achieve a viable product.

I assume, Kilroy said, that the viable product you're referring to is me and the people who live here.

Right. And you didn't turn out so bad, considering.

Thank you. I'll accept that as a compliment on behalf of all viable products.

You're welcome. But while bio-engineering you guys was

one thing, the real challenge was the geo-engineering. They had to build this place, for a start.

Kilroy sat up. Are you saying Landmass wasn't here before?

It was, but they elevated it to remain above the predicted water level. Right now, we're sitting on a layer of fresh alluvial soil fifteen hundred metres deep, which is why it's easy to grow crops, although the range is limited to what you can do with rain, wind and sun. There was a debate about leaving you some animals, but it was too complex to integrate them, so non-humans were taken out of the equation. Except for fish, of course.

And parrots, Kilroy said.

Cynthia laughed. The damn parrots! Nobody can figure that out. There must have been a breeding pair that survived when this whole place took a deep cleanse before the repopulation. It was human error, I guess, and that's how you got your African Grey.

Sorry, what did you call it?

African Grey. Why?

Oh. It doesn't matter.

Cynthia touched his arm. You'll get him back. He'll be all right.

I hope so. Meanwhile, I still haven't heard why that guy I had to shoot looked uncannily similar to me.

We're getting to that, but do me a favour, OK?

What?

Don't judge me. Not until you've heard everything.

Then I can judge you?

I'm pretty sure you're going to. But there's nothing I can do about that, so I'm just going to tell you what happened, and live with it.

You have my full attention.

At first, Cynthia said, there was no intention to do any genetic engineering. The plan was to build the environment, and leave behind a small population of volunteers, screened to optimise survival. Nice idea, but they saw pretty soon it wasn't going to fly. Conditions got worse more rapidly than they expected. They were constantly modelling outcomes, and none of them delivered overall survival rates at more than ten per cent, and most were lower. Like, zero. Rising water level wasn't the only problem. Atmospheric changes were kicking in, to the point that everyone had to wear breathing apparatus all the time. So, they switched to plan B, which didn't work either. It turns out you can't just give everyone a new set of lungs, plus a spare skin to deal with the unfiltered radiation that was cascading down. And even if you could, there were dozens of other issues that were basically going to make this place uninhabitable for a long time. For us, that is. The people we were at that moment. There was only one option left, and they took it.

They made new people? Kilroy said. I thought you told me—

Not new. Different. You've got to remember, the scientists who created this project didn't know if we'd be able to come back. There was a chance that whatever life they left down here might be all that survived of us as a race, and they wanted humanity to continue, in some shape or form, even if it wasn't entirely identical to their own. They got as close as they could, based on their own DNA. Which, by the way, is a molecule inside each cell with two chains that coil around—

Ribbons!

Cynthia looked at Kilroy in surprise.

We know about that, he said. They call them ribbons. It's a new field of research, and the church doctors don't release much information about it. But they can't keep it completely under wraps. It's like news about the skyflies – the drones – which they put out in controlled leaks, otherwise it gets out by itself, and ordinary people might get the crazy idea they're being lied to. Sorry, I'm interrupting you.

That's OK, Cynthia said, I'm interested in how these things are controlled. Like, how did the church end up running the military?

It's always been that way.

Do you know *any* of your own history?

Kilroy turned to gaze at the sinking sun. The church, he said, teaches us that you only need historians if you want to argue about the past. And why would you do that if there are accurate church records? And yes, I can see the problem with that. Like I told you, even when I was a kid we had more books. Not many, but more than now. They disappeared over the years, and this is the world we live in now. And when the world is a certain way, people who want to change things have a hard time.

What about what's been happening recently?

Maybe it's time for a change.

Is that why you want to help Sheba? Because she's found out the truth, and everyone has a right to know about it?

No. She was in trouble and I made it worse. That's all.

That's not true!

If you say so.

Cynthia slapped his face.

Kilroy rubbed his cheek. Fuck was that for?

Sorry. I don't know. This isn't the way it's meant to be.

OK, tell me how it's meant to be. And don't slap me again. Ever.

Cynthia took a deep breath.

Two gigabytes of information. That's what it takes to make a person. But they couldn't just replicate themselves, even if they'd wanted to. Firstly, they had to make adjustments for practical reasons, like the fucked-up atmosphere. Secondly, they needed to diversify the gene pool. Thirdly, there were moral considerations. Genetics happens to be my field, and there are dark avenues that open up when you get into cloning, by which I mean making replicas. There had been some big advances in the field just before the disaster, and researchers were facing tricky ethical challenges. Then the shit hit the fan, and some scientists decided the leash was off, and they were free to try anything that might work. They ran simulations – a lot of simulations – and eventually they came up with a human model that had a chance of making it, using the materials at hand. Long story short, that's where you came from.

If we're not replicas, Kilroy said, what are we?

Think of it like this: you have sixteen great-great-grandparents, right? And you get your genes from them. That's the model they used. Sixteen sources for each person in the original population, in different variations. They left embryos here. Those were incubated by AI systems programmed to decay when the first generation approached adulthood. There was some concern that by making the AI smart enough to do the job they might become autonomous, but they did what they were told, like good little robots.

OK, now you've lost me.

But you get the idea? The intention was to make everyone different.

Right. And I also know about good intentions, and the road to hell.

You have that expression? Interesting. That was the other

issue: culture. There was even more conflict over cultural heritage than there was about genetics. Some people even opposed restricting the range of skin pigment. But scientists want to solve problems: that's why we do science, and the skin-pigment adjustments weren't just about the cultural history I mentioned. They were also a response to anticipated extremes of temperature, and the need to achieve a robust dermatology.

And we couldn't have been other colours?

Maybe you could, but the range would have been restricted, whatever the choice, because of the practicalities. In the final year before everyone left, the overall temperature went up by eleven degrees.

Kilroy looked at his fingers. I'm happy to be this colour. I don't think pink would suit me. Or black.

Count your blessings, Cynthia said. At one point there was a suggestion that you should all be yellow.

Yellow?

It started as a joke, partly. But to understand why it's funny you'd have to know about a specific part of the popular culture back then, and the fact that the suggestion came from an endocrinologist called Simpson.

I guess you had to be there.

I guess you did. In the end they did their best, and here you are – as large as life and twice as handsome, sweetheart.

Cynthia planted a kiss on his cheek.

Thank you, Kilroy said.

You're welcome. But whichever way you look at it, the skin pigment issue had social and cultural implications. Which opened the door for the evolutionary psychologists, and the ethnographers, and the psycho-fucking-biologists. Cut to the chase, some of them proposed making changes to the brain. Mainly to modify the spiritual impulse, because throughout history there had been so much murder committed in the name of religion, they said. But the majority was adamant that without the possibility of spirituality the entire human experience would be vastly impoverished.

Kilroy grimaced. Could they really do that? I mean, did they have the ability to make those kinds of changes?

Nobody really knew for sure. It was accepted that certain parts of the brain are *associated* with experiences of spirituality, transcendence, and what have you. There had been work with scans, and probes, and drugs, but nobody had experimented surgically to alter the brains of living subjects. Leastways, nobody had admitted to it. Most scientists wouldn't have done it anyway, because it seemed clear that no single area of the brain is exclusively responsible for a particular experience. It's a network. But there's always that one person who thinks they know better, isn't there?

Uh-oh, Kilroy said.

Very much uh-oh. And the frightening thing is we still don't know exactly how he did it. But somehow he inserted himself into the execution of the project to influence the culture. He may have interfered genetically too. He hacked into everything.

Are we talking about Shadbold?

Yes.

Let me get this straight once and for all. Shadbold was a real person?

Yes, unfortunately.

Kilroy waited for her to continue. Her face was illuminated by the dying rays of the sunset, which faded as Kilroy watched her. She shivered.

Shadbold, she said, was trouble right from the start. He

was brilliant, and charismatic, and charming. He was also raving mad, it turned out. He was one of the founders of the project development team, and everyone always knew he was eccentric. He came across as being arrogant, too, but you could argue he had a right to be, because the breadth of his expertise was astonishing. The project might have fallen apart in the early days if he hadn't been such a driving force, and everyone was reluctant to face the truth when he started getting seriously weird. But he went completely over the top on the question of spirituality and religion. He was outraged by any proposal to interfere with what he believed was an innate propensity for spiritual revelation, and he insisted that religious artefacts and texts should be included in the cultural starter-pack. Seeds of faith, he called them. And when some people claimed they'd identified neurobiological receptors for religious belief, and wanted to suppress them, he went off the rails entirely. Not just yelling and ranting, but actual physical fights, in which he had to be restrained. Then he went strangely quiet, and got very polite. That should have raised a red flag, but everyone wanted to believe he'd had a change of heart, and you can understand why. When you're working twenty hours a day on trying to build a new human species while wearing a biohazard suit, who has time for nutty-professor shit? Anyhow, Shadbold seemed to cool down. He took a step back from the front line, and most people assumed he'd had a breakdown, and was keeping a low profile while he recovered. What he was really up to only emerged in the final stages, when it was too late: like, the anchor is up, the gangplank is being raised, the ship is sailing – that late. Maybe he thought the only way to make sure his ideas prevailed was to take matters into his own hands. That would be a charitable interpretation. But it's more likely he planned it all along. You know, people accuse scientists of playing god, but Shadbold took it further. He *became* god. He was a monster and a criminal, and he still is.

Kilroy wasn't sure he'd heard correctly.

Still is?

Yes.

You're telling me he's still alive?

Cynthia nodded. She looked unhappy.

So, Kilroy said, you're saying Shadbold is like…nine hundred years old?

Nine hundred and seventy.

Kilroy stared at her.

I know, Cynthia said.

But how can that even happen?

Surprisingly easily, it turned out. They should have guessed what he was really doing on the project, given that before he joined it he was deep into research on longevity, and people suspected he was working beyond the compliance parameters of ethical review boards. He was on the verge of something, then along came the perfect experiment. The largest scientific endeavour in history, with almost unlimited resources, and oversight that was unravelling under pressure, in conditions that positively encouraged risk-taking mavericks to do their own thing and face the consequences later. You couldn't ask for a better excuse to fool around with human genetic material in creative ways. Hell, they actually *needed* people to do that. It was all he could have wished for.

Kilroy stood up. He walked to the front of the barn and peered into the deepening gloom outside. His legs were stiff.

Cynthia said, Should we go?

Kilroy checked his watch. Soon.

He walked back to where she was sitting and stood in front of her.

All that stuff in the scripture, he said, about Shadbold being our saviour, and interceding with Upstairs Mum and Dad? He invented all that?

He did.

How did he do it? I mean, how did he…insert it…into our lives?

We don't exactly know. He definitely created artefacts and texts, and got them into the cultural starting materials. And it's possible he somehow intervened to reinforce neuronal functions that could tend to enhance religious belief, although it's hard to see how he could have done it. But that's the thing about Shadbold. He was way ahead of everyone, and there's no telling what he might have done.

Kilroy ran his hand over his chin. He needed a shave. Who knows about this? he said. I mean, how many people?

People here on Landmass?

Yeah. How many people know the whole story?

I don't think anyone knows the *whole* story, except Shadbold. But if you're asking me how many people know that most of the history you've been taught – about who you are, and how you got here – is a lie, the answer is just a handful. Until now, of course. Manfred blew the lid off the story, and now Sheba is out there turning it inside-out.

No wonder they're worried, Kilroy said. And if Sheba keeps trying to tell more people, they're going kill her for sure. Maybe they have already. You think so?

I don't think so. Not yet. Not until they know how far the material has spread.

Right, Kilroy said, they'll try to catch everyone who knows about it. Roll up networks, eliminate cells, sterilise pockets of infection. That's the procedure.

Something tells me she's alive, Kilroy.

Is that so? Is it something like an instinct, or something more like another weird little machine you've got in your pocket that I don't know about?

Please trust me.

Kilroy didn't reply. He turned away and began pacing around, but stopped abruptly.

Where is he? Where is Shadbold now?

Yeah, I need to tell you something about that.

What?

Why don't you sit down?

Kilroy sat down.

Shadbold is here, Cynthia said.

Kilroy suppressed the urge to look over his shoulder.

Here on Landmass?

I'm pretty sure, yes. Remember the guy you shot?

Let me see. Yes, there was something familiar about him. Oh, I know. It was because he looked like me, and it was creepy as fuck. That was it.

Not only like *you*, I'm afraid. He also looked like Shadbold.

Kilroy felt sick. OK, he said, that means Shadbold is… related to me?

Kind of. It's another line he crossed. The process I told you about? Sixteen separate donors providing genetic material for each person? The agreement was that once each unique variation was created, the blueprint was destroyed. But an agreement like that depends on all parties having a moral compass. It breaks down when one of those parties happens to be a criminal lunatic. See where I'm going with this?

Shadbold kept the material?

Not only that, he rigged the process so his own genes could emerge as dominant contributors, not just in the first population, but over many generations. You told me you believe there's something of everything in everyone. You're right, but there's more of Shadbold than there should be in some people. You, for example.

But that guy in the car didn't look exactly like me, did he? More like a rough approximation. And he didn't look happy about it.

Very true. He was falling apart even before you blew his face through the back of his head. Which makes me suspect Shadbold is improvising, without access to a proper laboratory. That clone of you was sketchy, and it was decaying badly by the time you made its acquaintance.

That is extremely damn disturbing to know.

Get used to it. There's more where that came from. Literally.

More versions of me?

It's possible.

But why? I'm just a cop. I was handed a case, and I'm doing my best to solve it. I'm not exactly a big wheel in the scheme of things.

Cynthia folded her arms. Come on, Kilroy, you know why this case was given to you, and not anyone else, don't you?

Yeah, I do. It's because I'm just smart enough to find out what they want, but not smart enough to cause much trouble.

Cynthia seemed taken aback. You really think that?

Isn't that what you meant?

No. I meant the connection with Shadbold.

Kilroy began to run his hand over his jaw again. He paused. Slowly he moved his hand away from his face and peered at it closely, turning it as he examined it.

It's freaky, he murmured.

What is?

That I look like him.

Cynthia shook her head. I didn't say you looked like him. I said there's a certain amount of him in you. There's a resemblance, but only in small ways.

And I'm the reason he's here?

Partly. But I think he's exploiting the whole situation here. It's volatile. Everyone's pissed off, right? Subversive ideas are gaining currency, and the more they try to stamp them out the more firmly they take hold. People want the truth, because they've got enough reasons to think they're being lied to. It's what happens when life become uncertain, and people aren't happy. When times are good, nobody gives a shit.

I can't argue with that.

And now, Cynthia said, there's a power struggle going on. It tends to come with the territory at a time like this, and Shadbold is somewhere in the mix, I'm sure of it. It's possible he influenced the decision to put you on this case.

If that's true, why did he send that…thing to kill me?

Right now, Cynthia said, your guess is as good as mine.

Kilroy regarded her thoughtfully. Maybe, he said, keeping his voice casual, it's true that Shadbold came here to exploit what's been happening. But you were here before all that. You've been here for a long time, haven't you?

Cynthia frowned. I didn't tell you that.

No. Sheba did.

What did she tell you?

Just that you knew her mother. But I'm guessing you were involved right from the start. Let me ask you: where did Manfred get all those ideas from in the first place?

Not from me.

Really? Convince me.

OK. You know he was an intelligence operative, right?

I thought he was probably with a special unit in the security apparatus.

You people, Cynthia said, have so many spies. Did you know that in the city where you live, approximately one person in four is an informant of some kind?

I didn't know it was that many, but I shouldn't be surprised.

Well, Manfred was a professional spook, in a city of spooks, and one day he received an order to investigate a very senior official. A top church doctor.

Kilroy snorted. They should have just handed him a nice warm mug of poison to drink. Who was the target?

Someone in charge of sensitive archives: a whole bunch of highly classified documents and records. Manfred is ordered to break into this official's home and retrieve whatever the guy is keeping in a strongbox in his basement. So, Manfred gets into the target's house one evening when he's out, and locates the strongbox. Which is much larger than expected, and when Manfred gets it open he finds it's crammed with files, too many to carry. Documents, pictures, papers of all kinds. What can he do? He starts working his way through this stuff, and before long he finds himself reading some very old documents, and the information they contain blows his mind. Next thing he knows, he's hearing the archive priest arriving back home, and he realises he's been in a trance for three hours. He grabs everything he can carry, and leaves by a back window just as the priest is walking in the front door. Next morning, he reports that he had to abort the mission because the target arrived back before he'd had a chance to crack the strongbox. He knows his story won't hold for long, but he doesn't even care, because he's so excited by what he's found, and so is his wife when he turns the whole stash over to her.

The wife? Kilroy said. The one who got killed?

Her name was Wanda.

I know. But why did he give the files to her?

Because it was the evidence she'd been waiting for. Wanda was a teacher, and something of a scholar, and she'd been working for years to unearth the truth about the history of Landmass. The notebooks were her work, by the way, not Manfred's.

I'm confused, Kilroy said. I thought it was Manfred who was trying to get this stuff out into the open, and that's why they executed him, and Wanda was collateral damage.

Is that what you call a woman getting her throat cut?

No, sorry, I didn't mean it that way. I just didn't realise she was the main player, which is what you seem to be implying. I thought it was Manfred.

Maybe that's what you were meant to think.

Who wanted me to think that? You?

Look, I'm not denying I was in contact with Wanda when all this was happening. But there's no way I would have done anything that put anyone's life in danger. The opposite, in fact. I tried to stop Manfred making everything public.

Yeah, Kilroy said, that's another thing: if he was part of the security apparatus what made him go rogue?

You've never been married, have you?

Me? No. Have you?

Never mind me. But people change in weird ways when they're close to each other for a long time. Maybe when Wanda married Manfred she was pretty happy about him being in the security apparatus. But over the years she became concerned about what was happening. Books disappearing from the schools, history lessons being restricted, any kind of imaginative expression starting to be treated as heresy. She finds herself turning into a dissenter, then a subversive. Which is what authoritarians call any intelligent citizen who wants to stand up for the truth and do the right thing. Or do you have a problem with that definition?

I hear you ma'am, and please step away from the lecture podium.

Sorry. I wasn't implying that you—

No offence taken. I just want to know how Manfred ended up getting terminated in the town square, and not Wanda.

The official story is that he went crazy.

But that was an act. Wasn't it?

Who knows? Maybe acting crazy is dangerously close to being crazy. And in the last couple of years Manfred was getting seriously conflicted. Every day at work he convinces himself he's doing a fine, upstanding job that's necessary to the stability of society, and every night at home his wife tells him he's supporting a totalitarian system. Some people can compartmentalise internal contradictions, but Manfred wasn't one of them, especially not after he found those documents, and realised Wanda was right. He flipped, and went at it with the zeal of a convert. He started shouting from the rooftops.

Maybe it felt good to him, Kilroy said, that he didn't have to fight with his wife any more, and he could prove he loved her by showing her he was on her side.

Or maybe, Cynthia said, he was just being a prick. Here's another interpretation of Manfred's flamboyant heresy: he does it to sabotage Wanda. He predicts that by making a big noise in public he'll force the authorities to step in and take control. Which is pretty much what happened, and Manfred gets what he wants.

At the cost of his life? Why didn't he just hand back the documents instead of giving them to Wanda, and simply denounce her, if that's what he wanted?

He may have miscalculated. Don't forget, there's a power struggle going on. The assignment he was given in the first place may have been a cover. Certain people may have wanted him to find those documents, and even expose them.

I've noticed, Kilroy said, that every time you explain something to me it gets more complicated.

I'll stop now. But whichever explanation is correct, the end result is the same, which is that it flushes Shadbold out.

And I have to take your word for all this, do I? That Manfred's heretical shenanigans exposed Shadbold, and Shadbold is a thousand years old, and is my kind-of-ancestor, and that you got interested in my investigation of Wanda's murder because you thought Shadbold might try something, and one thing leads to another, and now here we are, two unimpeachable individuals with an inspiring mission to save the world. Anything else I should take your word for?

Not right now, no.

Kilroy stood up again and walked to the front of the barn and looked out into the night. A gibbous moon hung low in the sky.

I need to ask you one more question, he said.

Go ahead.

Kilroy turned back to face her. How old are you, Cynthia?

Cynthia looked down. When she raised her head, her expression was blank.

Nine-hundred-and-thirty-eight, she said.

As a rule, Kilroy said, I don't usually go for older women. But I'll make an exception for you.

Cynthia stopped laughing and licked his ear. Let's lie down again, she said.

Not now. Kilroy gently removed her arms from around his neck.

Cynthia stepped away from him and looked out into the darkness.

It's getting late, she said.

We'll still get to the city before dawn if we leave soon. I just want to ask you something else.

That's not fair. A minute ago, you said you only had one more question, and I gave you the answer.

This is the second part of the same question.

Let me guess. Am I going to live for ever? The answer is no. I'm not.

How long, then?

Around eleven hundred years, probably. That's the best estimate we have. There might be new developments, but it seems there's a biological limit, for now.

Kilroy gazed at her intently. Shit, he murmured, I don't know.

What don't you know?

I don't know why I'm not as angry as I should be. Maybe I will be later.

What would you be angry about?

How could you do that? You and those other people were able to extend your own lives, but you gave us a limit. That makes you like…executioners. You get to decide when we die. I shouldn't be angry about that?

Not if you know why we made those choices. Think about it. People who live to be over a thousand years old are in no hurry to reproduce. That wouldn't have worked for the population we left here. We needed you guys to get down to it, create some turnover in the generations, put some evolution into the game.

In that case, Kilroy said, why not kill us off at thirty? Fuck it, kill us at twenty. Eighteen. Why do we need to stick around after we've reproduced?

That's not the way it works.

For who?

For you! Jesus, Kilroy it's not like we didn't think this through. There are social and cultural benefits to having three generations alive in any given time-frame, but if you live to be older than eighty – give or take – in this environment, there's a law of diminishing biological returns that kicks in. You people are almost disease-free, and we fixed it so you wouldn't need too much in the way of medical technology. Up to a certain age, it works out pretty well.

Not any more, Kilroy said. People have started to go wrong. Getting sick, dying before their span, that kind of thing.

Cynthia frowned. I know. We're looking into it.

Gee, thanks. Only if it's not too much trouble.

We're doing our best! All along, we've tried to get it right, believe me. You think it was easy, making decisions about when people die? We put a cap on your longevity because in the end it was the most compassionate course of action.

But that doesn't apply to you and friends, obviously.

Different circumstances. We had all the medical technology we needed, and we were able to take it with us. But we didn't have room to multiply quickly as a population. It's crowded. It makes more sense to live longer and reproduce much more slowly.

But you do still reproduce?

Theoretically.

Do you have children yourself?

Cynthia hesitated.

Kilroy walked over to her and stood close. Do you?

222

No, Cynthia said.

Are you married?

Yes.

How's that working out for you?

You've met him. Benedict, one of the two people who tried to capture me.

Holy shit. You two seem to be going through a rough patch.

Cynthia laughed. You could say that.

Is it about not having children?

No, it's not about that.

So why are you looking shaky right now?

Because it's a sensitive issue, but not for the reasons you think. Benedict and I separated a long time ago. Five hundred years. And our relationship, as you perceptively observed, has gone through some changes. And it's true I had an emotional response when you asked about children. But that's not about me. Or not just me. It turns out that not many of us can have children. And I can tell you why in one word. Shadbold.

Cynthia stepped out of the barn and gazed up at the sky. The stars were bright.

It was a long journey, she said, and he gave us a lot to think about en route. But he didn't tell us everything he'd done all at once. Where's the fun in that? First, he admitted he'd interfered in what we called the foundational process. He talked about the mythic origins of all religions, and the saviour who intercedes to end the sins and suffering of believers. Then he told us he was going to be immortal, and had established himself as the avatar of salvation in a religion that the population of Landmass would adopt. He let us chew that over for a while before his next pronouncement, that his immortality was real, and not just a legend he'd created for the foundational culture. He told us he'd undergone what he called a procedure. He conceded he wasn't talking about true immortality, but an extended lifespan of a thousand years plus, although he held out the possibility it could be extended much further, with more work. To within sight of eternity, was the phrase he used.

That's scary, Kilroy said.

If it seems that way to you, imagine how we felt about it, trapped on a fucking spaceship with this maniac.

Couldn't you stop him?

It was too late. And he made us an offer we couldn't refuse.

Why couldn't you refuse?

We didn't want to, and he knew it. As it stood, he was going to live ten times longer than the rest of us, and we couldn't reverse the procedure he'd undergone, because he was the only one who knew exactly what it was. He pointed out that his power and influence would only grow if we declined his offer. We would die off, and he wouldn't. He would be there all the time, as generations came and went, and they would be increasingly reliant on him. Basically, he was telling us he could enslave our descendants if he felt like it. He would not only control the future of the survivors on the satellites, he would also control everything that happened here on Landmass. The only way we could prevent that from happening was to accept his offer – his gift, he called it. And if the temptation of a tenfold increase in our lifespan wasn't enough, he made it seem like it was our moral duty to share his longevity, so we could keep an eye on him and stop him being evil. Like he was being selfless, and it would be better for humanity that way.

Didn't it cross your mind, Kilroy said, that it all sounded too good to be true?

Yes, and yet we all agreed to the procedure. Not everyone at once, though. We decided, in our wisdom, that we should all be free to follow our conscience. All it took was for one person to agree to the procedure, and then it became almost impossible for the rest of us to hold out. And he tricked us, naturally. All he cared about was our genetic material, and the procedure was a way to harvest it, and keep it for his own purposes.

His own purposes being, Kilroy said, to make replicas? Clones?

That and a few other little projects. But I don't think you want to know about them right now, and if I tell you anything more you're going to hate me.

Should I just shoot you now?

Cynthia's smile was strained. Maybe you should.

I won't. I don't want to have to deal with another dead body.

I swear I will help you bury your father, if that's what you want.

Thanks, Kilroy said. He looked up at the high moon. Let's go.

I'm ready.

Do me a favour, though.

What's that?

Change your colour back to what it was before.

Cynthia laughed. Shit, I forgot that!

Better do it, Kilroy said. I have a feeling people would notice.

Almost as soon as they swung onto the main road they saw the glow of an illuminated public screen about a kilometre ahead. A face filled it, huge and eerie in the midnight darkness. As they approached they saw it was Sheba.

There were no vehicles or people in the viewing area. Kilroy parked as far away from the road as possible. They switched on the car's audio and watched the broadcast.

Viewers were told that Sheba was a wanted criminal who had escaped from custody in an incident that was notable for its ruthless violence. The picture changed briefly to a shot of a chaotic street scene, with two crashed vehicles and some bodies on the ground.

That's faked, Kilroy murmured.

Sheba's face was replaced by another huge head shot. It was Curtis. The commentary informed the public that Sheba had been aided by an accomplice. It described Curtis as especially dangerous as she had been a state security officer who had now committed an unforgivable act of treason, and was capable of using her training to evade capture. In the interests of public safety, the authorities were issuing an edict that would permit her to be killed on sight. Meanwhile, an important message from the Procurator of the Faithful.

The broadcast switched to a studio, and a man who looked, to Kilroy to be in his late sixties. He had a bland face and an air of subdued watchfulness. He was introduced as Dr Glibbery, and Kilroy loathed him on sight. The man spoke with quiet authority:

These are dangerous times. We face a test of our faith. The dark forces of heresy, subversion and disorder are emboldened, and we must put our trust in Upstairs Mum and Dad, and the compassionate protection of the divine Shadbold, enacted through his servants in the church. It is the duty of every citizen to be vigilant, steadfast and, more than ever, obedient to the authorities at this time.

To ensure public safety an emergency edict has been issued, banning any public gathering of more than five persons. Individuals who flout this law are subject to immediate arrest. There will be an enhanced police presence on the streets, and their powers to detain and question any person they consider a threat have been increased. There is no telling how long this emergency will last, but by uniting in our rejection of heresy, we shall triumph over disorder, darkness, and sin. May we all remain safe, and free from contamination. Thank you, my friends. In the name of our Upstairs Mum and Dad, through the Grace of Shadbold, who is with us, and among us, and within us.

The broadcast switched back to the photos of Sheba and Curtis, and the commentary reminded the public that both these suspects were irredeemable heretics of the most dangerous and ruthless type.

The screen went black for a moment, then the loop began again.

Kilroy drove the car out of the parking area. He glanced at Cynthia and saw she was looking out of her window, her head turned away, seemingly lost in thought.

Hey, he said, are you OK?

She turned to him. Sorry, I guess I was shocked by how fast things are moving, even though I could have expected it. So, does this change our plan?

No, Kilroy said, but it raises the stakes.

He accelerated along the dark, empty highway to the city.

CURTIS

I was underground, and not just metaphorically.

Our centre of operations was in the basement of a Reform Tabernacle located in the southwest of the city. It was nearly four hundred years old, which meant it had originally been consecrated as an orthodox church a century before the Schism. When that conflict erupted, the tabernacle – as it now was – had sided with the reformists, and suffered the persecutions that followed. At that time the building was just outside the city walls, in an affluent settlement founded by a guild of engineers. The engineers were men and women whose skills were prized in a period of rapid urban expansion, and they worked on projects to serve the city's growing population, one of which was a new sewerage system. But they were also independent artisans with a long tradition of freethinking, which made them natural recruits to the reformist cause.

That's why, in addition to building the new sewerage system, which was still in use, they riddled the entire district with a series of secret tunnels. These were in constant use during the thirty years of persecution, which ended with the announcement of the Plan for Reconciliation, when the government – or a bright individual within it who possessed the rare ability to think rationally – finally realised there was a better way to deal with religious dissent than ruthless repression. After all, the theological differences that divided the reformist position from the orthodox were relatively minor. The main point of contention was whether Shadbold was physically present when we asked for his intercession, made manifest by our faith, or whether our prayers, if they were sincere, simply lent agency to his spirit, enabling it to work through us.

There was a more radical group of dissenters who maintained that Shadbold was not present at all in these transactions, and that we alone were responsible for our relations with Upstairs Mum and Dad. This outlandish heresy was condemned by both the reformers and the orthodox, allowing them to find common ground for a settlement. With the benefit of hindsight, it's easy to see that the extremists who professed such beliefs were *agents provocateurs* inserted into the conflict by the government. It can be very useful to both sides in a fight if they can agree – at the right moment – that someone else is more wicked than either of them.

And agree they did, although the authorities made it seem as if they were the ones making all the concessions. They understood it was more effective to permit the expression of mild theological dissent than to crush it. That way, they could channel any spirit of popular opposition into a single religious issue, where it could be policed, and in the process they provided the dissenters with a comforting illusion that they'd won a great victory. This had a wonderfully pacifying effect on the most obstreperous of them, who were inevitably the most conceited and self-important. And from the government's economic point of view, reconciliation was far cheaper to implement than repression.

After Reconciliation, other reformist congregations claimed they'd been just as rebellious as the engineers, and these churches were now proud of their alleged defiance, and incorporated rousing tales of heroism, daring and sacrifice into their histories.

But the engineers kept quiet. They resisted any temptation to talk about what they'd done, and although quite a few people knew about the tunnels, or had heard of them, details of their location and extent gradually faded from memory, and after about fifty years even their existence was largely forgotten.

Now, nobody knew about them, except a small group who had guarded the secret of the tunnels for many generations, along with another secret. From the beginning, there was an inner circle of activists within the community of dissenting engineers – a secret society – who were not just reformers, but revolutionaries. They'd been dedicated to overturning the established order, and especially the church, since long before the Schism. Reconciliation had effectively robbed them of the chance to make the profound social and political changes they wanted, but they knew their time would come again, and they kept the secret of the tunnels, and of the radical tradition, alive.

I was told all this by a young pastor, in the basement of what was still referred to locally as the Engineers' Tabernacle. The room had been a crypt when the place was still an Orthodox church, but after Reconciliation, when the relics and decorations which it had contained were cleared out, it became a meeting room for scripture study. That was the official story, anyway.

But the pastor, who was called Brocklebank, wasn't only a pastor. He was a revolutionary. You could say he was hiding in plain sight, because he was well known to be a rousing, firebrand preacher. That was an excellent cover. The authorities kept an eye on him, but they didn't keep a *close* eye on him. Why would they? They had his number, or so they thought. What they saw was a vocally reformist cleric, perhaps even something of a doctrinal radical. And if some of his preaching was borderline subversive, well, that was a passionate young reformist pastor for you. Just don't overstep the line, son.

The fact that Brocklebank was already way over the line completely escaped them, because the paranoid style of government, obsessed with complex deceptions and baroque conspiracies, looks in every direction except the obvious one.

Brocklebank was the inheritor of a secret tradition stretching back four hundred years, and his role was to be ready when conditions were finally right for a revolution. That moment had now arrived, he believed, heralded by Sheba and her message. There was an irony here that wasn't lost on Brocklebank and the other activists. They were dedicated to overthrowing the Church, and yet the emergence of Sheba as the catalyst for an uprising mimicked the religious model itself – of a patient, suffering people who would be redeemed by the appearance of a saviour.

We all had a good laugh about that.

Yes, we were a merry band, and I will admit to feeling exhilarated by joining a revolutionary network, many of whose members appeared, to my jaundiced eye, to be young, passionate, and remarkably good-looking.

Brocklebank and the others had decided to trust me, after subjecting me to an interrogation which I found laughably easy to deflect, especially as they wanted to believe me. After all, I'd helped Sheba to escape, and delivered her to them more or less single-handed, and they were ready to accept almost anything I wanted to tell them.

They already knew who I was, because they had moles in the security apparatus. In fact, when Kilroy arrived at my place with Sheba, they knew more about the operation to arrest her than I did, and they were able to have a couple of their people on hand when my place was raided, watching what went down.

But they didn't know much more than that, and I greatly enhanced my credibility by making what must have seemed like a full disclosure. I told them what I'd been ordered to do, and how I'd defied my orders, and taken matters into my own hands. I admitted I'd been motivated as much by concern for my own survival as by any ideology, or devotion to Sheba. As I'd intended, my honesty about my own self-interest only reinforced their conviction that I was trustworthy. My background as a security officer gave them something of a thrill, and made my apparent conversion to their cause all the more dramatic, and therefore convincing. I've always been intrigued by the willingness of idealists to embrace a defector, and to overlook the possibility that a turncoat is more, rather than less, likely to turn again. All told, I found it easy to infiltrate the network, and Brocklebank and the others were eager to welcome me for who they thought I was.

It helped, of course, that I had a pretty good story to tell.

Two days after I'd received my conflicting instructions from Allardyce, Pascal and Glibbery, I learned that Sheba was to be moved. This supposedly secret plan became common knowledge in the department, just as my superiors had predicted. The justification for the move was that Sheba was being allowed a visit to her brother on compassionate grounds. She would be taken from the cells, and transported to the outskirts of town, where young Roland, who was being cared for by his foster family, had fallen ill. That was the story, and I found out later that Roland was in fact genuinely unwell. He was probably being poisoned.

Allardyce had instructed me to exploit the disorganisation of the planned visit as an opportunity to kill Sheba, and to make it look like an accident occurring in a chaotic shoot-out, preferably caused by her rescuers.

Pascal, meanwhile, had ordered me to pose as a turncoat, help Sheba escape, and infiltrate the network so it could be shut down and its members eliminated.

Glibbery wanted the same outcome, with the difference that I was to embed myself in the network and discredit it from within, rendering it debased and contemptible.

I didn't trust any of them, and I suspected my own death was, if not an actively desired outcome, a perfectly acceptable corollary to all three plans.

Under normal circumstances I would look for a weak point, where I could gain leverage. My problem was that each of the plans proposed to me by Allardyce, Pascal and Glibbery was little more than a series of weak points, loosely connected by a thread of speculation. Having said that, each plan constrained me in the same way, by requiring me to engage with the rescue, and either kill Sheba or infiltrate her rescuers. Those conditions were not negotiable. So, I decided to act within the only matrix that offered me the chance of independent agency, which was the time frame. In other words, I would do what they wanted me to do, but not necessarily when they wanted me to do it.

The morning after my encounters with Allardyce, Pascal and Glibbery I went into work and did some research on Alexander, the custodian who'd taken me to Sheba's cell. I accessed data beyond my rank by pulling in favours, including from my boss and sometime lover, on the promise of hot sexual payback at some future time. I thought it was unlikely I'd ever get around to performing the depravities I whispered in his ear.

The plan I was hatching depended on whether Alexander was an authentic convert to Sheba's message, or a plant. I didn't expect him to be entirely uncompromised, seeing that his job was to detain state prisoners and facilitate whatever his superiors wished them to undergo. He would have witnessed brutality, even if he didn't dish it out himself. I discovered he was an informant, naturally. He'd seen and heard a lot in the course of his work, and he was pretty shrewd about how he used it. Sometimes he went over the heads of his immediate superiors, and reported to people higher up the chain who wanted to keep an eye on their subordinates. Occasionally he went outside the department, and fed information to other agencies in the apparatus. But Alexander wasn't playing for high stakes. He was simply trying to make the most of his resources, and increase his chances of a reasonably quiet life. That didn't mean I could trust him, but it was clear that none of the people he worked for considered him particularly important. So far, so good. But I still needed to find out whether he'd become a true convert to the cause. I learned he was married and had two children. I decided to drop in on him that evening.

Alexander opened the door to me and tried to conceal his surprise. Over his shoulder I caught a glimpse of his living room, where a couch was occupied by two small children in pyjamas, sitting on either side of a woman who held a storybook on her lap. Alexander stepped forward, blocking my view.

Look, he said, is this necessary? If you want to speak to me about something can't it wait until tomorrow?

No, it can't.

Why not? His face betrayed a spasm of fear. Unless, he said, trying to peer behind me, you've come to—

No, I said, I'm alone.

What's it about? If it's about the girl I'll deny everything.

Can I come in?

He stared at me. Wait a moment.

He half-turned to the room behind him. Take the kids to bed, he said.

As his wife hustled the children away he shuffled back to allow me in.

Sit down, he said.

After you.

He took a step towards me. Tell me the truth, he hissed, did you have a wire on you that night?

No, I didn't.

How about now?

Want to search me? I held my arms out and stood with my legs apart.

He looked me up and down, then shook his head. All right, he said, let's sit down for fuck's sake. Do you want a drink?

I left an hour later, convinced that Alexander believed in Sheba, and was a sincere convert to her cause. I like to think

I'm sceptical and objective, but the truth is I rely on instinct as much as everyone else, and everyone else relies on it far more than they admit. All you can do is gather information, test it as hard as you can, then go with your gut.

So, I decided to trust Alexander. I told him as much of the truth as he needed to hear, disclosing my orders from Allardyce, but not those from Pascal or Glibbery. I persuaded him that I too was a convert to Sheba's cause, and I wanted to spread her message. I asked for his assistance in thwarting Allardyce's orders to kill her. His willingness to do anything he could to protect Sheba seemed genuine.

He'd already heard a rumour they were going to move Sheba soon. I told him they intended to offer plenty of opportunities for an ambush, and I expected them to transport her in a lightly fortified vehicle with a couple of guards, and a motorcycle outrider or two. The convoy would take a route so vulnerable to attack that even the most half-witted ambush attempt couldn't fail, unless it was bungled to the point of derangement.

But my plan, and the reason I need Alexander to be part of it, was to rescue Sheba before the convoy even set off.

Two days later it played out pretty much as I'd predicted.

Allardyce contacted me and told me Sheba was to be moved the next morning, an hour after dawn. I was assigned to travel with her in the armoured vehicle, making it easier for me to kill her during the anticipated rescue attempt. Two guards would travel with us, and motorcycles would flank us. Two more agents would be in a backup car.

There was only one external entrance to the cell block, in an alleyway that sloped down from the main road. This was where detainees were transferred to and from vehicles, which parked directly in front of the reinforced gates. My orders were to join the armoured vehicle there. However, I persuaded Allardyce that I should be waiting inside the cell block, to supervise the job of getting Sheba into the wagon.

You never know, I said to her, they may make a rescue attempt before the journey even begins. We can't rule anything out where that girl is concerned.

Allardyce agreed. It helped that she, and everyone else, as far as I could tell, held Sheba in an awe that stopped little short of attributing supernatural powers to her. A myth had accumulated around her. Everyone seemed terrified of her, and Allardyce readily accepted that we should take no chances when this skinny girl of thirteen was escorted over a distance of a few dozen metres, under armed guard, to a waiting armoured vehicle.

I was outside Sheba's cell with Alexander a few minutes before the escort was due to arrive. The official plan was that we would get a signal when the vehicle was approaching, and open Sheba's cell. We would march her to the end of the passage, and when the team outside was in place they would bang on the gates, which we would open. Sheba would be put into the back of the vehicle by the armed guards, who would sit with her, I would join the driver, and we would pick up the motorcycle escort and the backup car when we reached the top of the steep alley and joined the main road.

Alexander had agreed to help me on the condition that it would look as if I'd forced him to co-operate. Although he was part of the network, he had a family and he wasn't yet prepared to go underground. Fair enough. We knew the cameras would be recording, and might even be monitored, given the paranoia surrounding Sheba, so we calculated everything to the last second.

When we got the signal to tell us the vehicle was approaching Alexander unlocked Sheba's cell. As soon as she was out I pulled a gun on Alexander. To make it look good, he tried to grab it and I whacked him in the face with the barrel, slightly harder than I'd intended. My pistol-whipping technique was a little rusty. I had a second gun, which I gave to Sheba. We walked Alexander to the gates, and instead of waiting to hear from the team outside that they were in place, we made Alexander unlock them immediately. As soon as they were open I gave him another tap with the gun, and he went down.

The timing was perfect. The gates swung open just as the vehicle reversed into place, the back doors opened, and the two guards stepped out to find themselves facing our guns. We hustled them into the passage, and I used Alexander's keys to lock them inside Sheba's cell. She and I ran to the front of the wagon and offered the driver the option of leaving the vehicle promptly or being shot in the legs. He made the right choice, and we got into the cab. I gunned the truck up the slope, and it shot out of the alley just in time to hit the two motorcycles that were pulling up. The riders went flying, and their bikes ended up blocking the street and preventing the backup vehicle, which was tooling slowly down the road, from chasing us. By the time the guards in the car had figured out what the hell was happening, and radioed for help, we were long gone.

Sheba played her part with remarkable self-possession.

As we drove away, I told her I'd burned my bridges, and I had to trust her. She said I could, and she trusted me too. I didn't know where we were going, but she did, and I followed her directions, driving fast but not recklessly. She told me about the tunnels, and where we could get into the system. When I asked how she knew about the tunnels, she turned away, and I heard what sounded like a stifled a sob. It was sometimes easy to forget that Sheba was a child who had recently lost both her parents to acts of brutal violence. I surmised that her mother and father had told her about the underground system, and now she was thinking about them. When she turned back to face the road, she was dry-eyed. She told me to keep driving, and that we'd soon arrive where we needed to be.

I was relieved to hear that our destination wasn't far away, as I wanted to ditch the vehicle as soon as possible. We turned into a side street, parked, and continued on foot. I was certain we weren't being followed, and nobody seemed to be paying us any particular attention. I found out later that the authorities had been obliged to delay issuing a screen bulletin about us until they'd faked up the street scene showing the aftermath of an alleged shoot-out.

Sheba led me to a small shop that housed the business of a tailor and a dressmaker, who were an elderly married couple. They also took in dry cleaning, fixed shoes and cut keys. It was a useful range of services, and it kept the shop busy with a varied local clientele. Who doesn't need clothes, repairs, dry cleaning, shoes and keys?

The shop wasn't open yet, but the owners were waiting for us, and let us in. The place had a friendly, cluttered feel, and the old couple gave the impression of being harmless, likeable types, with a smile and a good word for everyone. I discovered later that in order to protect the network the amiable old seamstress had killed at least one person with a pair of scissors, concealing the corpse by dressing it in a wedding gown and veil and propping it in a corner of the shop until her husband, the plump, jolly little tailor, dug a quicklime pit in a suitably remote location. My kind of people. They greeted Sheba with exuberant warmth, but they also seemed oddly respectful towards her, given that she was young enough to be their granddaughter. They accepted my presence unquestioningly, and seemed to find it unremarkable that I'd risked my life to bring the girl to them.

I began to understand that developments I'd assumed to be recent and unprecedented had long, deep roots. I was to learn more later, but right now it was time to descend into the underworld. Its entrance was behind a thin curtain which shielded one of three cramped changing rooms at the back of the shop. There was a full-length mirror on the wall of this little nook. The dressmaker hopped onto a stool and pressed a hidden catch behind the top of the mirror, while her husband engaged a similar mechanism in the next cubicle. The system only worked if it was triggered simultaneously in the two locations. The mirror swung away from the wall to expose a compartment no bigger than an upright coffin, standing over what appeared to be a gaping black hole. A flashlight revealed a set of metal rungs descending into a deep stone well. Sheba went down first and I followed.

That was my introduction to the network, and the tunnels.

The tunnel system was mainly accessed through hidden doors in private buildings, like the shop, but there was also a variety of other locations. For example, there was an entrance in one of the inspection pits of a suburban tram terminus, if you knew where to look, and a certain public toilet in a park had a cubicle with a false wall. There were a few more places like that. But the most important feature of the tunnels was that they didn't form a single, interconnected system. There were half a dozen independent minor systems that could be sealed off, so if one of them was compromised the others had a chance of remaining undiscovered.

A similar process applied to the network itself, which was organised in a classic cell structure. Each cell, which contained half a dozen people, was connected only to a pair of adjacent cells. Each member of a cell knew it would shut down in twelve hours if they didn't make their regular check-in. If they were captured, they just had to hold out for that long. Easier said than done. I knew it was exceptional for anyone to resist the itching test for more than a couple of hours, and as for other techniques, like the squenks, results were often achieved quicker than that.

But even if a whole cell was busted, the damage could be limited, and it wouldn't bring down the entire network. That was the theory. The problem was that the principle hadn't undergone a recent operational test. Now, however, the network was gearing up to fulfil its ultimate purpose – a full-scale popular uprising – and doing it at a time when the authorities were equipped with an arsenal of sophisticated counter-intelligence tools.

These matters were the subject of my discussions with Brocklebank, the young pastor, over the next few days in the Tabernacle basement. It was during these conversations that I learned about the history of the network, and why the sudden emergence of Sheba as a kind of prophet, bearing her startling news, wasn't really sudden at all. The network had long been anticipating her arrival, and it was the catalyst for an eruption that had been simmering for many years.

Among other things, I learned about the part played by Manfred and Wanda. The more I heard about them, the more it seemed Sheba had been trained for her role, especially by Wanda. At the very least, some planning had gone into what

Sheba was now doing. And what she was doing was extremely effective. Everyone who came into contact with her was captivated by her, and some were inspired to a kind of reverence that would have been creepy had it not seemed so natural.

I tried for a long time to put my finger on what made her so magnetic, but I couldn't, until I realised there was no extraordinary quality she possessed, and no ordinary quality she possessed in extraordinary measure. If anything, the opposite. She had *less* to her than most people. Less self-consciousness, less calculation, less artifice, less need. This created a kind of vacuum into which your attention and admiration were drawn – and perhaps your devotion, too.

Sheba was refining her message, and working on her delivery. She'd developed a compelling narrative that she could put across in just a few minutes. It was less comprehensive than the story she'd told me in her cell, but it packed a bigger punch. Nobody would ever be able to deliver it as persuasively as she could, and it was mesmerising to see her do it, even after I'd witnessed it several times, but the message was now simple enough to create a reliably powerful impact by itself, and even the dullest narrator would have had to work hard to bungle it entirely. As a consequence, it was spreading swiftly, along with Sheba's personal legend. The network was growing exponentially, which created an unintended consequence: the revolution was just too damn popular.

The network had been designed as a secret society, and now the committee couldn't control the way Sheba's message was gathering public momentum. The most recent converts were highly visible, but even as the authorities swooped down on them, more sprang up to take their place. We were fast approaching a moment when a single, concerted push from either side could be decisive.

If the speed of what was happening had taken the committee by surprise, they weren't the only ones. The security services were now in the same jam as the network, in that they had no previous experience of what was unfolding. The arrest and execution of Manfred, the murder of Wanda, and the attempt to frame Sheba – these had been manoeuvres conducted by comfortable strategists who were confident of their ability to control the outcomes. If the plans they hatched were only partially successful, or failed altogether, they had the time and space to improvise, or to change course depending on the consequence of this or that tactical move.

But a security apparatus that has effectively dominated its enemies becomes lazy and arrogant. It's easy to believe you're a master of the game when your opponent is deprived of the means to compete. You become a victim of your own success. But when the bullets start flying, or the bombs explode, or the barricades go up, and what's required is decisive, well-planned action, you're screwed. The game has changed, but you can't, because you've trained yourself to speculate, rather than act.

This speculative quality was exemplified by the plans my three superiors had laid out for me, although I found out later that Pascal, at least, had devised a backup plan. His idea was that if the ambush didn't happen, Sheba's visit to her brother would proceed, and during it Sheba, Roland, and his foster parents would all be assassinated, and I would be framed for the murders, then eliminated on the grounds that I was a dangerous fugitive. This plan was very similar to the scheme whereby Sheba had been framed for her mother's murder, and I suspected Pascal of being the originator of that idea too. It was clearly one of his signature moves when he needed to dispose of more than one person at a time. I still liked him, though.

But there was no time to think about that now.

I'd been wrong-footed by the speed of events, along with everyone else. My expectation was that after I delivered Sheba to the network they would slowly grow their movement underground, and build up clandestine support, so that when the moment for an uprising came, everything would be in place. I expected the process to take several weeks, perhaps months. I wasn't used to being completely mistaken, and it came as a shock.

I was kept abreast of developments by the reports that poured into the Tabernacle basement, which was now a command centre, operating around the clock. I'd been given a pair of rooms in one of the tunnel systems, adjacent to the basement. My little apartment was extraordinarily well-equipped, and the ventilation was so efficient I sometimes forgot I was under the ground.

Over the next few days I made a couple of visits back through the tunnels to the shop, to get a sense of the public mood, although I didn't venture outside. I stood behind the curtain of the changing cubicle with the hidden door, eavesdropping on people coming and going. Most were legitimate customers, unaware of the proprietors' secret roles, and some of these stayed to talk. The gossip was infused with urgency. Nobody knew what was happening. People were being arrested. The authorities were overreacting, some said. Others claimed it was important to maintain order. But most agreed it was wrong to treat ordinary citizens like criminals. It would end badly, they said, unless things changed, and maybe they would, seeing the way things were going, and about time, perhaps.

A few of these customers went further, and hinted that in

the event of an uprising they were prepared to support the struggle. It was hard to tell whether they were trying to make tentative contact with the network in good faith, or whether they were informants. A couple of times I spotted customers who were clearly agents, making casual enquires about activists in the area. The old couple maintained an impenetrable façade.

Nearly every time the shop door opened, I heard sirens in the distance, and occasionally close by. People passing in the street, individually or in small groups, walked quickly, and once or twice there was some running.

The shop was also visited by existing members of the network, bringing and receiving information. Occasionally they also delivered trusted contacts for whom life had become too hot, and who needed to go underground, via the changing cubicle and down into the tunnels.

That was how I made the acquaintance of Sheba's younger brother, Roland, in miserable circumstances. Someone came into the shop towards the end of the day, when it was quiet, checked the coast was clear, then brought the boy in. He was pale and silent. I was preparing to return down to the tunnels, so they asked me to escort Roland to the command centre, where he could be reunited with Sheba. I did as I was asked, but I couldn't get a word out of the boy as he followed me obediently down the deep access hatch, into the tunnels, and through the labyrinthine system. His lips remained clamped firmly shut, and his jaw was clenched. He was trying desperately to hold back tears.

He allowed the tears to come when he saw Sheba. He ran to her arms and they clutched each other for a long time in silence. He didn't want to talk to anyone except her, but I was able to hear most of what they said when he eventually began to tell her what had happened.

He'd been out on an errand, and he returned home just in time to see his foster parents being dragged from the house by security agents. Roland ducked behind a wall, and peeped around it to watch the couple being forced into an armoured wagon. The woman resisted. She was shot in the head, point-blank, there in the street in broad daylight. Roland ran to a neighbour he could trust, and from there he'd been brought to the shop.

Sheba remained strangely calm as he told her his sorry tale, especially given that the dead woman was a cousin. But after a few moments I realised she was simply exercising remarkable self-control. She was focused entirely on her little brother, and the comfort she could give him.

Meanwhile I was able to witness at first hand Roland's peculiarities. At one point he turned away from his sister and struck a declamatory pose:

I am consumed by woe, he wailed, and I believe my heart will break!

Then he threw himself into her arms again, and sobbed. I understood that when he spoke this way it didn't mean he was insincere – it was just his way of dealing with the intensity of his feelings, as if he were trying to tame them somehow by containing them in this weirdly formal structure of speech.

He was certainly an odd child.

What had taken place was a kind of turning point. Up until now the authorities had maintained a pretence, at least, of lawful process. Bad things, no doubt, were happening to people once they'd been arrested and taken away, and perhaps some of them were eliminated. But shooting a woman dead in the street was an unequivocal step towards a different state of affairs.

I was now faced with an urgent decision I'd hoped to postpone for a while.

Officially I was still an agent of the security apparatus. Just because I'd subverted the ill-conceived and contradictory orders I'd been given by three different superiors, that didn't change the fact. As far as Allardyce, Pascal or Glibbery were concerned, I might simply be working deeper undercover than they'd expected, going the extra kilometre for them. True, gigantic images of my face had appeared on every public screen, along with a declaration from the Procurator of the Faithful that I was a dangerous terrorist who could be killed on sight by anyone who felt like taking a shot. But that directive could – just possibly – be a smokescreen they put out to help my credibility with the network.

The likelihood of this interpretation being correct was reduced to almost zero when Glibbery disappeared. A further screen bulletin was broadcast about twelve hours after the first one, featuring a different church official, introduced as the Procurator of the Faithful. Which meant Glibbery was out, although there was no indication of whether he'd jumped or been pushed.

This turn of events concentrated my mind wonderfully. My fate, which was supposed to be held in Glibbery's hands, was now in free fall. I tried to remain objective. We were at a critical point, and things could go either way. If the dissidents could gain sufficient public support quickly enough, the resistance might bloom into a full insurrection, with a fair chance of succeeding, and perhaps toppling the government.

However, this didn't *quite* seem to be happening. The authorities were stretched, but they hadn't lost control, and were able to snuff out the small flames of disorder that sprang up before they spread into a wildfire. No matter how many activists emerged to replace the ones being detained, the movement wasn't achieving the critical mass that would overwhelm the forces containing it. For that to happen, large numbers of ordinary citizens would have to throw in their lot with the activists, all at the same time – and they weren't. The obstacle was communication. Sheba's message was compelling, and it was spreading, but not fast enough. When you first heard it, you got excited, and maybe you felt inspired to do something about it, but unless that feeling affected a large number of people simultaneously, the impetus to act could dissipate. The revolution needed a big, angry swelling mob, and what it got was a series of unconnected outbreaks, each of which was crushed, or spluttered out of its own accord. Word of mouth wasn't enough.

Meanwhile, no matter what I thought or felt about what was unfolding, and how it would play out, I had a powerful desire not to be on the losing side.

Then something decisive occurred, and it was all down to my old friend Kilroy.

K
I
L
R
O
Y

Cynthia broke the silence:

You know that woman?

Yes, Kilroy said, I know Curtis.

Did you know she was a security agent?

Sure. We didn't discuss it, but I knew. And she knew that I knew. I knew all along.

Really? OK, if you say so.

Kilroy glanced at her. What do you mean by that?

Cynthia shrugged. Nothing. Forget it. But what makes you think that picture they showed was faked? The one of the shoot-out she's meant to have caused.

Didn't you think it looked faked?

Yeah, I thought it was probably bogus. But can you be sure?

Kilroy shifted his hands on the wheel. What are you asking

me? How well do I know her? Can I be sure she's not capable of doing something like that, and murdering a bunch of bystanders?

Approximately, yes.

For what it's worth, I think she'd be quite capable of doing it. But if you're asking me whether I slept with her, just go ahead and ask.

Did you?

No. We were using each other, but not in that way. It was a kind of working friendship, if that makes sense. But I like her, I'll admit that.

Good for you.

Kilroy didn't reply and they drove on in silence.

After a while Cynthia drew her feet up beneath her and angled herself towards Kilroy. I'm sorry I slapped you, she said.

Kilroy smiled. I forgive you.

Have you changed your mind?

About what?

About not getting involved with the big picture.

Why would I change my mind about that?

Isn't it obvious? If that broadcast is anything to go by, it looks like an uprising is about to happen. It's probably started already, and my guess is that everything will move fast. Maybe it's time to take sides.

Why do you think I haven't taken sides?

You said you weren't concerned about getting Sheba's message out, and you just wanted to save her because you felt guilty.

Maybe I wasn't being honest when I said that.

And maybe I wasn't being honest when I slapped you.

It felt pretty honest.

Cynthia squeezed his arm. I'm sure you've had worse.

That's true.

So, are we going to do something?

You obviously think we should.

And you do too. I know you do. So, let's think it through. The next few days are going to be critical. It looks like Sheba has gone underground, with the help of your friend Curtis. Does it worry you that Curtis might be playing a double game?

Curtis? A double game? No shit. I'm not ruling it out, believe me. But I'm not going to worry about it. Because what are we going to do? Try to contact Sheba? Not advisable, even if we knew how to do it. There's a risk we'd get picked up, or lead them to her. If we're going to do something, we need to do it independently.

Agreed, Cynthia said, and if there's going to be an insurrection I can guarantee you the weak point will be communication. There's only one channel of mass communication around here, and the government controls it. But that monopoly could turn out to be their biggest weakness.

I can see where you're going with this, but –

Wait, bear with me. Those broadcasts on the screens reach everyone, right? I mean people are actually obliged to watch the damn things. It's compulsory. So, what if they suddenly start broadcasting Sheba's message, and calling on everyone to join the uprising? What if I told you I could override their system, and do that?

Kilroy shook his head.

What, Cynthia said, you don't believe I could do that?

Oh, I believe you. But let me tell you something. The problem with those screen broadcasts is that nobody pays them much attention, and even when they do pay attention they don't trust them.

Why not?

Kilroy laughed. Because it's the fucking government! Who trusts the government? Look, just because we have to do what we're told, that doesn't mean we've given up thinking. We're under tight control, and most people don't like it, but they're only going to risk an uprising if they think there's a chance it could work. If they see messages about it on the public screens, you know what they'll assume? It's a trap, or a ruse, or something like that. You're telling me you can break into those broadcasts, and I believe you, but most people will be suspicious.

OK, but how else can we get to them? It's the only way.

Nope. There is another way.

How?

The written word.

What do you mean?

I mean write it down, Kilroy said, and let people read it.

Are you serious? Apart from the logistics of that idea, why is reading something going to work any better than seeing it on the screens?

Because people trust writing.

Cynthia gazed at him in silence. Okaaay, she said finally, tell me more.

It's about value, Kilroy said. Remember what I told you about the books disappearing? It's given written words a scarcity value. People trust them. That's why the church always distributes printed versions of their edicts, as well as broadcasting them. There's something about holding that sheet of paper in your hand and reading it. It feels more real. More…true.

But what are you suggesting? Printing thousands and thousands of leaflets?

Yes, now you mention it.

How do we do that? And more to the point, how are we going to distribute them?

Maybe we can use those things up there, Kilroy said, jerking his chin upwards.

Cynthia looked out at the night sky. The drones?

You said there were a couple of hundred of them up there.

That's for the whole of Landmass. There are probably fifty within range.

But could you—

Yes! Wait, wait!

What?

I'm thinking. And actually… yes! They have grabs underneath them. We use them to pick stuff up all the time, and sometimes drop things off. They could easily carry bundles of leaflets. And be programmed to drop them in a progression so they don't all drop like a bunch of bricks. The weight would be critical. And I could probably get control of those fifty units, now I've got two pads, for a limited time. It would be a narrow window. I'd have to figure it out.

So it could work?

Cynthia's excitement subsided abruptly. Wait, she said, what about actually printing the things? Have you thought about that?

I have, as it happens. Let me tell you an interesting story.

Around eight years ago, Kilroy said, I was sent to provide extra muscle on a raid.

It was below my pay grade, but someone was sick, so I went along. It was a raid by the interior ministry. By that time, all the printing presses were meant to be under government control, and the days of independent publishers had long gone. But for a year or so after the requisitioning was enforced, the authorities were still occasionally unearthing small operations, hidden away in various nooks and crannies of the city. The place we'd been sent to that day was typical. It was a little storefront business, in an area a long way from the centre of town. Old, narrow streets, dirty buildings, cheap rents, and people minding their own business – except for whoever snitched on this printer. The interior ministry agent in charge of the raid was a mid-level time-server. Not too bright, not too dumb. Mediocrity personified. He'd done some research, and the guy we were busting was just an elderly man with an old electric machine in the shop. As far as anyone knew, he was printing low volumes of harmless stuff like children's books, just to make ends meet. But he'd ignored a few demands to report to the ministry and hand over the business, so it was time to shut him down. Nobody anticipated any trouble, and it was just me, the agent, and his subordinate, who was little more than a kid. All he wanted to do was pick his nose, and he was barely competent to find it on his face.

The little shop was at the end of a narrow, cobbled side street, and it would have been easy to miss even if the whole storefront hadn't been caked in grime. But the printer turned out to be a stubborn bastard. He said he was too old to give a fuck about what anyone thought of him, including the government, and he didn't see why he shouldn't be allowed to scrape a meagre living from the trade he'd pursued for more than fifty years. I could see his point, frankly. But he was full of piss and vinegar, and he wasn't coming quietly. I stood aside while the agent and his spotty sidekick handcuffed the old geezer, which didn't improve his disposition. He gave them enough trouble to keep them busy, and while they were getting him under control I noticed the most recent job that was lined up on the press, ready to roll. There was already a sample in the tray. It was a single-sheet leaflet, setting out the old man's grievances about the authorities in no uncertain terms, and pretty salty language. To be honest, he was lucky he was being arrested for nothing more than running an unauthorised business, because if he'd printed that leaflet and distributed it, even to a handful of neighbours, he would have been looking at charges of blasphemy and sedition.

I didn't say anything about the leaflet. While my colleagues were wrestling the old man into the back of the wagon, kicking and screaming all the way, I took the shop keys from a hook by the door, and locked up. I pulled down the shutters, and padlocked them. Then I got into the front of the wagon with the agent, who was driving, while the kid got in the back to keep our prisoner company. We'd only driven fifty metres when there was a terrific commotion from the back. We slammed on the brakes and ran around to look. The old printer was lying in the road, stone dead. The kid hadn't locked the back doors properly, and the moment we set off the prisoner leaped up and kicked them open, and flung himself out. Unfortunately, he'd broken his neck. We'd stopped the truck just before we reached the main road, and it looked like nobody had seen what happened. We got the old man's body back into the wagon, slammed the doors, and stood there staring at each other, breathing heavily. The kid was scared shitless. I knew the agent was the type who would do almost anything for a quiet life. They were both looking at me, and I could tell they were praying I wasn't going to make trouble. I let them stew for a while then I sucked my teeth and tipped my hat back.

All right boys, I said, this doesn't have to be as bad as it looks.

They both relaxed considerably.

I told them to get the handcuffs off the body right away, and find a rope or something else to make a ligature with, wind it around the old man's neck, and make it look he'd hanged himself, and say we'd found him that way in the shop. It wouldn't fool a state coroner who was diligent and sober, but I happened to know one who was neither of those things. He was also on the verge of retirement, and would consider a small gift of money to be in excellent taste. I kicked in a couple of banknotes, and told the agent and the kid to top it up to a decent sum. They didn't object, unsurprisingly. They were only too eager to get off the hook. I told them which coroner to contact when they got to the morgue, and suggested they then mislay all the paperwork. I figured it should be pretty easy to bury the whole case for ever, as it was hardly a top-priority crime. A cranky old guy was running a small-scale local business in a tiny shop, printing harmless kid's books, and he'd decided to hang himself rather than take any more shit from the authorities. Nobody would give it a second thought. As for the shop itself, I told them not to worry about it, and I would take care of it.

Which I did. I kept the keys, and a few weeks later I quietly transferred the ownership to myself under a different name. I also assigned the utility bills to the same name, and one night I went back into the shop, left a couple of lights on, and locked up again. I pay a negligible power bill every quarter, and nobody asks any questions. And it turned out the printer held the lease on the entire building. So, you're talking to the proud owner of a small printing business, and the landlord of six apartments over the shop.

Cynthia chuckled. You're full of surprises, aren't you, Kilroy?

I try to keep up with you.

You think you can work that printing press?

I guess we'll find out. How hard can it be?

That's the spirit, team. OK, let's say we can pull it off, and we can print a whole bunch of leaflets. But we also need a place where I can guide the drones down, to pick them up. It needs to be a wide, flat surface. Ideally, somewhere high up.

Well, the building I've – inherited, let's say – has a flat roof. And you can access it from the apartment on the top floor, which I happen to rent. From myself, in a different name, naturally.

Another different name?

Uh-huh. To muddy the trail.

And what do you do with this apartment?

Various things. It's my secret hideout.

Your *what?*

Kilroy smiled. My secret hideout.

Cynthia laughed, and leaned over and kissed his cheek. You've got it all figured out, haven't you?

Not entirely, Kilroy said. For one thing, I'm worried about this car.

Don't be. You said yourself it can pass for a government vehicle. That's because it is one. But the license plates aren't registered to any specific department, and anyone who checks on them won't get far. They'll just come up with a notification that the car has a top security clearance, and an instruction to back off. Do not investigate.

That's nice. How did your friends work that?

They have connections in high places. But maybe not for long. And here's an irony for you: Benedict and Gabrielle, and their friends, are determined to stop me intervening here. So, what have they done? They've intervened. Hilarious, no?

Ask me again when this is over.

I look forward to it.

They reached the suburbs at five in the morning.

There was no traffic on the roads as they wove their way into the city, and twenty minutes later they arrived at the narrow, cobbled backstreet that housed the printer's shop. Everything was silent and still.

Kilroy parked with the nearside wheels up on the sidewalk outside a nearby apartment block, easing over the steep kerb with a barely perceptible effect on the car's cushioned suspension, leaving just enough room for another vehicle to pass.

As they walked along the street to the little shop Kilroy glanced around, checking out the vicinity. He caught Cynthia's eye.

What do you think?

Feels weird, she murmured, like something waiting to happen.

They reached the shop and Kilroy took out a set of keys.

We have to get in through the front, he said. There's a door from the back of the shop into the rest of the building, but I've always kept it locked from the inside.

As Kilroy leaned down towards the padlock at the bottom of the storefront shutters, he paused. He straightened up, and stepped back.

The entire surface of the shutters was covered in fresh graffiti that almost obscured the faded layers of earlier efforts.

That's new, Kilroy said.

Cynthia read out one of the slogans: 'Uprising now!'

Shit, Kilroy said, look at this one: 'No more lies, the truth will set you free!'

They're going for broke, Cynthia said.

Kilroy held up his hand. Hold on. Listen to that.

There was gunfire in the distance. Two quick bursts. Then silence.

Kilroy got the shutters open quickly and raised them just enough to unlock the shop door. They both ducked inside. As he reached back and lowered the shutters behind them a wail of sirens erupted a few streets away.

Everything was exactly the way the old man had left it.

Kilroy and Cynthia examined the printing press that squatted in the middle of the shop. It appeared to be in working order, and the controls seemed straightforward. Everything was still set up to print the leaflet the old man had prepared, before his arrest halted the job.

Kilroy switched the machine on. It clicked and whirred for a few moments, then settled down, emitting a faint hum of anticipation.

Cynthia checked the supply of blank paper in the feed system. Kilroy set the controls to print a dozen test copies, and pulled the start lever.

Nothing happened for a second, then the machine sprang to life. It disgorged the leaflets all at once, then paused abruptly, ticking and hissing quietly, as if its appetite for work had been awakened, and it was eager to continue.

Kilroy picked up one of the leaflets and handed it to Cynthia.

Seems good to me, she said, turning it over in her hands.

OK, I'll reset the text for what we want to print. How many are we aiming to make?

It depends on the weight, Cynthia said. If we use the same paper as these leaflets here, single sheet, same size, each of the drones could carry a few thousand. Say five to be safe. If I can commandeer all the drones within range, I'll be able to operate around fifty. There'll be a few I can't reach, and we should assume some will be shot down, maybe before they can unload. With luck I'll be able to get forty drones under my control for a limited time. Call it two hundred thousand leaflets. Think that will be enough?

I don't know. If it's the right message, dropping all over a city that's on edge, maybe ready to erupt, I would say there's an even chance it's enough.

Cynthia grimaced. Let's hope for better odds than that.

She walked to the back of the room, where several long rolls of paper were stacked, and began to inspect the labels on them.

Shit, Kilroy said, I forgot about the paper. We need to cut it up.

Relax, there's a machine in the corner. It's already set up to cut these rolls for the size of those leaflets you ran off. I just need to find the right grade.

Kilroy watched her getting to work. OK, he said, I'll compose the text, right?

You do that.

I may need some help with it.

She smiled at him. I'm sure you'll do a good job, Kilroy. Get going.

Half an hour later Kilroy became aware of Cynthia standing beside him.

He was hunched over an upturned crate, using it as a work surface. It was strewn with sheets of paper covered with his handwriting, dense with amendments and deletions.

Can I have more time?

Nope, Cynthia said.

This isn't really my thing, you know.

Show me what you've got.

Hold on, Kilroy said, let me just explain what I'm trying to do here. I'm not used to this type of work.

Cynthia gave him an amused look. All right, tough guy. Tell me all about it.

OK, Kilroy said, here's what I thought. I liked what was written on the shutters out there. No more lies. The truth will set you free.

Interesting. That idea has been around for a long time. It's a quote: Then you will know the truth, and the truth will set you free.

Who said it?

Someone called John, allegedly. But I like it because there are two ways you can think about what it's saying. Like, hearing the truth is powerful, for sure, but you know what also sets you free?

Kilroy smiled. Telling the truth.

Right. Put it at the top. No more lies, the truth will set you free.

That's exactly what I was thinking. Big letters. Look.

Kilroy handed her his most recent draft.

Cynthia looked it over. It's good, she murmured. Strong and simple. I like the part about trusting each other, and doing what you know is right. And the list of all the ways they've been lying. It works.

Is there anything you want to change?

Let me read it again.

Kilroy looked down, trying to hide his nervousness while Cynthia scanned the sheet carefully. She nudged his shoulder.

He looked up quickly. What?

It's perfect. Run it.

It was late in the evening when they finished.

Kilroy unlocked the door at the back of the shop. It opened

onto a cramped passageway next to the stairs that led up to his secret apartment.

Sorry, he said, no elevator. We'll have to carry them up to the seventh floor.

Cynthia eyed the boxes into which they'd packed the printed leaflets.

I'm a strong girl, she said, and you're in reasonable shape, from what I remember. It should only take a few trips.

Before we do it, I need to go out to the front again. The shutters should be padlocked from the outside. I'll do that, then come back in through the street door.

He dangled his set of keys. Cynthia nodded.

Kilroy raised the shutters enough for him to duck under them, then rolled them down behind him. He looked around. A few street lamps were casting pools of light on the empty sidewalk, emphasising the blackness beyond them. The surrounding buildings loomed dark and featureless, except where the occasional glowing thread of yellow betrayed curtains that weren't tightly closed.

As Kilroy bent down to padlock the shutters, he glimpsed a group of hunched figures hurrying across the mouth of the lane, along the main road. The trams didn't appear to be operating, and there seemed to be no other traffic. He closed the padlock, let himself back into the building by the street door, and rejoined Cynthia in the stairwell.

It took them five trips to ferry the boxes full of leaflets up to the seventh floor. On their final journey, as they passed the fourth floor – yet again – the door to the apartment opened. A very old lady in a vivid purple dressing gown peeped out.

Who's that? she said.

Kilroy backed down the stairs to her level. It's me: Mr Oliver, from the top floor.

She craned forward and peered at him. Are you related to the landlord?

You mean Mr Gladstone? No, I'm not. Why do you ask?

You look like him. Although I haven't seen him for a long time. Years. He must be still alive, though, because he seems happy enough to take my rent. Not so happy to repair my window frames though.

She gave a wheezing chuckle.

I see him occasionally, Kilroy said. Would you like me to mention it?

The old lady frowned. Well, perhaps it's best not to bother him. He might put my rent up. It's very reasonable at present. No, I'll manage. Best to leave things as they are.

Kilroy nodded. All right, then I'll say goodn–

What are you doing?

Kilroy looked around. What, now?

Yes. What's in the boxes?

Food, Kilroy said. He nodded up towards Cynthia. My... sister is coming to stay, and we needed to get some food in.

Are you expecting a siege? You've been tramping up and down the stairs all night.

Kilroy gave her his most charming smile. Perhaps, he said, we can invite you up to share a meal with us one evening this week, Miss...?

Mrs Rollington. And I wouldn't blame you if you *were* preparing for a siege. I haven't been outside for two days. It's not safe. What's happening out there? Are they killing them yet?

Killing who, Mrs Rollington?

Who do you think? The government.

I don't think it's that bad, to be honest, Mrs Rollington.

It will be soon, mark my words. I talk to my friends. I know what's going on. People have had enough, and they're fighting back. Good luck to them. And I don't care if you tell anyone I said that. I hope they string those bastards up from the lampposts.

She smiled sweetly and closed the door.

Cynthia looked around the apartment. I like what you've done with the place, she said, which appears to be nothing at all.

Kilroy laughed. I'm a big fan of minimalism.

You'd better show me the roof.

Kilroy led her up four steps in the corner of the living room, and out through a glass door onto the roof.

She nodded approvingly. This will be fine.

Kilroy walked to the edge of the roof and looked out over the city. Cynthia stood beside him. The streets were deserted. Nearly every government or municipal building had a searchlight mounted on the roof, and occasionally a passing official vehicle – a car or truck – was pinned in the momentary sweep of a beam before slipping beyond its range, and back into the darkness.

Every so often a reddish light bloomed in the distance and they heard an explosion, and sometimes gunfire. These outbursts were sporadic and uncoordinated. It was if the city was feverish, tossing and turning under a hot, heavy blanket it couldn't throw off.

Let's get inside, Kilroy said.

There was nothing to eat, but plenty to drink. Kilroy poured them both a large whisky, and they sat on the couch.

Cynthia nestled against him.

How long, Kilroy said, is it going to take the drones to pick up those leaflets once we get them onto the roof? Like, all laid out and ready?

Not too long. A matter of minutes. I just have to prepare the drones.

Can you do any of it now?

Not even if I wanted to, Cynthia said, pressing herself closer. I'm too tired. But we need to decide what we're going to do after we drop the leaflets. Whatever happens, whether it works or not, we'll need to get the hell out.

What if I want to stay?

Then you're fucked, sweetheart. Revolution or no revolution, this city is going to be a dangerous place for a cop who works for the regime.

Used to work for the regime.

Good luck with convincing an angry mob where your heart lies, when they're stringing you up from the nearest street lamp, as your adorable elderly neighbour put it.

I can try to get to Sheba.

How? Do you have a plan to reach her?

Kilroy gazed down at his drink, swirling the liquor around in the glass. Finally, he looked up at her. OK, he said, you're right.

And, she continued, if the whole uprising fails, you'll need even more luck to stay out of prison, at the very least, when your former employers catch up with you. Which they will, if they're still around. They'll want to find you, and they'll want to punish you.

I know all that, Kilroy said. But where can I go?

Come with me. We can hide out and wait to see what happens. I can't stay here either, and wherever I go, I want to be with you.

Thanks, but hide out where?

I know a place. Trust me.

Cynthia drained her glass and set it on the floor. She pressed herself against him, stroking his hair. She turned his head gently towards her and kissed him.

Kilroy came up for air. Just one thing, he said. Can we bury my father?

Cynthia pulled away and studied his face. It's in the wrong direction, she said.

You made a promise. I'm holding you to it.

All right. We'll go and bury your dad. But now let's go to bed.

Kilroy stood up and offered her his hand. She grabbed it, and pulled herself up and into his arms. They shuffled into the bedroom, locked in an embrace, undoing their clothes as they went.

Kilroy and Cynthia stood on the roof and watched the dawn.

They were surrounded by fifty neat stacks of leaflets, laid out in a grid formation on the flat surface. Each stack was held together by a narrow strip of paper. A breeze began to stir the exposed edges of the topmost sheets.

Cynthia reached into her pocket and took out the slim, book-shaped device she'd been using when Kilroy first met her, and from her other pocket she extracted the pad she'd taken from Gabrielle.

All I need to do, she said, is take a picture of one of these stacks, and I can program the drones to grab one stack each, and release the leaflets in staggered batches. What height do we need to go for? Fifty metres?

Maybe higher, Kilroy said. High enough to spread the leaflets over a wide area, but low enough to minimise the risk of them all getting blown in one direction or another by the wind. I'd say a hundred metres.

Fine, I'll extend that by ten metres each way and program a variable vector to skitter within that bandwidth unpredictably. Make it harder for them to be shot down.

That makes sense, Kilroy said, although I don't understand any of it. Does that also make sense?

Sure. What you're saying is that you have perfect confidence in me. OK, here goes for the master shot.

Cynthia stood over the nearest pile of leaflets, with her feet on either side of it. She raised one of the devices, and Kilroy heard a series of clicks. Cynthia looked at the screen and smiled. Here, she said, showing it to Kilroy.

It took him a moment to grasp what he was seeing. It was a three-dimensional image of the brick-like stack, allowing him to view every surface, from every angle, as Cynthia tilted the screen this way and that.

Amazing, he said. Now what?

Now I do some serious coding. I need to link these tablets so I can take control of all the drones at once. And I have to build a defence code, to stop anyone overriding me when they realise what I'm doing, although they'll crack it pretty quickly. I'm guessing I can keep them out for around thirty minutes. An hour, maximum. OK, I need to get started. It'll take a few minutes.

Don't let me stop you.

Cynthia squatted down and began working with the tablets.

Five minutes later the shooting began.

It seemed to break out all over the city at once. After a few moments there was a series of explosions. Plumes of smoke rose up in straight, narrow columns through the crisp, early-morning air. There was a heavy concentration in the southeastern district.

That's not good, Kilroy said.

Cynthia looked up. Why? What's happening?

Government munitions, Kilroy said. Last night I was hearing all different types of weapons, but those explosions are from heavy mortars used by the military, unless someone's managed to steal them. I can't hear much other – whoa, hold the phone!

Kilroy ducked instinctively as a huge flash was followed by a booming pressure on the eardrums. A column of debris erupted only a few blocks away.

Correction, Kilroy said, that was definitely freelance. Improvised, but pretty sophisticated. And hear that shooting? That's non-military firepower out there now.

Kilroy dropped to a crouch and scuttled to the parapet at the edge of the roof. He raised his head warily and listened for a moment, then ran back, keeping low.

Plenty of resistance, he said, but it's random. My guess is the authorities have launched an offensive, and they'll try to end it all with a sweep of the whole city in the next few hours. Neutralise the whole thing.

Cynthia stood up. It's now or never, then.

Stay down! Have you finished what you need to do?

No, but I'm close enough. We need to go for it. Say goodbye, Kilroy, your babies are leaving home.

Kilroy glanced down at the leaflets and read the bottom line he'd written:

NOW IS THE TIME. AS SOON AS YOU READ THIS, FIND EACH OTHER. JOIN TOGETHER. WE ARE STRONGER THAN THEM. RISE UP NOW AND WIN!

He became aware of a heaviness in the air above him and heard a muted throbbing sound. He looked up to see the sky filled with a flock of sleek black drones. They converged, and plummeted down so swiftly he flinched, fearing they'd crash onto the roof. At the last moment they stopped. Each drone hovered above a stack of leaflets, then settled on it tenderly. Slender articulated arms sprang out from the underside of the drone and gathered the stack to its belly with a delicacy that struck Kilroy as maternal.

The drones were motionless for an instant, then they all rose up at once with stunning speed, and peeled off in every direction. In a matter of seconds, they'd all vanished, except for a handful that were still visible as dark specks, poised above nearby districts.

Cynthia stood up. Ready?

Kilroy got to his feet. He gazed around, taking in the view of the city.

Do it, he said.

Cynthia tapped at one of the devices. Done, she said.

Kilroy saw a drone less than half a kilometre away begin to disgorge its leaflets in a stepped cascade, like a fluttering staircase falling through the sky. The drone moved away, trailing the arc of falling leaflets behind it, and suddenly increased its altitude, then just as abruptly dropped to a height lower than before, continuing to jinx up and down as it moved away.

They got one, Cynthia called from behind him.

Kilroy turned in time to see a distant puff of smoke and shrapnel dispersing on the other side of town.

Cynthia checked some data on her device.

Who got it, Kilroy said, your guys or mine?

Yours. My defence is holding, so far. Let's go.

They ran to the fire escape at the edge of the roof without looking back.

Kilroy drove like hell. Caution was no longer appropriate.

The apartment they were leaving behind was in a district at the edge of town, and although they needed to swing around to head due east, they could do it without driving any closer to the centre of the city. Kilroy knew the backstreets, and he sped through them, calculating and adjusting the route as he went.

They saw leaflets on the ground, but they also saw them being passed around among groups of people clustered on street corners and outside the cafés that opened early. More people were emerging onto the streets all the time.

Kilroy began to wonder where the cops and the military were. He reached a junction with a main road. He decided to risk using the wide thoroughfare for a few blocks before taking to the side streets again, but as soon as he made the turn he saw a big armoured truck coming to a halt up ahead. A special forces unit swarmed out of the back of the vehicle, guns at the ready, while a squad of ordinary cops pulled roadblock barriers from the back of a second truck.

Oh shit, Kilroy said, keep the pistols handy.

Cynthia squeezed his arm. Breathe in, she murmured.

The special forces agents saw the car approaching and moved forward. As it got closer they paused, then took a respectful step back, signalling to the cops with the barriers to wait.

Kilroy slowed down, lifted his hand in a casual salute, and pulled away fast.

Cynthia exhaled.

A few more blocks took them to the edge of the city. Just when Kilroy thought they were out of danger he made a turn and was confronted by a group of at least fifty people striding towards them, spread across the road, heading for the city centre.

Kilroy reached out an arm to restrain Cynthia as he slammed the brakes on. The car screeched to a halt, and without pausing Kilroy threw it into reverse, swinging it back around the corner and clipping the kerb. From the corner of his eye he saw the crowd break into a run as he accelerated away, and in the rear-view mirror he watched them stop and cluster at the intersection, realising pursuit was futile. A few rocks were flung at the departing car, all of which landed in the road well behind it.

A few minutes later they crossed the city limits, heading east along back roads. After half an hour they were travelling through what Kilroy thought of as real countryside.

They approached a roadside screen that was blank.

Kilroy nodded towards it as they passed. No news is good news, right?

That's the fourth one, Cynthia said, by my reckoning.

Really? I didn't notice the ones in the city. Were they dead too?

The ones I saw were either blank or jammed up with static.

I wonder what that means.

I can find out, Cynthia said. First, let's see how many of our birds got the job done, and are still on the team.

She tapped at one of her devices and peered at the screen.

That's good, she said, they only shot down four. Mission accomplished by all the rest. We seriously snowed on that town, Kilroy. And I can access the birds that are still aloft. Here goes.

She made another adjustment and Kilroy heard the sound of crowds and gunfire. He glanced over at the screen and saw an overhead view of an open space he didn't recognise. It was full of people, surging like a wave against barriers with trucks and military behind them.

Good god, Cynthia said, it's all kicking off.

Where is that?

A park in the south of the city, according to this. Want to stop and watch?

I don't think so, Kilroy said, checking the rear-view mirror. The road behind them was clear and he wanted to keep it that way.

I'll record this, Cynthia said, and we can watch later. Wait. Oh shit.

What is it?

Lost control. Let me try another…nope, that's gone too.

She tapped at the screen for a moment, then shook her head.

All gone, she said. They're overriding me. Well, I did pretty good, even though I say so myself. It's taken them nearly an hour to piss on my bonfire. I'd better shut these down, before they get a fix on us.

She deactivated both the devices.

Hey, Kilroy said, look at that up ahead. Signs of life.

They were approaching another roadside screen, on which a disjointed image was flickering sporadically, as if the picture were struggling to assemble itself.

When they were three hundred metres away the flickering stopped, the screen went dark, and lines of white-on-black text appeared.

Kilroy slowed down so they could read them as they passed:

Emergency. Martial law is in force. Remain calm. Follow orders from the legitimate authorities without question, or risk severest penalties. Go to your homes. Stay there until further notice. An announcement will be made shortly.

They drove on. Kilroy glanced at the dashboard and tapped a dial.

Just what I was thinking, Cynthia said. We need juice?

Yeah, we'll have to charge up soon.

You think the power will be working OK?

I don't see why not. I guess if you wanted to cause disruption you might try to knock out a local supply. But that would jam everyone up, including whoever did it. I don't see anyone trying to cripple the whole grid. I'm not even sure it could be done.

It's phenomenal, Cynthia said. That's one area where you people have succeeded spectacularly. Such a robust system.

It was all upgraded, Kilroy said, around thirty years ago.

But the infrastructure has been there for what, a hundred years?

Search me. It's all just been there, way under the ground, for as long as anyone can remember, and it's always worked. Nobody even thinks about it.

It's what we hoped for, Cynthia said. Interdependent systems, solar, wind and hydro, oscillating between sources. Nice work, Landmass.

She fell silent for a moment, then she spoke quietly, almost to herself:

We ruined everything. And now maybe we're doing it again. I don't know.

Kilroy glanced at her and saw she looked tired. He rested a hand on her leg. Don't beat yourself up, he said. It's a waste of time.

She patted his hand. If you say so, Doc.

We'll stop at the next juice point. One recharge will take us to my father's place, and around two hundred K beyond that. Will that be enough? Because I hate to nag, but you still haven't told me where we're headed, and I'd dearly like to know.

We're going south.

To the south coast? Why the hell would we go there?

Because I know a place where we'll be safe. The only place, in fact.

Kilroy waited. Is that all you're going to tell me?

That's it, for now. Hey, is that a charging point, up ahead?

It is. Keep your eyes open while I juice up, and keep hold of that gun.

Kilroy swung the car into the driveway of his father's place.

Want to get the car under cover? Cynthia said. She pointed to the woodland lining the driveway, where Kilroy had left the motorbike on his previous visit.

Kilroy nudged the car into the treeline as far as it would go.

That's about as much cover as we can get, he said, and if you don't want to do this, and you don't think we should be here, just tell me.

No, let's do what we came for. Sorry, it's just that I'm worried. We're vulnerable now I've lost the drones again. People are going to be trying to find us. And I don't like not knowing what's happening in the city.

But the fact the screens aren't working is a good sign, I'd say.

Maybe. But I keep thinking about Shadbold. The longer I don't see any sign of him, the more nervous I get. He's not the type to walk away.

Kilroy opened his door but didn't get out. He took a deep breath.

Hey, Cynthia said, I'm sorry. I know this must be difficult for you.

It's OK. I'm just wondering what I'm going to find. Or not find. Whoever moved the body the first time may have come back and done it again. What the hell was that about anyway? People will never cease to amaze me.

The corpse was still in the hole. It was partly covered by the tarpaulin, which was bunched and tangled up, probably as a result of Benedict struggling to free himself from it when he woke up after the tranquiliser shot. Sylvester's body appeared undisturbed.

Cynthia took a step back from the edge of the hole. Don't take this the wrong way, she said, but that body is definitely decomposing.

Kilroy laughed. It happens to the best of us. You can stay up here if you like.

No, it's going to be quicker if we both do it.

OK. If you go and fetch a couple of shovels from the shed around the back of the house, I'll get down there and wrap him in the tarp. Then you can help me get him up. I'd like to bury him over by those trees where the bench is. He built that. We'll put him just on the far side of it, in the shade.

Cynthia nodded. Sounds like a plan.

Kilroy patted down the mound of earth gently with the back of his shovel. He stepped back and gazed around.

Want some time on your own? Cynthia said.

No, that's all right. Let's get going. And thanks for helping me do this.

You're welcome.

Kilroy looked up abruptly. I'll be damned. Come here, Creek!

He held out his arm and the parrot flew down from a branch above him. It landed on his wrist and fluffed its feathers, then hopped up his arm until it reached his shoulder, where it bobbed forward and bowed, so Kilroy could rest his cheek against the top of its head. It made a soft, contented clucking sound, and pushed its head forward. Kilroy stroked the bird's body gently.

He's looking good, Cynthia said. Better than when we last saw him.

There's grain around, and he's pretty resourceful. Hey Creek, say hello to Cynthia.

Kilroy straightened his arm and the bird hopped back down to his wrist, where it allowed Cynthia to stroke its head.

He approves of you, Kilroy said.

I wonder if he's been here all the time.

I think so. I think he's been guarding the body. He doesn't need to stay here now, though, so I guess he'll be happy to come with us. You all right with that?

Cynthia hesitated.

What? Kilroy said.

Nothing. It's fine.

Kilroy lifted his wrist and brought Creek up to his face. OK with you, buddy?

The bird clacked its beak. Then, with uncanny clarity, it spoke:

Damn sweet, it said.

Kilroy drove for an hour until they reached the main highway going south. They crossed over it, then Cynthia took the wheel so Kilroy could navigate, using a map to guide them along minor roads. Even though there was barely any traffic on the main roads Kilroy wanted to avoid them. Occasionally he glanced back to check on Creek, who was under a blanket in the space behind the front passenger seat, apparently content to sleep through the journey, sometimes clacking and muttering softly in his parrot dreams.

For the next hour the public screens they passed were still displaying the same message as before, about martial law being in force, then it disappeared, and there was nothing to see except an occasional burst of static.

Cynthia was amused by Kilroy using the map. She told him there were orbiting drones, way above them, that could navigate any route she wanted, but she would need to switch on her device to access them, and that would almost certainly betray their location.

Kilroy didn't entirely believe her. It was better to rely on a map, he told her, than some machine in the sky that could maybe mislead you.

They were still arguing the point good-naturedly when Kilroy saw Cynthia frown at the rear-view mirror.

Kilroy craned around. Far behind them a pair of figures had appeared in the road. Kilroy waited for them to diminish the distance, but they didn't. If anything, they got closer. appeared to be running after the car.

That's not possible, Kilroy said.

Cynthia checked the mirror again. Uh-oh, she said, this could be bad.

Where did they come from, anyway?

Kilroy scanned the surroundings. They were driving on a narrow country road, beginning to ascend an incline. On either side of them densely planted crops, over three metres high, were growing to within a metre of the verge.

Give her some juice, he said.

Cynthia accelerated, but when Kilroy looked back at the road behind them he was astonished to see the running figures were catching up with them.

The car swerved. Shit! Cynthia said.

Kilroy whirled around.

They'd nearly hit a person who'd suddenly appeared at the side of the road. As they pulled away the figure began to run.

Oh no, Cynthia said.

More figures were appearing on either side of them, emerging from the rows of tall crops.

Kilroy looked over his shoulder. A dozen runners were pounding along relentlessly behind the car, gaining on them all the time.

Now more people were spilling out from the rows of crops, and running alongside the car. Cynthia was driving as fast as she could, but the runners kept up with them.

Then Kilroy saw their faces.

¹ᵛ hell, he whispered.

⁻ᵉm looked like him. Not exactly like him, but : Kilroy feel terrified and sick. He glanced at was pale and her face was slick with sweat.

.n, Kilroy said. Swerve into them! Hard!

.hia gripped the wheel but didn't turn it.

The figures on either side of the car had now assumed a formation, like an escort of military recruits on a training run. Through the closed windows, and above the noise of the engine, their voices could be heard:

Hup, hup, hup, they chanted as they ran, eyes front, arms pumping, steady and disciplined. There were now at least thirty of them. They were showing no signs of stress or fatigue, and even though the car was travelling at well over a hundred kilometres per hour, they remained alongside it effortlessly.

Kilroy grabbed the wheel and pulled it sharply towards him.

Dammit! Cynthia yelled.

The car smashed into three or four of the runners on Kilroy's side, then he released the wheel in time for Cynthia to keep the car on the road.

The runners beside Kilroy who'd been hit by the car were lurching and stumbling, but they regained their balance quickly. One of them had a badly damaged arm, and another's head lolled grotesquely from a broken neck, but they all kept running and they didn't slow down.

There was a thud as the car absorbed an impact from the rear.

Kilroy turned to see that the runners behind them were now a solid wall of bodies, pressing against the back of the car.

Hit the brakes, he said to Cynthia.

I am! It's no good! They're pushing us!

Oh fuck, Kilroy said, as he saw what lay ahead. The crops were receding, and the incline they'd been ascending was levelling out. In front of them the road ran along the side of a hill, and on Cynthia's side the terrain began to drop away into a valley.

The runners surrounding them changed formation. The phalanx alongside Cynthia put on a burst of speed, outpaced the car, and swept around in a tight, curved wave to fall into place next to the line of runners on Kilroy's side.

He saw what they were going to do.

Cynthia pumped the brake pedal but even with the wheels locked the car continued to be propelled forward by the mass of bodies behind it.

Now the runners next to Kilroy began to lean in against the car. He reached over and tried to help Cynthia keep the wheel steady, but the car was being edged over to the side of the road where the drop was becoming more precipitous every moment.

Kilroy took out his gun and began to open the window on his side. He knew it was hopeless. There were now dozens of densely packed runners, three ranks deep, pressing against the entire length of the car, in addition to around twenty behind it. But he was damned if he was going down without a fight. He got the window open and levelled his gun, but before he could fire, one of the runners closest to the car exploded. Then three more of them came apart, disintegrating into clouds of flesh and pink mist.

The car began to skid. Cynthia still had her foot down on the brake, but the pressure from behind the car had decreased. She released the brake and hit the accelerator. Kilroy turned around to see the runners behind them falling away, four of them exploding as he watched. He turned to Cynthia.

What's happening? he said.

The car was back under her control, and she was glancing between the road ahead and the sky.

Up there, she said.

Kilroy saw two drones hovering about fifty metres above the road. They were firing weapons of some kind, picking off clusters of runners in rapid bursts.

Twenty seconds later the car was clear, pulling away from a long stretch of road strewn with bodies, and parts of bodies, and pools of gore.

The drones had disappeared.

Kilroy craned forward to try and see them.

He turned to Cynthia. Have they gone?

No. We're going to have to stop.

A moment later one of the drones dropped down directly in front of the car and hung in the air, keeping pace with it. Kilroy didn't need to check to know the other drone was behind them.

He saw something glowing in the pocket of Cynthia's coat, and heard a muffled command:

Stop the car, Cynthia.

Cynthia's knuckles whitened on the steering wheel.

Hey, Kilroy said, how did they switch that thing on?

Cynthia, the voice said, stop the car please. Don't make us do it.

Slowly the car rolled to a halt. Cynthia leaned forward and rested her head on the steering wheel.

They got us, she said.

Kilroy and Cynthia sat on a rock at the side of the road. Cynthia held the screen so they could both see Gabrielle's face on it. There were shadows beneath her eyes, and Kilroy thought she looked exhausted.

Let's just agree, Gabrielle was saying, that we need to compromise. We don't have many options and we're running out of time. The situation is getting dangerous.

No shit, Cynthia said.

Gabrielle rolled her eyes. Whatever, Cynthia! And by the way, any time you want to thank us for just saving your skins back there, feel free.

You wouldn't have needed to, Cynthia said, if you'd done what you should have done about Shadbold a long time ago.

Kilroy heard a voice from somewhere behind Gabrielle on the screen, muttering something in which the only word he heard distinctly was bitch.

Gabrielle glanced over her shoulder. Shut up Ben, she said, and just do your job.

Hello there darling, Cynthia said sweetly, are you fucking things up, as usual?

Gabrielle sighed in exasperation. Please, Cynthia, give it a rest. Let's just admit that we all made mistakes, OK?

Kilroy saw that Cynthia was clenching her jaw. He leaned

over and waved at the screen. Hi Gabrielle, I'm happy to admit I've made mistakes, if that helps. And so has Cynthia, but she's pissed off at you.

Thank you, Kilroy, Gabrielle said wearily, now let's just get everything straight, OK? Cynthia, you listening?

You know I am.

So, here's the thing. None of us can stay here.

Whoa, Cynthia said, if you think I'm going back now—

Nobody said anything about going back! Just listen, OK? We should make for Landmass Two, and regroup there. We'll put everything to the council, and agree to arbitration, and try to salvage the best outcome from all this.

Which council, Cynthia said, the one you're trying to subvert?

We're not trying to subvert anything. Stop being so paranoid! Just stop, Cynthia!

Stop the car, Cynthia, another voice said.

For a moment Kilroy thought the voice was coming from the screen, then he caught a flash of colour beside him, and saw that Creek was out of the car, strutting up and down beside it, looking pleased with himself.

Stop the car, Cynthia, the parrot repeated, perfectly mimicking not only Gabrielle's voice, but also the slight electronic distortion produced by the speaker in Cynthia's device, and even the muffled quality of the sound, the way Creek must have first heard it, when the device was still in Cynthia's pocket.

What the hell is that? Gabrielle said.

It's a parrot, Kilroy said.

What? A parrot?

Cynthia laughed. Long story, she said.

Gabrielle stared out from the screen expressionlessly. Then

the ghost of a smile appeared on her face. Of course it is, she said. Of course it's a parrot, and of course it's a long story. And you know what? It's not even the craziest thing that's happened in the last few days. Not by a long way.

You got that right, Cynthia said with a chuckle.

Kilroy realised both women wanted to use the moment as a chance to relax their mutual hostility. They were recognising a truce.

We can work this out, Gabrielle said, but we can't do it here. You've just seen what can happen. And believe me, Cynthia, we're in as much danger as you are.

Where are you?

We're on the move. But we— oh shit!

What is it?

Gabrielle's face tilted on the screen and Benedict said something urgently in the background. The screen went grey for a second, then Gabrielle's face reappeared, close up and slightly blurred.

We have to go! she said. We'll see you on Landmass Two!

What's happening?

Get out, Cynthia! Go now!

The screen went dead.

Cynthia drove as fast as she could, skidding on some of the tight turns that took them down into a valley on the far side of the hill.

The terrain levelled out and the road ran straighter as they descended onto the southern plain. After fifty kilometres the vegetation became denser, and soon they were travelling through thick forest. There was no habitation here, and the roads were increasingly rough. The last public screen they'd passed was two hours behind them.

You can put the map away, Cynthia told Kilroy, I know the route now.

The route to where, exactly?

A place on the coast. I know where it is, but I don't know the name. It may not even have a name. It's just a little cove, very remote.

And that's where the boat is?

Cynthia didn't answer. She frowned up at the sunlight that pierced the forest canopy, as if making a calculation.

Kilroy prompted her. The boat, right? That's where it is?

I didn't actually say it was a boat. I said it was like a boat.

Kilroy watched the trees going past, dappled with sunlight.

And I didn't actually say I was coming with you.

Are you serious?

I still have a job to do. It may have changed, but I belong here. I don't want to run away now. There's probably a revolution happening, and I need to be here.

And I need you to come with me!

Cynthia kept her eyes on the road, but Kilroy saw they were glistening.

Look, he said, I like you a lot, but these things don't always work out the way we want. I wish we could be together, believe me.

It's not about that, you idiot!

Cynthia turned to glare at him, and Kilroy had to grab the wheel to keep the car on the road. Cynthia pushed his hand away and steadied the car, dropping the speed a little as she wiped her eyes with the cuff of her coat.

Don't flatter yourself, Kilroy, she said. You think I'm in love with you?

Oh. OK, now I feel like a fool.

Well, don't. But I'm talking about something bigger. I want

you with me because I need an ally. I'll admit I prefer an ally who's a good fuck, but that's not the point.

Kilroy laughed. Thanks for the compliment, but what happens when I reach my span, around forty years from now? You'll need to find someone else to fuck for a couple of hundred years.

We could fix that. There's no reason why you shouldn't undergo the procedure and live as long as me. In fact, it could be even easier for you. Just a matter of switching off a couple of genetic inhibitors.

So I could...not die? I mean, not like everyone else. Everyone else here.

Why, does that make a difference to your decision?

I don't know. I really don't know. I'm going to have to think about it.

Kilroy was still thinking half an hour later when he caught a glimpse of the sea.

Nearly there, Cynthia said.

She turned the car onto a narrow track. Foliage on both sides brushed the bodywork, and gradually closed in on them until they could go no further. The track continued as a barely discernible footpath.

Cynthia waited until Kilroy got Creek out of the car, then began walking along the path, forcing her way through undergrowth in some places. The parrot sat on Kilroy's shoulder, shifting nervously from one foot to the other.

Cynthia glanced back at him. You look like a pirate, she said.

The path opened out abruptly and the sea filled the horizon.

They were standing at the top of a gentle incline that led down to a beach. The coastline around them was uneven and jagged, with sandy patches between promontories of rock. In places the sea was calm, but it crashed against the rocks where they formed blunter cliffs, surging into narrow inlets, and cascading out of them in foaming waves.

This way, Cynthia said.

She led Kilroy down the slope and headed right, clambering over a series of rocky outcrops. The shoreline began to curve, and Kilroy saw they were approaching a small, sandy cove where a pristine beach met a placid, shallow waterline.

Cynthia continued along the sand for a hundred metres, then stopped and pointed to the low cliffs at the top of the beach.

Look. That opening in the rocks? This is the only vantage point you can see it from, because of the way the cliffs overlap. That's where we're going. See it?

Kilroy scanned the cliff face. No, he said, what am I looking for?

Pretty much in the middle of the rocks, right at the top of the beach there. A kind of slit, not quite vertical, sloping down from right to left. See?

OK, got it. I wasn't looking for something that narrow. I mean, there's no way you'd get a boat in there, even a small one. So I was looking for something bigger, because of, you know, the boat.

I know, but I'm not going to explain it, because it's going to be easier to just take you there and show you. OK?

The entrance was just wide enough for a person to get through, at a slight angle. Cynthia went in first.

As Kilroy began to edge himself in behind her Creek squawked loudly in his ear and fluttered his wings.

Kilroy paused. I get it, buddy. Wait out here if you like.

The bird took off, and found a nearby rock to perch on,

from where it could keep a beady eye on the cave entrance.

See you soon, Kilroy said, and squeezed himself through the opening.

He found himself in a space the size of a prison cell that could conceivably be comfortable for one inmate, if you were the type to get comfortable in a prison cell, but a little crowded for two. Cynthia used the screen of her device as a flashlight, swinging it around to illuminate rough, damp walls. The roof was a looming overhang of dripping rock with a metre of headroom for a tall man.

Cynthia trained the light on the back wall, and it disappeared. The light was simply swallowed by an area of darkness. It was the size and shape of a large doorway.

There it is, she said. Watch this.

She killed the light from her device, and Kilroy could see nothing at all. It was pitch black. He looked behind him and saw a faint glow from the cave entrance, but the light that seeped inside didn't get far. He turned back, and saw it. Or rather he didn't see it. The doorway-sized aperture was even darker than the darkness around it. It seemed to devour not only all the available light, but the surrounding darkness as well. It was blacker than black, and emanated a kind of energy because of the absence it created: an actively negative space. Kilroy shuffled towards it, trying to see inside.

Cynthia grabbed his arm. Not too close, she said. Not yet.

What the hell is it? Some kind of tunnel?

You could say that.

And you expect me to go in there with you?

I don't expect you to do anything. I'm asking you.

What will happen if I go in there?

Come outside. Let's talk.

They sat on the sand in the sunshine.

I can imagine how you must feel, Cynthia said. All hell is breaking loose here, and if I were you, I'd want to stay. I know you think I haven't been listening when you keep telling me you have a job to do, but I hear you, Kilroy. And it's the same for me. I have a job to do, too.

Then maybe, Kilroy said, we need to go our separate ways, and do our different jobs.

Cynthia linked her arm through his. If you stay here, she said, you'll be one fighter among many. But I'm going back to face a battle I can't win without your help. Even with plenty of other people on my side, and maybe Gabrielle and Benedict seeing sense now they've understood what can happen if we don't intervene here, I'm still up against powerful opposition. If you come with me it gives me a much better chance, because your voice is worth a hundred of theirs. You can do more good that way, believe me.

Kilroy picked up a handful of sand and let it sift through his fingers.

If I go with you, he said, would I…come back?

Yes. And that's another thing. We're all going to be coming back some time. We can't stay where we are forever. Even if we could, there will be huge pressure to return here, because pretty soon it's going to be a different place. Look at this shoreline. Ten years ago, that water was above the level of the cave we've just been in. It's receding fast. This place is stabilising, if you can call it that. We're going to come back. We won't be able to resist the urge to repopulate, and that's going to cause a whole new set of big problems. From our point of view, we'll simply be coming home, but for you we'll be colonists. And we *will* be, except we'll be re-colonising the place we lived in to begin with. But we need to be building bridges before that, and I want to start now. With you.

I don't think I'd make a good diplomat. I'm a cop.

I don't need a diplomat. I need a good, honest man who wants to do the right thing.

That's me, your average, simple bozo.

You have no idea, Kilroy! Do you know how many good, honest men I've found in my life? The answer is between zero and one, and the one is you.

Thanks. But this is my home, Cynthia. This is where I live.

Cynthia rubbed her temples, then lay back on the sand and gazed at the sky.

What do you want me to say, Kilroy? That I love you? I don't even know what that means, and I say that as someone who's had several hundred years to find out. All I know is that I want you to stay with me.

Kilroy was silent.

Give me a clue, Cynthia said.

I wish I could, Kilroy said. And I wish I could say yes without needing to think about it, but I can't. Maybe it would help if I knew what was happening back in the city, and whether there's a fight I could still be part of.

Cynthia sat up. I'll be straight with you, she said. If you stay here, for this fight, there's a strong chance you won't survive. That's going to be true no matter which side wins here, because you're in a different fight, that you didn't choose, and you can't win. You're up against Shadbold, and you have no conception of the kind of enemy he can be.

I still don't know why Shadbold is such a threat to me. I mean me personally, compared to anyone else. Why?

Because he's inside you, like I told you. But maybe what I should have made clear is that you're inside him too.

Kilroy gazed out at the sea. Does that mean we're the same?

Yes and no, Cynthia said.

Thanks, that's a big help.

OK, think about your dad. Are you exactly like him?

I hope not.

There you go. As it happens you *are* kind of like him in some ways, although I know you don't want to hear that.

Damn right.

But you're totally unique, that's the point. There's some of your father in you, but you're unlike him in many ways. And you're probably like your mother in some ways, but not in others, and the same with your ancestors, and so on.

And with Shadbold?

Right. Which brings me to a tricky question I need to ask, since we're talking about families. Just tell me this: do you have children?

No, I...I don't think so. Pretty sure, in fact.

Are you sterile?

That's a hell of a personal question.

I know. But I'm asking for a good reason. Are you?

Kilroy nodded. Almost certainly. I've been with plenty of women who could have conceived, if it was going to happen, and they've conceived with other men, but not with me.

Yes, I was pretty sure you'd say that.

Why is it important?

Because Shadbold found out. He must have done. He didn't know about it when he contrived to send you hunting for Sheba, but he found out, and it changed his plans.

What plans? And how would he find—

Kilroy stopped. He pictured a quiet house in the suburbs, where he'd sat at twilight with a nice married couple, and delivered a stern but kindly warning to their young son about his habit of writing deceitful letters to the police. He saw the woman's face – her name was Gloriana, he remembered – as she gazed out of the window at the setting sun, and asked him if he had children of his own. And when he said he didn't, the man, Frobisher, asked him if it was his choice, and Kilroy had surprised himself by his readiness to admit he was unable to have children. The couple had struck him as decent people. Ordinary, decent informers.

What's up? Cynthia said.

I'm just thinking about something that could fit with what you're saying about Shadbold getting that information. But why would it change his plans?

OK. You probably like to think you're not easy to shock, am I right?

Try me.

Shadbold sent you to find Sheba because he had plans to mate the pair of you.

To do what, excuse me?

He wanted you and Sheba to reproduce. To breed.

Holy hell, I'm nearly forty, and she's thirteen!

Fourteen next week. But if you're both fertile, that's all he cares about. Then he discovers you're sterile, and now he needs to get you out of the way, and replace you with a clone – a version of you – that's able to impregnate the girl.

Wait, wait. How does Sheba fit into this?

So far, Cynthia said, there are three people I've seen here on Landmass who unmistakeably look like they share more of Shadbold's genes than most of the population. One is you, and another is Sheba.

And the other one?

The man we saw on the screens, delivering the emergency decree. The one who was introduced as Procurator of the Faithful. He called himself Doctor Glibbery.

He's Shadbold?

Not entirely. He is, and you are, and Sheba is. But he's got the most of Shadbold in him, out of you three. He's the one I can look at, and see that bastard behind his face, with absolute certainty.

How about you, Kilroy said, is he in you?

Yes, but not so much. There's more of Shadbold in everyone here than there is in me, because he's had hundreds of generations to experiment in this population.

It's like the prayer says, then.

Which prayer?

The blessed Shadbold, who is with us, and among us, and within us.

Cynthia shook her head with a bitter smile. Evil, she said.

I don't know about that, Kilroy said. Leastways, I stopped thinking in those terms some time ago. Good and evil. It doesn't cover the vast range of complicated ways people fuck up, and the weird, wonderful reasons they do it. But if you're right about what Shadbold planned for me and Sheba, and me impregnating her, that gets pretty close to evil, I have to admit. Why would he want to do that, anyway? Some kind of twisted experiment, for the hell of it?

Not for the hell of it. Never that. Shadbold never does anything without a practical purpose, and he plays a long game. I believe he's trying to produce an heir. A successor, or perhaps a whole breed of successors: a new generation he can work on. And he wanted to do it biologically, if he could, for whatever reasons. But he's amended his plan, because you can't do the job. To put it bluntly. Sorry.

Don't apologise. Hell, I'm glad about it. But I wouldn't have done it anyway, you know that, right?

I know you wouldn't have done it willingly, or knowingly.

What does that mean?

There are things he can do to people that you can't imagine, and things he can make people do. So, I'm glad, too. I'm glad you're out of the running.

And now he's going to use one of those…things to do it? Those abominations that look like me?

That's what I'm guessing. Did you notice something about those clones that tried to run us off the road?

Kilroy grimaced. Ugly motherfuckers.

Sure, and what else?

I don't know. No, hold on, they were younger, weren't they? Younger than the one I shot in the car. He looked like he was ready to die, and I did him a favour. But the runners on the road looked like they were thirty, maybe less.

Exactly. And they'll probably get even younger as Shadbold perfects them.

And then the girl will be…like, ready? Willing?

Cynthia smiled sadly. Put it this way: whatever happens, it won't seem so unnatural, will it? A teenage girl and a handsome young man only a few years older than her. It may be wrong, but it won't seem depraved.

Shit. Doesn't that make it even more important to stop him?

No, it makes it even more dangerous, especially for you. You have to understand that now Shadbold has given up on using you to breed with Sheba, he's going to eliminate you. You, and everything that carries your genes, so the field is clear for the people he's making, the replicas of you.

Everything that carries my genes? What does that mean?

Cynthia took his hand. You may as well know, since you hate him anyway, but I'm pretty sure it was Shadbold who had your father killed.

You're saying he gave the order? OK, but who pulled the

trigger?

Cynthia gripped Kilroy's hand harder and tried to draw him towards her.

Oh no, Kilroy said. Was it one of them? No, no, no. That means the last thing my father saw was someone who looked like me firing a gun at his face. Fuck! Why? Why kill an old man that way?

It's horrible to say it, but from Shadbold's point of view your father amounted to a loose end, genetically.

He was nearly eighty!

I know. But he could still reproduce.

Damn all of you to hell! Kilroy wrenched his hand away and sprang up. He felt an overwhelming urge to leave, to run, to be in motion.

But there was nowhere to go.

Kilroy stood at the edge of the sea, looking out at the horizon. He felt Cynthia's breath on his neck. She put her arms around him and pressed herself against his back, muffling her voice as she hugged him:

I know you want to kill him, she said.

Kilroy shifted around in her embrace, turning his back on the waves and tilting his head back to look into her eyes.

More than anything.

I know. And your chances of being able to do that will be much better if you come with me now, and work with me, until we have the power. I promise you.

Kilroy pulled away from her gently. He turned to look out at the sea once more, and took a series of slow, deep breaths. When he faced her again, his expression was calm.

Maybe you're right, he said. Serve it cold. I could live with that.

Cynthia kissed him. What more can I tell you?

You can tell me how that thing in the cave works. That tunnel, or whatever it is, that's supposed to take us to Landmass Two. It's not a damn boat, I know that.

It's a means of transport, Cynthia said, and it's quicker than a boat. As for how it works, I don't even know myself, not in any technical detail. But you remember when I described some of the science we did, when we were trying to figure out how different scenarios here could play out, and I mentioned simulations? We were working on simulations, and we came up with some solutions that make it easier to get from one place to another.

Simulations. Are you saying all this is…fake?

No, I'm not saying that. What does this feel like? Your life. Does it feel real?

Yes, it feels real.

Then it's real.

And what about you? Does this feel real to you?

A flicker of unease crossed Cynthia's face, then was gone. She smiled.

Kilroy took her by the shoulders. What? What is it?

Nothing. Believe me. It is real.

Kilroy scrutinised her face. She held his gaze.

All right, he said. Just give me an hour.

To do what?

I want to write something. I want to write down what's happened. Think of it as an unofficial report.

And what are you going to do with it?

Send it to someone.

Curtis?

Yeah. I want someone to have an account of everything, from my side of it. I don't know why, but I do. Maybe I can do it in half an hour, if time is an issue.

No, take an hour. But listen, were you planning to send it with Creek?

Kilroy looked down and swallowed hard. He nodded.

OK, Cynthia said, but I have a better method for you. I can give you a recording device. It's really small. Look.

She fished something out of her inside coat pocket. It was grey, and about the size of a child's thumb. It was curled in on itself, and looked like a seashell.

Kilroy took it from her. How does it work?

You put it in your ear.

Whoa! I saw what happened when you put one of your gizmos in your ear. Am I going to turn green or something?

Cynthia laughed. No, don't worry. You simply place it in your ear and start talking, and when you finish, just take it out. When someone else puts it in their ear, it automatically starts to play. It can hold a thousand hours of audio, and it's no heavier than a few sheets of paper. It's even got these little flexible loops, see, that you can use to tie it to the bird's leg. OK?

All right. Do you mind if I go and sit on those rocks, and do this by myself?

Of course not. Take your time.

Kilroy sat facing the sea, telling his story. He felt embarrassed at first, sitting there talking to himself, but soon he got engrossed in the narrative. When he'd finished he was surprised to find he'd been talking for over two hours.

He took the device out of his ear and stood up, shaking his legs. As he looked around for Cynthia he saw her emerging from the entrance to the cave. She smiled at him.

Kilroy held out his arm. Creek flew over to him and perched just above his wrist. All the time he'd been talking, the bird had been pacing around on the sand nearby, glancing at him occasionally.

Kilroy lowered his head and whispered to the bird.

I have a job for you, buddy. It's a very important job.

The bird moved its head from side to side, looking at Kilroy from the corner of its eye. Kilroy stroked its back, and gently tied the little recording device to Creek's leg with the threadlike fibres that were attached to it. The parrot clucked and whistled.

Kilroy began to walk up the beach towards the cave.

I want you to go home, he said to Creek. You hear me? Go home.

He stopped a few paces from the cave entrance. The parrot shuffled up Kilroy's arm and bowed. Kilroy rested his forehead on top of Creek's head for a moment, then kissed it softly. Say goodbye, he whispered.

The parrot shook its head slowly.

Kilroy raised his arm and looked the bird in the eye. No? OK, have it your own way. But go home.

The bird didn't move.

Go home!

Creek spread his wings but didn't take off.

Please, Kilroy said, go home. Go!

The parrot flapped its wings once, twice, and took off. Kilroy watched as it flew up and circled above his head, passing close to the cliff.

Kilroy dropped his gaze and walked towards the cave. He didn't look back.

As Kilroy squeezed through the entrance Creek soared up into the sky, hovered for an instant, made one more wide, slow circle, and flew away.

CURTIS

I can't be certain the leaflets tipped the balance, but I know they played an important part in deciding the outcome of the struggle.

Perhaps the rebels would have rallied even without the encouragement that fell from the sky that morning, but in its absence the government might have contained the fighting that was breaking out all over the city, and survived for longer. I believe the uprising would have succeeded in the end, but the conflict could well have been bloodier and more prolonged if Kilroy and his friend hadn't done what they did.

The timing was perfect. Kilroy wasn't aware of the government's plan to launch their attack just after dawn that morning, or that we in the network knew about their intentions and had made our own hasty plans accordingly. And yet, just as the masses were mobilising as best they could, and we were struggling to maintain our lines of communication, and hoping our lack of readiness wouldn't sink us, that manifesto fluttered down and did its work.

Kilroy and Cynthia had pinpointed our weakness, and their answer to the problem, in the form of a strong, simple message to inflame the uprising, arrived at precisely the right moment. It was almost uncanny.

We had a couple of other things going for us.

Brocklebank turned out to be a fine leader. He was a shrewd strategist and a gifted organiser, and I was increasingly impressed by him. He was a good-looking young man, as I've mentioned, and we had a warm rapport, and interacted well. On one or two occasions, as the uprising was getting into its stride, I was able to meet with him alone, in his private quarters. We were both living on our nerves, excited by the events that were unfolding, and our encounters reflected that reckless energy.

My only problem with Brocklebank was that despite his sterling leadership qualities and his dedication to the cause, he was, like so many idealists, hopelessly naïve. He understood the importance of neutralising the government's military power, and also its instruments of social coercion and control. However, he was slower to grasp that a revolution must protect itself with robust security measures of its own. This is particularly true in the early days, when conditions tend to be fluid and chaotic, and the movement is vulnerable to counter-attack by both external forces and internal enemies. It's vital to eliminate any potential threat from spies, infiltrators, double-agents, appeasers, cowards, centrist rabble and suchlike, and to maintain unceasing vigilance against treachery of any kind.

Naturally, once a new, stable administration is established, these measures can be relaxed, somewhat.

But it quickly became clear to me that Brocklebank had given little thought to policing, intelligence, counterintelligence, and other aspects of security, and I was able to make myself helpful. In fact, I soon found myself becoming indispensible to the success of the cause. I was in the right place at the right time, with the right background, and I took on the task of overseeing what was necessary.

Policing wasn't too much of a challenge. The police force was not politically engaged, and was focused on ordinary crime. Frankly, the police were of secondary importance while the fighting was still going on. I was confident we could rely on the existing infrastructure, and most of the personnel, to serve the interests of the people. At some point in the future I would probably need to purge some senior officers, but the rank and file posed no particular threat.

My main concern was the security services. The military could be fought head-on and defeated in the open, and, unsurprisingly – to me, at least – many soldiers surrendered or defected in the first stages of the fighting. We were a people's uprising, and most of the soldiers were ordinary people. They were as dissatisfied with the way things had been going as everyone else, and for the most part they didn't have lifetime careers to think about, or dark deeds in their past to account for. Special forces units fell into a slightly different category, with personnel more closely involved in the security apparatus, but the number of units was relatively small, and they'd each developed a highly distinctive culture. This made them almost insanely secretive, self-regarding, and jealous, and I predicted they would end up fighting each other, rather than presenting a serious impediment to the uprising.

There was also the church to consider, but I was interested only in its uppermost echelons, and the senior clerics who were deeply embedded in the machinery of the state. If the theology that underpinned the church itself were to collapse as a result of the populace accepting Sheba's message, as seemed likely, the average churchgoer, and the priests who ministered to them, could be left to their own devices, for now.

The security services, however, had everything to lose. I knew those people, because I was one of them, and my background gave me an insight into how they would be thinking and feeling. They knew they could expect little mercy from the people they'd spied on, terrorised, and controlled for so long. This may seem counterintuitive when you consider the number of ordinary people – in the city, probably one in five – who'd acted as informants at some time or another. You might think they'd be reluctant to turn against those who knew their secrets. Quite the opposite. While the average informant will rationalise what they do, and devise a narrative that not only justifies it, but actually casts them as a morally superior actor, somewhere in their heart they despise themselves. But they despise those who suborned them even more, for showing them who they are. That's a simplification, of course, and the relationship is often a complex interplay of conflicting dynamics. But when the relationship breaks down, informants frequently take the opportunity to smash the mirror that shows them everything they hate most about themselves.

Another factor I had to consider was the vast trove of information in the possession of the security services. From my point of view this data was priceless. I was anxious to secure it before it could be destroyed, and I knew the authorities would set about doing this once the tide began to turn against them. Every piece of information that is procured clandestinely betrays as much about the person who obtains it as about its subject, and sometimes more, if the method by which it's acquired is particularly nefarious.

The security services knew all this very well, and I expected them to fight hard. I told Brocklebank and the others we should make it a priority to deal with this issue. However, they were reluctant to devote much manpower to the task, and they considered it less important than the need to organise and deploy all their resources in what looked, to them, like the main fight – the military effort.

But I was persuasive, and I made it easier for them to agree with me by offering to take full responsibility for the project myself, and volunteering to select individuals from among the ranks of the uprising to assist me. I probably made it sound as if I would simply pick a few fighters here and there, almost at random, and organise them into a loose unit to launch a one-off attack on the security apparatus. In this I was, perhaps, being a little economical with the truth. In fact, I vetted each selection carefully, and chose men and women partly based on their value in the current conflict, but mostly on their potential usefulness to me in what I planned to establish after the fighting was over, namely a People's Security Division.

As soon as I'd assembled my primary team we attacked the building that housed the central headquarters of the security services. I found it strangely gratifying to be revisiting my old workplace in this capacity.

The battle was fierce, and casualties were heavy. I played no part in the actual combat myself, as my personal mission was to secure the data stored in the building, including my own files. I instructed my forces to defeat the enemy by whatever means necessary, and reminded them of the ruthlessness and brutality with which their opponents would certainly treat them, given the opportunity. I ordered certain individuals to be taken alive if they were found, including Allardyce, Pascal and Glibbery.

This ambition met with limited success. Allardyce played a major role in the building's defence, and I was told later that she displayed great courage. When she was finally cornered she refused to surrender, and fought to the death. I regretted this outcome, as I would have liked to talk to her, one last time.

But there was no sign of Pascal or Glibbery, and when the fighting was over I toured the area, reluctant to accept that both had slipped through my fingers. The mopping-up operation was underway, with its inevitably disagreeable sights and sounds, some of which were a consequence of our unfortunate lack of medical resources to treat enemy wounded. In addition, the excessive zeal of certain combatants under my command, to whom I may have given insufficiently strict orders regarding the humane treatment of prisoners, also played a part in some of the more distressing scenes being enacted.

I detected no trace of the missing men. I did, however, come across the corpse of my old boss and erstwhile lover, and gave it an affectionate kick in the crotch.

Later that day I received good news. Pascal had been captured as he attempted to leave the city in a government car, crashing through a roadblock with no regard for anyone's safety, including his own. He was, his captors reported, remarkably composed, despite being held in conditions which they themselves admitted were far from comfortable. I asked for him to be brought to the building we'd just overrun, and which I would soon be repurposing. I had particular plans for the cells in the basement, and I thought it would be appropriate to confine Pascal in one of them, to await my interrogation.

I decided to postpone this treat for a few days. I looked forward to seeing him again, and to making a decision about whether he should work for me. Whatever I put him through down there in the basement he would, naturally, swear to serve me faithfully, so it was simply a matter of assessing how much I could trust him. I was also excited by the prospect of reinvestigating, and perhaps resolving, the erotic tension I'd always felt between us.

Glibbery, unfortunately, seemed to have vanished entirely.

Our other great asset was Sheba herself.

Each time I spoke to her, or even saw her, I was struck afresh by what I can only describe as her magnetism. I was reminded forcefully of this when I watched her address a large gathering, the evening before the real fighting began.

We knew what was coming, and we suspected the government would strike the next morning. Brocklebank proposed that Sheba should address the movement's leaders and key members, to fire them up. He wanted to stage a rally in the Engineers' Tabernacle, above our basement headquarters.

I thought this was a very dangerous idea, and I tried to dissuade him. It would put all the key players in the uprising in one place, at a time when the authorities were trying to track them down. By bringing them all together Brocklebank was creating a situation in which a single traitor could betray the entire movement. If it weren't for the fact that I'd made my plans by then, it could have been me. But I was now on the side of the insurrection.

Brocklebank was adamant. The uprising, he said, is happening. We've gone way beyond the point of no return. The government knows it's coming, and we may be just hours away from a concerted effort by them to smash us to pieces.

We're not ready. This thing has grown so big, so fast. Our infrastructure is shaky – chains of command, communications – but there's nothing more we can do about that now. In these circumstances, what's the only way we might be able to make a difference at this stage?

Give them Sheba, I said.

Exactly, he said, I believe the fight could be decided by morale. Literally, by the strength of our spirit, and the courage of our convictions. A relatively small number of people can make all the difference. We can bring nearly two hundred leaders here, many of them seeing and hearing Sheba in person for the first time. We know what she can do. Think of all those leaders, returning to their teams, inspired and uplifted by her. That's going to have a huge impact, I'm convinced of it.

It's extremely risky, I said. What if there's a raid?

We're going to be staging a whole string of diversions, all over the city. The authorities are jumpy, and they'll have to respond to every incident we stage – even just a few random gunshots somewhere – in case it's the start of the uprising. They can't risk *not* responding. And the bottom line is we have to do this. It's all we've got left.

And so it went ahead.

When Sheba began speaking to the packed church, she was mesmerising, and by the time she finished people were weeping and embracing. It was as if she could unlock a door inside you, and release something that had been waiting to be freed. She spoke simply, using no rhetoric, and her sincerity was like an irresistible moral force, undeniable and unsullied. Her delivery was impassioned without being oratorical, and she was able to make everyone feel she was addressing them personally, with great warmth and candour. Another way of putting it might be to say she filled the room with love.

She spoke of the need to know the truth. To expose the lies upon which our beliefs had been based, and the cynicism with which religious faith had been exploited as a tool of repression. She asked where our books had gone, and why we were being kept in ignorance. She told a story of light being quenched by darkness; a darkness in which a powerful elite was able to act without accountability. She demanded an end to being spied on and controlled by the state, and said we should be free.

She'd said all this before, although never so compellingly. But then she said more. She called for a fresh beginning, and a government that would truly serve the people. The security state must be dismantled, she said, and in its place a system must arise, organically, from the people and for the people. She proposed committees, communes, meetings. Everything must be transparent. She wanted free and fair elections, as soon as the battle was won. She offered a wonderful, irresistible vision.

I could see I was going to have trouble with this girl.

*

A combination of guilt and curiosity prompted me to visit Kilroy's apartment.

I thought I'd better call in to see how the parrot was doing – if it was still there and still alive – and I wondered if Kilroy had left any kind of message for me. The last time I'd seen him was that morning when he showed up at my place with Sheba, and we'd barely spoken to each other before I traipsed off to betray them.

I had no idea where he'd gone after he avoided being taken into custody, and I found myself thinking about him a lot, and what he'd been doing in these interesting times. I had a hunch he'd probably be supporting the uprising without actually joining it. Kilroy wasn't much of a joiner.

Creek was standing on the table with his eyes closed when I walked in.

The kitchen window was open, and it looked like the parrot had been coming and going as he pleased. I got the feeling he wasn't asleep, and knew I was in the room, but he didn't open his eyes. He appeared to be in good condition. He was a resourceful bird, and if Kilroy left the window open when he was away, as he sometimes did, Creek was perfectly capable of going out and foraging for food. Whenever I agreed to Kilroy's requests that I go and feed the bird, I knew he was really asking me to go and provide Creek with a little company.

Nonetheless, I opened the container in which Kilroy kept the food he gave Creek, and rattled some into the bird's bowl, and topped up his water, too.

The parrot opened its eyes. It hopped to the edge of the table and tapped a claw next to a small object that was sitting there. Closer inspection revealed it to be an earpiece of some kind. A few shreds of twine were beside it in a neat pile, and I figured the earpiece had been attached to Creek's leg before he chewed off the twine. I picked it up and warily inserted it into my ear. Creek hopped away from me and pecked at the food in his bowl.

I listened to Kilroy's story, and I've incorporated what I heard into this account.

By combining the data in Kilroy's recording with what I already knew, I've been able to fill in some gaps, and to include new information. Some of the story is speculative, like the assertion that Glibbery is Shadbold, or partly Shadbold, or working with Shadbold, or all of the above, or some other freaky hybrid possibility involving science that I understand only a little better than Kilroy did when Cynthia described it to him.

Which brings me to Cynthia, and here I must make an admission. While I haven't changed the narrative Kilroy recorded in any substantial way, I've embellished certain elements. He isn't particularly forthcoming about his relationship with Cynthia, and what went on between them. He makes it clear they slept together more than once, but doesn't supply the kind of details that would bring a little excitement to his account of the proceedings. I've taken the liberty of enhancing his somewhat laconic descriptions.

In this respect I may have indulged myself, and let my imagination off the hook in some parts of the story. In reality Cynthia may not be quite as ballsy and sexy as I've portrayed her, although Kilroy implies that's what she is, and so you could say I've simply fleshed out the character a little.

As for the rest, your guess is as good as mine. I'm inclined to believe most of it is true, with certain reservations. I won't dispute the idea that Shadbold is real, is alive, and poses a potential threat to all of us, but I prefer to remain more sanguine than Kilroy and Cynthia (if, that is, Kilroy gives an accurate picture of her attitude) about what he might do. I've trained myself to look at all sides of any situation, and I believe there's a possibility Shadbold could play a valuable and constructive part in our immediate future. While I never assume someone is my friend without solid grounds for doing so, I also prefer not to conclude I have an enemy without sufficient evidence. Shadbold's plans, whatever they were, have clearly suffered a setback, but he sounds like the type of man who's always prepared to make new ones, and he's likely to be looking for allies. Who knows how things may play out?

Meanwhile, Kilroy has gone. He believes, as far as I can tell, that Cynthia is taking him to Landmass Two, where he may undergo some kind of longevity treatment, and continue to be her lover, as well as becoming her ally and ambassador, if and when the mooted re-colonisation project ever happens. So, they may return, with company.

However, that may all be a bunch of crap. It's equally possible that Cynthia looks on Kilroy as a scientific specimen, and plans to use him as the subject of some kind of experiment, and has been exploiting him for this purpose all along, and manipulating him cleverly. I have no proof of this, but neither does Kilroy have evidence to support his interpretation of what Cynthia has told him.

A word of caution here, however. Even assuming that Kilroy has told the truth, his account ends with him sending the recording back home with Creek, and him about to step into the cave. But he may have changed his mind. He may have omitted important information from the story. And he may have told any number of lies. As it happens, I've recently begun to receive reports that Kilroy, or someone very like him, has been sighted in several different locations in the city and far beyond it. Make of that what you will.

All I really know is that Kilroy was here.

And I've got his parrot.

END

THANKS

I would like to thank Scott Pack for his steadfast support and editorial advice; Sara Davies for her feedback and encouragement; Clio Mitchell for her meticulous attention to text and story, and Nell Wood for a great cover.

GOSPEL

The Landmass Gospel

Chapter One

1. In the beginning was the Water. And the Light moved upon the face of the Water, and the Light was Upstairs Mum and Dad.

2. And the Light brought forth Life from the Deep.

3. Upstairs Mum and Dad moved ceaselessly upon the face of the Water, and looked with favour upon the Creatures that thrived within it, and that were fruitful unto their kind; as the Glud, the Urfish, and the Slider.

4. Then Upstairs Mum and Dad grew weary, and they sought a Place that they might rest, but they found no Place, for the face of the Water was without end.

5. And they went forth accordingly into the Deep and raised up a pillar; and the pillar was made of the mud of the depths, and it was strong. And the summit of the pillar was raised above the face of the Water, and its Mass divided the Water.

6. The Mass was broad in its measure, even unto one third part of the Earth, and it was firm beneath the foot; and it was pleasant to behold.

7. It was Landmass, and it was a resting place for Upstairs Mum and Dad.

8. And so Upstairs Mum and Dad rested, and it was a hundred thousand days.

9. When Upstairs Mum and Dad had rested, they rose up and looked about them, and they saw that Landmass was an empty Place.

10. Accordingly, Upstairs Mum and Dad lay down, one with the other, and joined together their loins in the way of joyful propagation, as it was seemly.

11. And their loins were fruitful, and from them sprang the first Beings.

12. The first Being was without parts.

13. The second Being was with the parts of a Man.

14. The third Being was with the parts of a Woman.

15. The fourth Being was with the parts of a Man and a Woman.

16. The Fifth Being was with parts that were neither of a Man nor a Woman, and yet were of both, and was sufficient unto itself. And this was Shadbold.

17. And Upstairs Mum and Dad looked upon Shadbold and they were well pleased. See, they said, we have wrought a Being that shall be blessed, for he is as a blessing unto us, and is our truly beloved Son.

Chapter Two

1. Then Upstairs Mum and Dad lay together once more, and their loins were again fruitful, and they brought forth children.

2. The children of Upstairs Mum and Dad were in number one hundred thousand, and they were made in the image of Shadbold, who was perfect in their eyes.

3. But no other child was as perfect as Shadbold, for they had the parts of a Man, or the parts of a Woman, or the parts of both Man and Woman, but yet they were not sufficient unto themselves, as Shadbold was.

4. And the children who were not sufficient unto themselves cried out in hunger, saying: Behold, we are empty, even in our bellies, and surely we will perish.

5. Accordingly, Upstairs Mum and Dad caused the ground of Landmass to bring forth food in great abundance, and of many kinds, and the number of different kinds was one hundred thousand.

6. They caused also Beasts to spring forth from the ground, each unto its kind; as the Skroal, the Flappers of the Air, and the Thuds.

7. Thus was the hunger of the children assuaged, and likewise their thirst, and they were well satisfied.

8. And the children of Upstairs Mum and Dad dwelt in peace, one with the other, and joined their loins together when it was seemly, and were fruitful.

9. They gave thanks to Upstairs Mum and Dad, and to the Blessed Shadbold, who was first among them.

10. In this manner did the children of Landmass thrive and prosper, and the time of their prosperity was one hundred thousand days.

Chapter Three

1. After this time, some among the children of Landmass grew dissatisfied, and permitted greed and covetousness to spring up within them.

2. And these same children of Landmass became hasty in their harvests, despoiling the ground, and were unmindful of the hearts of the Beasts, even unto using them in the manner of those who would themselves be beasts.

3. Thus were the seeds of strife sown among the children of Landmass.

4. Then Shadbold spake unto them, teaching them to honour Upstairs Mum and Dad, and to fear their displeasure.

5. But the children raised up their voices, saying, Why should not we ascend Upstairs and taste of its delights? For where are Upstairs Mum and Dad, and what gifts can they give us that we cannot take ourselves?

6. And Shadbold said unto them, Raise not your voices, for if you are humble, you shall ascend Upstairs when your span is complete, as it was promised to you, but if you are proud you shall surely not ascend Upstairs, but will perish

without comfort. This is the covenant of Upstairs Mum and Dad.

7. But the children of Landmass heeded him not.

8. Then Upstairs Mum and Dad beheld the ingratitude of their children, and spake unto Shadbold, and said, Go, tell them to repent of their depravity, for we will surely punish them, even causing them to go wrong.

9. And Shadbold told the children of Landmass, but they heeded him not.

10. Then Upstairs Mum and Dad waxed wrathful, and spake again unto Shadbold, and said, Lo, we shall cause a great punishment to fall upon them, and they shall be destroyed, in all their number.

Chapter Four

1. Then Upstairs Mum and Dad caused a great Flood to arise.

2. And the children of Landmass saw that the Flood would destroy them, even all their number, and fell into anguish, and repented of their ingratitude, and cried out in a great

voice, pleading with Upstairs Mum and Dad to spare them.

3. But Upstairs Mum and Dad heeded them not.

4. Then the children of Landmass cried out to Shadbold, and begged him to intercede with Upstairs Mum and Dad, and to plead for their Mercy.

5. And Shadbold spurned them, for their ingratitude was an affront also to him, as it was to Upstairs Mum and Dad, who loved him well.

6. Then the children cried out to him again, and again he spurned them.

7. But when the children cried out a third time his heart was moved, despite his righteousness, and he told the children of Landmass he would stand before Upstairs Mum and Dad, even as a sacrifice, to be punished in their place.

8. And the children of Landmass fell down before him, and were grateful.

9. Then Shadbold went to Upstairs Mum and Dad and begged them to show Mercy to their children, and offered himself as a sacrifice in their place, and fell down before them, and bared his neck, that they might smite him, and sever his head from his body.

10. But Upstairs Mum and Dad raised him up, for they were well pleased with him, and saw his heart was noble, for which they loved him.

11. Then they spake unto him and said, We cannot be deaf to the voice of our beloved Son, that pierces us to our heart. Accordingly, we shall not destroy our children utterly, but even so we must visit punishment upon them, so they will learn the error of their ways.

12. And Shadbold asked them what manner of punishment they would visit upon their children, and begged them to be merciful, as they found it seemly.

13. And Upstairs Mum and Dad said unto him, We will spare a part of Landmass, being one tenth part of its measure, and the Flood will not engulf it.

14. In the same manner, we will spare a number of our children, and the number will be one hundred thousand, being the same number that first We brought forth, before they joined together their loins, and were fruitful.

15. But we will destroy the Beasts of Landmass, that they have no succour from them. Likewise the manifold foods, leaving only three kinds; namely, mizzet, spood and farge, and from these alone must our children take their succour.

16. And we will dwell only in our Upstairs kingdom until our children have expunged their errors in full, and we will not hear their prayers, for we will hear only the prayers of our beloved Son, and You shall be their emissary.

17. And so it came to pass.